DATE DUE

1944

GAYLORD   PRINTED IN U.S.A.

WE AIN'T THE BRONTËS

WE AIN'T THE BRONTËS

ROSALYN MCMILLAN

URBAN Renaissance

www.urbanbooks.net

Urban Books, LLC
78 East Industry Court
Deer Park, NY 11729

ISBN 13: 978-1-60162-243-3
ISBN 10: 1-60162-243-0

First Printing February 2011
Printed in the United States of America

10   9   8   7   6   5   4   3   2   1

Distributed by Kensington Publishing Corp.
Submit Wholesale Orders to:
Kensington Publishing Corp.
C/O Penguin Group (USA) Inc.
Attention: Order Processing
405 Murray Hill Parkway
East Rutherford, NJ 07073-2316
Phone: 1-800-526-0275
Fax: 1-800-227-9604

Dedication

I wish to dedicate this book to my five grandchildren, Dominique, Malik, Alyce, Noelani, and Darren.

Acknowledgments

Putting God first in my life is my mantra. I thank God for blessing me with the talent to write. The Lord knows my heart, and He knows that writing is my passion. Some way, somehow, I knew that God had not forsaken me. He's blessed me in so many ways and now He's blessing me again. I pray that my faith stays strong and that I will continue to earn God's precious grace.

I'd like to thank my agent, Dr. Maxine Thompson, for her patience and hard work. Without her input and suggestions this novel wouldn't have been published. She is an expert in her field with her own internet radio show as well as being an accomplished author. I couldn't have dreamed of a better agent.

Carl and Natalie Weber are two professionals that I thank God are on my team. I want to thank my publisher, Urban Books, for believing in my work and giving me the opportunity to make a comeback in the publishing industry. This company is a class act.

I want to thank all of the Book Clubs who supported me over the years. Their allegiance is endearing. Equally important is all of the Black Bookstores that kept my books in stock long after the shelf life had expired. Thank you.

Family is an important part of my life. My sisters, brother, cousins, uncles and aunts, and my four children, Vester, Jr., Shannon, Ashley and Jasmine, never lost faith in me. They encouraged me to keep writing until I received a new contract.

As always, I save my husband, J.D. Smith, until the end. He is my rock, my strength, my special soul-mate who keeps me grounded and humble. We never know how much one loves till we know how much he is willing to endure and suffer for us;

and it is the suffering element that measures love. I thank God for blessing me with my husband's love and passion. I cherish my "old man" and pray that we will have many many years together this side of eternity. And afterwards, I pray that our love will still exist and grow in the lifetime of the Almighty.

1

It's the first week in June and the city looks like a postcard for tourism. I love visiting California this time of year. My big sister, Lynzee Lavender, paid for my first class ticket to come to the Bay Area. Lynzee has been very generous to me and my twin sons, Javed and Jamone, since she made the New York Times bestsellers list more than twenty-five years ago. I'm very proud of her accomplishments and hope that one day soon, I will be in the same position. I write contemporary fiction. But something just doesn't seem right about the timing of this visit. Is Lynzee being her usual benevolent self, or does she have something else on her agenda?

I decide not to worry about it since I'm so excited about attending the Essence Awards with Lynzee tonight. It took us three hours to get dressed. I'm wearing a brand new, long black lace empire dress with a hot pink under-slip, which Lynzee let me borrow. She even bought me the Sonya Rykiel black pumps to match it.

We're in Lynzee's bedroom and the two of us are checking out our images in her full-length antique mirror. Lynzee has on a beige Richard Tyler slack suit with an antique white lace blouse. She looks fabulous, but something's amiss. I rush into the bathroom and retrieve her fluffy powder brush and compact. I use the brush to blot the oily splotches on her nose and forehead. I step back and assess her face. Perfect.

I haven't been to Oakland in nearly two years, and I'm having a great time. Lynzee has a wicked sense of humor and for the past half hour she's told me non-stop jokes about some of her fan mail. My sides ache from laughing so hard.

I look forward to the awards ceremony, featuring Denzel Washington and his wife Juanita, Queen Latifah, Larry Fishburne, Angela Bassett, Bill Cosby, Vanessa Williams, and Halle Berry. Although the ceremony is being held three hundred sixty miles away in Los Angeles, Lynzee hired a limousine service to drive us down. She could've flown us in, but she loves to ride high on the hog in a limo. With the extra leg room we have, our clothes never get wrinkled.

"Charity? Are you ready to go? The driver is waiting," Lynzee tells me, looking up the staircase.

"Just let me put on some lip gloss and I'll be right down." I hurry and finish, then rush down the stairs.

"I'm ready." It's a sunny seventy-five degrees outside, so we don't need wraps.

Lynzee checks her watch as she grabs her purse. "It's almost a six-hour drive, so let's get going. I don't want to be late." She pauses and fingers one of my tendrils. "You look good, sis." She kisses me on the cheek.

"You look pretty swell yourself."

I pick up my purse. "Now, let's go."

We hurry outside to the waiting car and allow the driver to open the door for us. Inside the limo it is lush and spacious. Like most limos, a full bar is located on the rear of the driver's seat. I don't drink, and watch as Lynzee scoffs down a couple of vodka shots. She exhales, and pours another double. I'm irritated when she lights up a Kool cigarette and blows the smoke right in my direction. She's pissed about something, so it's going to be a long ride; that is, unless Lynzee takes one of her famous naps.

And we're off.

"How's the twins?" Lynzee asks me. Javed and Jamone are sixteen.

"Happy. They just sold one of their pieces for five grand."

"You know, I never heard of artists, especially twins, who paint together. That's pretty cool."

"Yeah, it is. Jett is pretty proud of them too." Jett is my husband of twenty-seven years.

I pause, and then say, "So, where is Tyler? I miss her."

"She's visiting a college this weekend."

"I'd almost forgotten. Don't forget to tell her that I said hello and that I love how she redecorated her room."

We talk about our children going to college and their love lives for a good piece before Lynzee starts yawning.

"Sleepy?" I ask.

"A little."

"Go ahead and take a nap. I'll be fine."

It doesn't take much coaching. Lynzee is fast asleep five minutes later. I admire the lush palm trees, tropical yucca plants, and the beautifully landscaped azaleas. The contemporary homes in the subdivision look like they belong in *Architectural Digest*. We navigate our way through the narrow streets of Lynzee's subdivision until we get on the 580 East freeway. Then we take the 5 South, which will take us into L.A. I sit back, relax, and enjoy the ride.

Something is bothering me, though. Lynzee hasn't asked about my book contract. Usually, it's the first thing that she asks. As we make good time on the freeway, I try to think of a good lie to tell her. It's none of her business where my career is headed.

I don't realize that I've fallen asleep, too, until the driver knocks on the window and says we're only thirty minutes away.

It's pitch black outside. Lynzee turns on the interior lights so that we can touch up our makeup. While Lynzee's face is obscured from mine by her compact, she finally asks the question. "So, how's your book contract coming?"

"Slow."

"Do you have a new agent?"

"Yes."

"What's her name?"

"I'd rather not say."

"Why not?"

"Because you know everyone in the business and you're too judgmental."

"Well, all I'm saying is not to expect the same money that Mitchell and Montague paid you last time." Mitchell and Montague were the publishers on my fourth novel, *New Collar Blues*.

"I never told you how much I got paid."

Lynzee closes the compact and rolls her eyes at me. "It's my business to know what's happening in the publishing industry."

"I don't like that about you, Lynzee. You've always tried to get in my business."

"Well, baby cakes, I have to look out for my name."

"Your name? I thought it was our name."

"Your last name is Evans, remember?"

"I remember that before Mama died she told me to use my maiden name. You agreed. Why all the drama now?"

"Because your publishers are trying to capitalize on my name and I don't like it. Face it: your books haven't been selling well. Your sales are way down, possibly because they won't give you a senior editor to work with."

"So, you know about my sales, too?" I seethe.

"Like I said. It's my—"

"Business to know," I finish. "You know, Lynzee, I wouldn't be having all of these problems with editors if you'd lift a finger to help me. I've never asked for your help. I'm asking you now." My heart is quivering inside, worrying if she's going to tell me "hell no!"

"Change your last name on your next book and I'll see what I can do." She leans back and crosses her legs. Then she folds her arms across her breasts. She gives me a look that says not to fuck with her.

"My answer is hell no."

Lynzee looks out the window. "Then fuck you and your career. You have no fucking idea what you're doing."

"Isn't that why it's obvious that I need your help?"

She leans forward. "Look, I'm not budging on your last

name. Your unprofessional writing style is ruining my reputation. I worked too hard to get where I'm at. You think you can just waltz in here and steal the show. I know you want to outsell me. Don't tell me you don't, because I heard all about it. You told a bookseller that you want to be the first African American to sell a million hardcover books." Her mouth bunches together. "Admit it. Don't lie."

Of course she's telling the truth; however, I didn't think the bookseller would go back and tell Lynzee. I feel trapped. In my heart I know that our mother wouldn't want us to compete with each other.

"So I said it. I was just kidding."

"The hell you were." She snickers. "Your writing is so bad you'll be lucky if you ever sell a hundred thousand books."

"Oh, now the truth comes out. So, you think I'm not a good writer."

"Fuck no. And if it wasn't for my last name, no one would have ever given you a contract in the first place."

"You're a real selfish bitch, Lynzee." I can't help it. Tears form in my eyes.

"And you're the bitch who's trying to ride my coattails. I wish you would get the fuck off and get your own career before you ruin mine."

Back in the day, when we were in our early thirties, Lynzee and I were close. She said she loved the idea that I wanted to be a writer and follow in her footsteps. But after our mother died, Lynzee changed from a lamb to a tigress. To my horror, Lynzee trumped up one demand after another. When I wouldn't give in to her threats, she wrote me the nastiest letter that a sister could write to her sibling. She said that I was the Latoya Jackson of the family, shut out. I cried for days, but I refused to back down. I have fans, women and men who love my writing and identify with my characters.

Fuck her. Latoya's got pizzazz.

Finally we arrive at the Chinese Theatre. Bright lights abound at the entrance and red-carpet walkway. I'm hurt and don't want to spend another second with Lynzee. When the driver opens the door, I pull back.

"I'm not going in. I'm going back to your house to pack and get the hell out of here." I exit the limo and try to find another driver to drive me back to Lynzee's house. I don't have enough money on me to pay for a taxi, so I barter with a limo driver who will accept my credit card.

Lynzee comes up to me as I'm getting into the limo. "Suit yourself. It's embarrassing for me to be seen out with you anyway, so go on home, hussy. You won't be missed. Most of the people here are my friends, and they don't like you anyway." She slams the door and gives the driver instructions.

Now the tears fall. I'm hurt over Lynzee's hateful words. How can she be so heartless? Plus, I'm disappointed that I won't be able to see Denzel Washington. He's my favorite actor. Lynzee told me earlier that we could probably get backstage passes so we could get Denzel's autograph. Damn, another disappointment and another reason why I should have kept my black ass at home.

The drive back home passes quickly. Once there, I ask the driver to wait so that he can take me to the airport. Thank God I have a key to her house. I rush upstairs and pack my things. I'm back in the limo in thirteen minutes. While riding to the airport, I call Jett. I tell him everything that happened.

"I told you not to trust Lynzee. She's your sister and she loves you in her own way, but she's not going to help your career."

"I know that now." Fresh tears cloud my eyes. "I'm going to have to fly home standby, so listen out for my call so you can unlock the door. I forgot my house keys."

"Okay. And, Charity, don't you shed any tears over Lynzee. Ever since she started making big money, she's changed. Knowing her, she'll probably call you and apologize anyway. You know you two can't stay mad at each other for too long."

"No. I don't want to hear from Lynzee. And it's going to be a frigid day in hell before I call her."

I feel a little better after having talked to my husband. There's been some tension between us lately because our finances our tight and the stress is getting to him, but still, he's a great listener whenever I have problems with my sister.

While I wait at the airport, I watch CNN. The next thing I know, my cell phone is ringing.

"It's me."

"What do you want, Lynzee?"

"I'm sorry."

"I'm not. I meant everything I said."

"That's too bad. I hoped we could come to a truce."

"If that means changing my last name, you can go fuck yourself." I hang up.

I manage to get on the next flight out to Memphis. I can't help but to start crying again. Both of our parents are dead and we have no other siblings. Should I totally cut Lynzee out of my life and never speak to her again, or should I give her another chance to redeem herself?

My cell phone rings again. It's Lynzee. I don't answer. There's no quick fix to our problems, and talking on the phone is not going to remedy the problem. No, she's going to have to come and see me in Memphis. If she cares anything about me, she won't let this argument fester. If she's the money-hungry, star-struck selfish bitch that Jett thinks she is, I won't hear from her again.

I don't know how I make it home. My eyes are blurry as I drive down the highway. As soon as I walk into the house and see Jett, I break down into tears.

Jett is a devilishly handsome creature. He's as chocolate as a moist brownie with skin that is tender to the touch. He has a long, narrow face, whisper-light eyebrows, small eyes, an average nose, and Michelangelo lips. His bright white, perfectly formed teeth merely highlight his sexy smile. At six foot six, he's a lady-killer. I should know; he slayed me.

It's good to see him, but I need to vent. "That Lynzee—" I shout, throwing down my purse on the sofa. "She'll fuck up a wet dream."

"Calm down, Charity, before you have a stroke." Jett comes over to me, but he doesn't hold me. "Forget that rich bitch. She's always been nasty to you. I don't see why you even fool with her."

I sob and sob as I protest, "But you don't understand. Sisters are supposed to love each other."

"She ain't never gave a shit about you. She ain't nothing, so stop sweating about her. Besides, she's jealous of you."

"Jealous of me? Why? She's got all the money."

"Yeah, but can money hold you at night? Yeah, that's right. She's mad because you got a good man who loves you."

Slowly, I start feeling better.

For once in my life, I'm going to try to act like my mother. She'd tell Lynzee to go fuck herself. Will I be able to stick to my guns, or will I allow Lynzee to take advantage of my kindness once again?

"We need to talk," Jett says to me one night while we're in bed a few days later. I know he's mad because I refused to have sex with him, but tonight's Wednesday. We only have sex on Friday or Saturday night, and he damn well knows it.

"I spoke with my attorney this morning," he tells me.

I turn on the lamp on the nightstand and face him. I am totally alerted to his tone of voice. I instinctively know that Jett is dead serious. "What the hell is this about?"

"I'm considering a legal separation." His voice is stern and I know that he's been thinking about this for some time. "I love you, but I can't tolerate all of the pressure I've been under. I feel ten years older than I am. My blood pressure is high, as well as my cholesterol. If I continue to live this way, I'm going to end up in a nursing home."

I hold my breath. If this is a dream, somebody please wake me up. When I look at him, his face looks like the auditor's at the Internal Revenue Service.

"Why, Jett?" I am too hurt to ask the unspoken: *Have you stopped loving me?*

"Like I said, my health, for one. Number two is money. I'm sick and tired of being broke. We're in debt up to our nostrils. You should have saved money from your contracts and then we wouldn't even be in this mess. I'm tired of you being so selfish about your writing career—"

"But—"

"Let me finish." He gets up and put on his robe. "I'm going to say this one time: Either you give up writing books and sell this house, or I'm outta here."

"Have you forgotten that it was my career and my money that provided us with this lavish lifestyle? A lifestyle that I know you've come to love."

"You're wrong. I want a normal life. I don't need this huge house."

He was telling the truth; he had never been as excited about our house as I was. He didn't even want to live in this state at first.

We built the house when Mitchell and Montague was paying me well. I was the one who insisted we go to Memphis. Lord knows I didn't want to build our home in Mississippi. When I was in grade school in Port Huron, Michigan, the students from the North used to laugh at the kids from down South. The myth was that they were slow, and were usually put back a grade or two.

I'm sorry, but it's the truth.

Since the 1980s, the schools in Mississippi have been the worst in the nation. You rarely see a recording artist perform in Mississippi. And going to see a play? *Forgetaboutit*. And to make matters worse, there are no professional sports teams. Both Jett and I love to watch football, basketball, baseball, boxing, and golf.

We settled on Memphis, Tennessee, and purchased 4.1 acres of land in an exclusive subdivision in Shelby County to build our dream home.

Eighteen months later, our 12,500 square foot home was finished. Neither Jett nor the twins and I could comprehend our good fortune. The house made a statement and our builder, as well as several of our neighbors, thought so too.

Our four-level contemporary brick home, built high on a hill, boasts six bedrooms, a library, dining room, nine bathrooms, two kitchens, three family rooms, exercise room, six fireplaces, a huge office, and a six-car garage. There are two saunas and an indoor hot tub. In the foyer, there is a twin staircase with wrought iron railing that borders a granite star design that cost over twenty grand. Jett argued that it was overkill, but I insisted that I had to have it.

Jett did agree to one more extravagance, the wrought iron fence that frames our lot. Two electronic gates that are interlaced with prancing lions secure the circular drive. An intercom for entrance to our property is a short distance away. Because our home is so elevated, we designed two circular wrought iron staircases installed in the rear of our home, to gain access to the backyard from the kitchen and master bedroom.

I was so excited about the work the wrought iron company completed on our home that I had to share it with someone. Of course, I called Lynzee. At the time, she was considering building a new home too.

I conveyed to Lynzee that the same wrought iron company that worked on Jett's and my home completed the ironwork on John Grisham's home in Oxford, Mississippi. "Can you believe it?' I asked her.

"Uh-huh, that's nice, Charity."

I should have known she'd be jealous. However, my feelings were still hurt. Couldn't she be happy for me for once in her life?

I shake the ugly memories of Lynzee from my mind to focus on the issue in front of me. My husband wants a separation. I am stunned. Now that we might be facing divorce court, even I'm not sure how I feel about our dream home anymore. Maybe we never should have built it. But there is one thing I am sure about: my career as a writer.

I tell him, "I will never give up on trying to become a *New York Times* bestselling author."

"Even if it means our marriage will suffer?"

I roll my eyes at him. "Our marriage has never been in jeopardy. You're beginning to sound like Lynzee." Oops, I didn't mean to say that.

"What has Lynzee got to do with our marriage?"

I haven't had a contract in over a year, and Lynzee keeps telling me to give up. Now here Jett is telling me to choose between our marriage and my writing career. I'm blindsided by his talk of separation, because as far as I'm concerned, we've had a calm, normal marriage.

Our weekdays always begin at six with fresh-brewed coffee, bagels, and the morning paper. We exercise between eight and nine. Then I change and go to my office, and Jett works on his two motorcycles, works in our yard, or does volunteer work with high school basketball players. Dinner is served at five, and we're in bed by nine. I pay the bills and shop for groceries on the first of every month. This has been our schedule for the past seven years. Up until last year, we had more than $190,000 in the bank. We have season tickets for the Grizzlies basketball team. We attend plays at least once a month at the Orpheum Theater, and can't wait to go to a concert at the Fed Ex Forum or in Tunica, Mississippi, where artists have finally began to perform at the crowded casinos. We vacation twice a year, once with the twins and then by ourselves. Our last trip was eight days in China.

We've built a life together out of these little routines. Now all that I love is being threatened.

Just to know that Jett is thinking about a legal separation is enough to piss me off to no end. Who does he think he is, leaving me? I made him the man he is today: a man who is now world traveled; a man who plays golf with celebrities; a man of leisure who was able to take an early retirement from his job as a superintendent from Champion Motors. It wasn't some skank welfare bitch who made him. Not somebody who only knows how to buy Happy Meals from McDonald's and doesn't know how to use a vacuum cleaner. No, Jett got the top of the line. And if he doesn't respect who and what I am, then some other man will. Hell, maybe I should be thinking about a separation. After all, he's damn near sixty. Why shouldn't I give a man in his forties a whirl?

I refuse to continue this conversation with him. I will not talk about a separation. I roll over and turn off the light. Maybe he'll wake up in the morning and have forgotten all about this nonsense.

2

"Charity, it's me." She's whispering.

"Lynzee?" I'm sitting at the computer in my home. Dozens of research papers and character profiles litter my desk.

"Yes, fool," she says scathingly. "I'm at Memphis International Airport."

"At the airport? Why?" It's ten-thirty in the morning and I'm typing away at my computer, working on my new novel, *Shattered Illusions*. I'm highly irritated that she's interrupting my flow. With the ultimatum Jett gave me, I'm writing at a feverish pace now, trying to get a new contract.

"I need you to come here right away."

What the hell is going on now? Is she ready to apologize so soon? It's only been a week. "I'm really busy. Can't you rent a car and drive out here?"

"No!"

"Why not?" I finally stop typing.

"Jett might be home. Is he there?"

"Yes. He's mowing the lawn." I stretch and yawn.

"Why am I not surprised? Look, I'm at the Rendezvous Café in Concourse A. Be here in thirty minutes." She hangs up.

That Bitch! What the fuck is it now?

I grab my purse and keys, get into my car, and head for

Memphis International Airport. It's twenty-three miles from our house, and I make it there in seventeen minutes.

The flowers are in perfect bloom in June. The air is heavy with the scent of floral magnolias and crape myrtles. Birds are chirping louder than ever, and my beautiful surroundings nearly make me forget where I'm headed.

Besides, my mind is on why Jett wants a legal separation. I wonder how much is really my fault. He wanted us to put a third of my salary from my two contracts in the bank. I didn't listen, and only managed to save a tenth of what I'd earned. It wasn't enough to pay all of our financial obligations without the benefit of a new contract.

I am too embarrassed to tell Jett that since last September, I haven't paid my credit cards on time. I don't want to withdraw any more money from our dwindling savings. Since I haven't been able to make any deposits, I don't feel that any of the money is rightfully mine. When Jett isn't at home, I manage to intercept the creditors' calls and make payment arrangements.

Presently, my finances are so bad I don't even have the credit to finance a doghouse. Even so, I can't let my current situation reduce me to living like a panhandler.

I'm so preoccupied that I don't notice until I get inside that I've lost my parking ticket, probably somewhere in the parking lot. I don't know how I'm going to cash out when I exit the airport today. I make it to the Café with two minutes to spare.

Lynzee is sitting there with a casual smirk on her face. She's wearing a Donna Karan olive green suit with a white knit T. She has on caramel Ferragamo pumps that I guess cost about twelve hundred bucks. And the purse she's carrying is a Hermes. That's at least thirty-five hundred. She oozes money and doesn't make any excuses about it.

I'm told that fame is the perfume of heroic deeds. If that's true, I haven't caught the scent.

I, wearing my jeans and pink T-shirt, take a seat next to the rich bitch and park my sixty-dollar purse on the table between us.

Lynzee has magnificent, warm cognac coloring. Her skin is

smooth and clear, except for tiny lines around her eyes and mouth from years of smoking. She has a small, pointy nose, large eyes with lush lashes, and bubble gum lips. Her best feature is her apple cheekbones. They make her look youthful. She has a beautiful cleft in her chin that I have always been jealous of. Some people say we look alike. That is totally untrue. I wish I could look half as good as Lynzee does.

On the phone we sound exactly alike. She's four inches taller than I am, but we wear the same size shoes, a nine medium. Unlike me, Lynzee has long legs, a short torso, and a small waist. She usually keeps her hair dyed black with blond highlights. Whoever told her that this look was attractive on her is a liar. She looks much prettier when her hair is a rich cayenne.

Lynzee is fifty-two years old, four years older than I am.

Lynzee is taking her time to speak. Finally she says, "I've got something important to talk to you about."

"Is it about my last name?"

"No. Something a little more important."

"Good. I'm not changing my mind." I cross my arms and stare right into her cold eyes.

A waitress stops by our table. I order hot tea with lemon. The small café is filled with customers, and I'm uncomfortable talking about personal matters in such a public setting. I wish she had come to my house like I'd asked. "Please tell me why you couldn't talk to me over the phone."

She stalls for a minute. I debate getting up and leaving. She finally says, "This needs to be said in person."

I gesture with my hands. "In front of all of these people?"

"They don't know who we are." Lynzee signals the waitress and orders a double vodka with orange juice.

Until now, I hadn't noticed the empty glass beside her. Apparently, she's already had one drink. Now, I observe that her eyes are reddened a bit. Has she been crying? I'm immediately in sister-mode. What's wrong with my sister?

"Thank you," I say to the waitress after she places the hot tea before me.

"I don't know how to say this," Lynzee says. I notice that her hands are shaking as I empty two packets of Equal into my brew.

I burn my mouth as I take a sip of tea. Something inside me begins to churn, and I can sense that Lynzee is going to be melodramatic. "Just say it, Lynzee."

"Jett and I had a daughter together." She can't look me in the eye.

Now my hands are shaking as I lower the cup from my lips. "Is this some kind of sick joke? Because I don't like the implications." Is it my imagination, or are the people sitting around us suddenly listening in on our conversation?

She raises her hand and crosses her heart with her index finger. "I'm not lying. Jett and I did the wild thang in my senior year in high school." Her face suddenly looks grotesque to me. "The only reason he began dating you four years later is because he couldn't have me."

That does it. I jump up and throw my hot tea dead in her face. "You low-down cunt. I hope you die." I grab my purse. I have such an intense feeling of hate for her, I feel like I'm on fire. We hate some people because we do not know them, and we will not know them because we hate them. I will never know Lynzee. My hate is raw. The incident with Siegfried and Roy and the white tiger was like a minor scrape in comparison to what I'd do to Lynzee.

"Sit down, Charity," she demands. "I said sit down." She retrieves a napkin and begins wiping the tea from her face and blouse.

Now everyone *is* looking at us and whispering. I take a seat. No matter what happens next, the damage is done.

"Jett doesn't know about our daughter. I never told him because I put the baby up for adoption."

I barely hear a word she's saying. I am envisioning Lynzee and Jett making love, and the snapshot I see is making me nauseated. I focus on the words "doesn't know" and "adoption." I feel numb. I feel betrayed. Jett has lied to me. He has never told me that he dated Lynzee before we got together. A feeling that I'm not familiar with surfaces: I feel threatened. My marriage is in jeopardy. Sooner or later, I will have to confront Jett with the truth. What if he denies it? What if he doesn't? Will his confession kill the trust between us, or will the humiliation of being second best trump my feelings toward him? And since this is a girl child, will he leave me so he can be with the daughter he has always longed to have?

My words sound hollow. "You say that Jett doesn't know about the child?"

"No. He doesn't."

"Where is the child? This girl?" I calculate that this girl must be about thirty-four years old now.

Lynzee drinks the vodka in one long gulp. "She's trying to locate me. She's left several messages with my agent. I've been avoiding contacting her. Eventually, we'll meet and I'll have to tell her the truth."

"Why?" I plead. "She doesn't have to know about Jett. You could lie and tell her that you don't know who her father is."

"Why should I lie?" She screws up her face and her pointy chin suddenly looks like a witch's.

Tears fill my eyes. My entire life is at stake. I can't let this lovechild come between Jett and me. I can't let Jett and Lynzee's sleeping together come between us either. Can I?

The waitress is back. "Would you like another cup of tea?"

"No. Thank you." She looks at Lynzee, then back at me. "Can I get you two anything else?"

"No, just the check," Lynzee says all businesslike.

When the waitress is gone, Lynzee just stares at me. She doesn't say a word. Her stare says so much. It says, "See, you've never been better than me at anything. See. I've got proof: birthing his first-born child. See. See."

The blood in my veins feels like acid. I am so hot, I can barely breathe. What in the hell am I going to do?

"Let me tell you what's going to happen, Charity. You're going to tell Jett about our daughter. I'll give you a few months or so. By then, I'll have met with April." She smiles. "Did I tell you that her name is April?"

"No," I whisper.

"Well, I'll have met with April by then. She, Tyler, and I, have a lot to talk about. Eventually, we'll get around to discussing her real father. I expect Jett to come to California and meet with us."

"You can't be serious. What if he refuses?"

"He won't."

The waitress returns with the check, and I sit with my mind reeling. There are so many questions I want to ask Lynzee. How long did she and Jett date? Why did they break up? Why didn't she ever tell me about them? Did our mother know? Then it hit me. Mama had to know. Why didn't she tell me?

In truth, I don't want to know the answers to these questions. Truth hurts, and my mind is still in denial. Lynzee has no proof that she and Jett had sex. But the proof is the child, isn't it?

"Lynzee. I have a solution. I need to see the child for myself. I want to talk to her before I tell Jett."

"No." She picks up the check and grabs her purse. "You do what I ask, or I'll have to resort to Plan B."

My heart is leaping. She's thought this shit out. She already knew what I'd say. *Ain't that a bitch?*

I follow behind her to the cash register and wait while she pays the bill. When she finishes, she heads out into the concourse.

"What's Plan B?" I ask timidly.

"If you don't tell Jett, I will." She walks away and leaves me with my mouth hanging open.

3

I move through my small world as if I'm on remote control. I can't write. I can't look Jett in the face, and I can't make idle conversation with my twin sons.

I find myself doing deep soul searching. I've got to think about my possible courses of action and their ramifications. At my very core, I want to confront Jett, go off on him, cuss his ass out, yet something holds me back. I think I'm afraid of losing Jett.

In my mind, I am going over every day of Lynzee's and my life back in 1975. I can remember most of her friends, and I thought I knew all of her loves. I tagged along after her so much, I thought she'd get sick of me, but she didn't—until that one time, when Lynzee was crying nonstop. She had started dating this college dude in January, and wouldn't tell me his name. I remember that she gave up her virginity to him. He was on the basketball team. I was only thirteen then and didn't realize the seriousness of her actions.

They dated for several months and then he broke it off with her. I remember the conversation well. We were in the kitchen. I was washing dishes. Lynzee was on the phone.

I heard her say, "You're not serious!" Pause. "No, please don't," she begged. Another pause, this time longer. She dropped to the floor and covered her eyes. "Please. I deserve another chance." Pause. "I'm begging you. Please don't let it end this way." There was another pause, and then I heard her scream. She hung up the phone, began crying profusely, and ran upstairs. I ran upstairs, too, but she made me get out. I remember her crying all night long.

Now I wonder, was that Jett she was talking to? Had he been that cruel to her? Then I remember Jett told me that he played basketball in college.

I remember that Lynzee went missing for a few months in her freshman year of college. She didn't tell my mom and me where she was going; only that she needed some time to herself. She said she didn't realize that college would be so stressful. Looking back, that must have been when she gave birth to her daughter.

I catch myself feeling sorry for Lynzee. Then I think, why should I care? The horny bitch probably deserved every heartache she got.

But why did they break up? Lynzee didn't say why their relationship ended, and now the why is killing me. She said that I was Jett's second choice, but if my memories are correct, that can't be true. He'd broken up with her long before he and I got together. As far as I'm concerned, Lynzee is lying.

I think back to our early childhood. We had a few fist fights, which, up until I turned twelve, Lynzee usually won. I guess the sibling rivalry started when I was a child. I was a straight A student and Lynzee was just an average student, making Bs and Cs. She hated the praise our mother always lavished on me. Moreover, Lynzee was the attractive child, so in an effort to compensate, my mother dressed me better. Lynzee was always jealous of the pretty clothes I wore. My mother felt I needed the edge.

Even so, we were close. When she wasn't putting me in my place, Lynzee always looked out for me. To this day, she still tries to maintain the role of "the big sister." Never in a million years would I think I'd be confronted with an issue like this. Lynzee has a daughter by my husband? I don't want to believe it.

I think about Lynzee's recent demands that I stop writing under my maiden name. I truly believe she's jealous that I'm a writer too. She wants to see my career fail. Have I been blind to my sister's true feelings about me? Jett has told me she can't stand that we've been married for so long. Does she just want my life? Is her jealousy so deep that she would make up a story as preposterous as this?

For the next few days, I watch every move Jett makes. I even watch him when he's sleeping. I can't sleep. I'm deeply depressed. I feel all alone. I can only reminisce about the bad old days and see ugly pictures inside of my head. Jett really has a temper, and although he's never hit me, I don't want to think of how he'll react if I confront him. If Lynzee is lying, will he be angry at me for believing such a negative story about him? And if he truly does have a daughter he doesn't know about, will he be angry that I didn't tell him as soon as I knew?

Is my marriage over? Who is Jett? Is he the cruel lover who hurts virgins and casts them aside, or is he the kind and benevolent man that I've learned to love? Do I even know my husband?

I toss and turn all night, unable to decide what I should do.

4

As if all the drama in my personal life isn't bad enough, I receive a call from my agent, Arlene Meeks, that throws me for a loop. "Gene liked this proposal much better than the others. He made an offer."

Gene Sloan is my editor at Mitchell and Montague.

My heart feels like it's going to burst. "Tell me!" I say like a real smartass.

"Fifty thousand."

I have no heart, I have no soul. I feel like I've been raped. A part of me feels like I'm dying. "He can't be serious. They pay first-time authors more than that."

Arlene is serious as hell. "Not anymore they don't. That's it, Charity. I'm sorry."

"But why? You said that he liked my story."

"Yes, but their argument is that your sales are down and you haven't earned out your advance on your last five books. They're not willing to spend that much money on you again until you prove yourself."

I can't speak. I only envision the bank foreclosing on my home. With Mitchell's pitiful offer, I can't pay my house notes, I can't pay my car notes, I can't pay my housekeeper, I can't buy clothes, and I can't take a vacation. What in the hell am I going to do?

"If I were you, I'd take it," Arlene says. "I've been checking around, and I don't think any publisher is willing to shell out another million dollars for your work right now."

Damn is she blunt.

"What about self-publishing?" I ask nervously.

"I wouldn't. But can you afford it anyway? Do you have about forty grand lying around?"

"Hell no."

"Then take it."

I am humbled beyond words. How am I ever going to face my husband and kids? How are they going to feel about me when I tell them that we're going to have to move? "I'll take it, Arlene. Call me back and tell me what happens."

Not an hour later, Arlene calls me back. "Charity, this is going to hurt like hell. I'm sorry, honey, really sorry. I don't know how to say this—"

"Arlene, will you stop stuttering and tell—?" I stop. Suddenly, I'd rather be horsewhipped than hear the rest. My heart is in knots, and I feel like knocking my computer off of my desk.

"It's no deal. Gene said that Mitchell and Montague don't want to sign you after all. For any amount of money."

"Why?"

"They say that you're difficult to work with. You're too much of a diva."

"That's not true and you know it."

My tears are like syrup streaming down my cheeks. I can't speak. My hands are shaking like an addict's when I hang up the phone. I feel so alone, isolated from life.

I want a drink. I want to get sloppy drunk and pass out. I want to forget that I ever dreamed of becoming a writer. I want to forget that I'm now considered a failure. I don't want pity from my husband and my sons.

I get a call from my friend Herman, who's a mortician. He's also what some people nowadays might call my "gay husband." When he's not at work, he loves to hang out with me. We've been friends since I moved to Memphis. Jett isn't crazy about him for some reason. He says there's just something about him that doesn't feel right. I think Jett is just jealous of all the time I spend with my friend. Either way, Herman doesn't come to our house very often.

"Hey, what's up, Charity?"

"Life and all of its problems. I can't seem to get a publishing contract. I can't understand what's happening. My work is good. I know it is."

"It's not your work. It's something or someone else that's stopping you from getting a contract."

"Do you know something, Herman? Tell me."

"You're not going to like this, but I heard that you've been blacklisted."

"What the hell!"

"I got this from a good source, so trust that this is true."

"Blacklisted! Dammit, by who?"

"Your old agent."

"Oh no, not Hilda."

"Yes. And you're not going to like this, but rumor is that Lynzee was involved in it too."

I think about it. Herman is an avid reader, and his former college frat brother/roommate is an editor at Simon and Schuster, who keeps him up on the publishing industry scoop. First Jett and Lynzee's alleged baby, now the blacklisting. I never had any inclination that Lynzee could be such a cold-hearted bitch. Obviously, I don't know my sister as well as I thought I did. She's nothing less than a she-devil, inflicting pain on family because she's so miserable.

Suddenly, my heart is on fire. I feel faint, like I'm having an out-of- body experience. Herman keeps talking, but my mind has tuned him out. Does Lynzee really hate me that much? Does she feel that threatened by my writing? Is she trying to ruin me so she can get back with Jett and they can be a happy family with their daughter?

5

I decide that the smart thing to do is call a private investigator. One, I want to know if there is a child, and if so, is this Jett's child? Two, I want some information on Lynzee. Did she blacklist me? If so, how? Sitting in my office at my desk, I pick up the telephone book. I flip through the pages until I find what I need. I check out the big and small ads. Then I spot one that says "Budget." Lord knows that I don't have too much money, but it's something that has to be done. I dial the number.

"Hello?" the man asks.

"Hello. My name is Charity Evans. I'm looking for an investigator, but I'm kinda short on cash."

"I'm Winston Norman. Please give me an overview about your problem, and then we can talk about costs."

"Well, my problem began back in 1975. . . ." For the next fifty minutes, I tell him as much as I know about Lynzee and Jett. Then I tell him about a child that was born as a result of their relationship, possibly in North Carolina, when Lynzee was in college.

"This sounds like quite a quandary. Tell you what. Can you come down to my office?"

"Yes. What time?" I check my watch. It's 1:15 P.M.

"How about four?"

"Can you give me a clue as to how much this might cost me?"

"We'll discuss that when you get here. Don't worry. I handle cases like this all the time and my clients are very happy with the results."

"Okay. I'll be there at four."

I'm so nervous when I walk up the steps to Winston's office. My hands and face are sweating like mad. When I reach the door, I knock. He buzzes me in.

I extend my hand. "Mr. Norman?"

"Yes, please follow me." He leads me into his small office and asks me if I would like any coffee. I decline. The room is done up in various shades of brown, with dusty files on the floor and desk. The space reeks of cigar smoke.

I take a seat. "I hope you can help me."

Winston leans back in his chair. "I made a few calls before you came. I've got a constituent in North Carolina that can do some snooping around for me. That'll save me the cost of flying down there myself."

"Is this guy reliable?" I hold my purse to my chest.

"Yes. I've known Ralph for over ten years. You'd be surprised how hard he'll work for five hundred dollars."

"That's my concern, Mr. Norman. How much is this going to cost me?"

"I'll need you to write me a check for twenty-five hundred. That's enough for two weeks' work. I believe we should have all of the information you need by then."

"Wow. Two weeks?"

"Guaranteed. I've been in this business for over twenty-five years. Trust me. Your case isn't all that unusual."

I open my purse and retrieve my checkbook. I fight back tears as I write out the check. This could be the end of my marriage, and it all comes down to a lousy twenty-five hundred bucks. If only I could find the courage to confront Jett; then I could save this money, but I feel so threatened I go ahead and pay this man. Meantime, I'm hoping against hope that this isn't his child.

I hand him the check and stand. "You'll keep me informed with your progress?"

"Absolutely. I aim to please." He smiles and I notice brown teeth and an overbite.

"You're sure about the two weeks?"

"Ma'am, I'd stake my reputation on it." He shakes my hand. "Now, let me do my job. I'll have some news for you in a couple of days." He lights up a Black and Mild cigar and the small room fills with smoke.

I wave away the smoke. "I'll wait for your call. Good-bye, Mr. Norman."

I leave. Once outside the door, I rest my back against it and close my eyes. I want to cry out to my mother. I want to slap Lynzee's face. I want to spit in Jett's face. In a matter of days, my entire life could change. What I don't know is what in the hell I'm going to do about it. Part of me is wavering, wondering if I even want to save my marriage considering the state it's in.

Jett was born in Corinth, Mississippi. You know, the sovereign state that has more dirt roads than paved ones and not an office building in the downtown area that's higher than three stories. He is an old-school Southern soul that believes he's a woman's dream. Initially, I bought into this assessment of his self-worth, but now I'm not so sure. I slave like Celie in *The Color Purple* to keep him satisfied. Am I happy? Who in this world is truly happy? What is happy? Does anyone really know? I sure as hell don't know.

What I do know is that I wouldn't be dealing with any of this if it weren't for my jealous bitch of a sister. I consider again that maybe Lynzee's playing some kind of sick joke and all of this will blow over. After all, she's never even met the child—if there is one.

Even if the private investigator finds out that Lynzee did have a child and put it up for adoption, I don't have to believe that the child is Jett's. Why should I? Lynzee has always been a shit stirrer. On the other hand, if he finds out that this is Jett's child, is the love for my children, my home, and Jett enough to withstand such a betrayal? Can I face this child and welcome her into our home with open arms?

I have to say no. I'm hurting too deeply. I'm embarrassed be-yond words. How would I ever tell my sons that they suddenly have a sister—who is also their cousin? Did Jett realize that his selfish actions would one day come back to haunt his family forever?

6

In an effort to save our marriage, I convince Jett to apply for a home equity loan from Hallmark Bank, enough to last us for almost two years. Hopefully I will get a new contract before then.

Unfortunately, Hallmark doesn't approve our loan. That same day, Jett states emphatically that we should be putting the house on the market. I don't agree. The tension between us is terrible. Is this the penalty I get for not telling Jett the truth about his alleged daughter? I don't want to do it because it will upset our lives more than they already are. Should I tell him and get it over with, or should I stall?

To my dismay and heartache, I hear back from the private investigator. He learned that Lynzee stayed at Churchill's Girls' Home. It's a facility that houses unwed mothers. She lived there for five months, from January to May, had a daughter, whom she ultimately gave up for adoption. She then went back to Chapel Hill in North Carolina and continued her studies.

It hurt to hear the truth, but I had to know. Still, there was nothing linking Jett to the child—that is, until I saw the pictures of April that Winston sent me. I fall to my knees. It's even worse than I imagined. She looks just like Jett chewed her up and spit her out! She could be his female mirror. As far as I am concerned, these pictures are proof of Jett's complicity.

Hurt and angry, I make a decision. I'm going to keep this information to myself. There's no reason to let Lynzee or Jett know that I know the truth. After all, I need to protect my sons from this farce. I try to convince myself that Jett will not want to be bothered by this turn of events. April could have children, and I know that Jett is too vain to admit that he could be someone's grandfather. Maintaining my marriage and family takes priority over a mistake that happened more than thirty years ago. Silence is my salvation. Ignorance is my middle name. To my advantage, Lynzee has not followed up with her threat to tell Jett—so far.

Lynzee hasn't gone forth with Plan B because she's facing some type of health challenge, At this point, she hasn't shared with me what it is. I'm just grateful for the reprieve.

In addition, Winston has given me the low-down on the blacklisting fiasco. My second agent, Krystal Collier, and Lynzee both colluded to make my name mud. They called every reputable agent in New York and California and told them that I was a bitch to work with and a closet alcoholic. They told the agents that I was loaded on Crown Royal when I did the editing on my manuscripts, and that's why they had so many errors. In turn, each agent said that they would call the editors that they were tight with and tell them that they should treat me as if I had the bubonic plague. Finally, they told the agents that my last five books didn't earn out my advance and they would be losing money on me if they offered me a lucrative contract.

I was outdone with this information. I didn't know that two people felt so much hatred for me in this free world. I didn't know that I was of that much importance to any sane soul. Is it any wonder that finding out this information would give me the biggest craving for a drink that I'd had in years?

But I won't give in. I'm going to sell my new book if I have to walk on burning coals and drink jalapeno water. I'll be damned if my career is over.

I can't decide if I'm going to confront my old agent and Lynzee or not. I also can't work up the nerve to tell Jett the truth about my career or the truth about April. In the meantime, I decide I better use what my mama gave me to keep Jett from selling our house.

Like an entranced feline ready to pounce on her prey, I wait for Jett to come out of the shower. I admire his wet, naked body as he skillfully towels himself off.

I lie in the bed, plotting, planning on how I will seduce my man and get what I need. I reach over on the nightstand and turned on a Barry White CD. When Barry's sexy voice wafts through the bedroom, Jett enters right on cue. I wink at him and turn off the television set.

"You have something planned, baby?" he asks as he slips between the sheets.

"I don't have to plan to make love to my husband. I just do it." I kiss him boldly on the lips. He faces me and caresses my face and lips.

"Aren't you tired? We've had a busy day today."

I put a finger against his lips. "Shhhh. Let's not talk about nonsense. I need you to show me how much you need me."

Jett pushes his hands between my thighs and sees that I am already lubricated. "Damn, you're hot." I can feel his smile.

"Why, thank you, darling."

Slowly, his lips come down on mine, until they brush. Just barely touch. That one point of light friction is more of a tease than a kiss, and I love every second of it. I raise my head and loop my arms around his neck to draw him closer to me, lips and tongue, warm flesh to hot heat. In the darkness, I can still see that he has that look, the one that could melt wax. Predatory. He has me then. He knows it and I know it.

He caresses my body like Casanova's ghost. It is a cyclone of hot breath on naked skin, hot breath and warm kisses in all the right places. I arch my back and let his wet fingers perform their magic.

"Tell me that you want it."

I stall and reach for him down low. I begin a symphonic stanza on his pulsating member, until I feel the warm fluid melt against my fingers. Ahhh. "I want you, sweetheart."

Just as I am about to make my move, Jett rolls on top of me.

I wiggle and wiggle my buttocks until I leverage myself to be on top. I laugh.

"I'm running this show tonight, mister."

He is about to laugh too when I begin rolling my hips in a way that pops his eyes out of his sockets. He gets serious.

"Show me what you got, baby."

I ease him slowly inside of me and suck in my breath. I begin to ride him like the best rodeo rider in Texas. I can hear his heavy breathing. The harder he breathes, the more he turns me on. My timing is perfect. My hips roll like they've been oiled. Sweat coats our bodies like diamond dust. When I know he is ready, I suck in my breath even deeper and call on my pussy muscles to suck the life out of him. Even though my legs are beginning to feel numb, I don't lessen my pace. I can feel him stiffen. I have him.

"That's it. Fuck me. Fuck me," he says.

I know it is mere seconds before he or I will sizzle and melt. I come first. He follows two seconds later. I fall on top of him, breathing like a banshee.

We lie there for what seems like an eternity, until our breathing calms. Finally, I roll over and lie on my back.

The final treat for Jett is to clean him off with soapy hot water. I go into the bathroom and retrieve a cloth. I soap it with hot water and ease back into the bedroom. By the way he is breathing, I can tell his eyes are closed and he is relaxed. I take my time cleansing and massaging him.

"How do you feel?"

"Like the luckiest man in the world."

I rise, and come back to rinse him off twice. I cleanse myself and get back into bed. I can hear him lightly snoring. I nudge his shoulder. "Baby . . ."

"Hmm. What?"

"You want to keep your wife happy so that I can keep making you happy, don't you?" I kiss his neck.

"You know I do, baby."

"We've got to get to the bank and apply for a new loan." I kiss him on the lips. "It's important to me, sweetheart."

"I know."

"Can we go tomorrow? I can call in the morning and make an appointment."

"Okay." He pats my buttocks. "Now let me get some sleep, baby."

"All right." I pull up the sheet and tuck it around his shoulders, then give him a kiss on the ear. "Sleep tight, sweetie."

I lie on my back with my arms folded beneath my head. I smile to myself. Yep. That did it. After tonight, there's no way that I'm putting this house up for sale. No fucking way. I turn on my right side and wrap my arm across Jett's waist. When I fall asleep, there's a smile on my face a mile wide.

I knew I've only momentarily sidetracked my husband's demand to sell the house, but the bitch in me ain't worried about shit.

We apply at Signature Bank, where we have another account. They turn us down. We are, in fact, turned down by several banks, which will ultimately make us late on our mortgage payments. I try to hide this from Jett. If he finds out, he'll be furious. He lets me handle all the finances, and up until recently, I was a pretty good money manager. But like the old adage, you can't get blood out of a turnip.

I am tempted to ask Jett to pawn his prized 1966 convertible Mustang. This morning I called the pawnshop. He can get at least fifteen thousand dollars for it. Then I stop myself. I can't believe I'm that desperate.

Finally, we get a call from Consumers Bank. "Mrs. Evans, my name is Dion Hill. I have good news. My manager at Consumers approved the loan for ninety thousand dollars."

"Thanks, Mr. Hill."

"No, thank you. We welcome clients like you and Mr. Evans."

"I'm so pleased, as well as relieved. Are there any stipulations to the loan?" I ask.

"No, except, of course, that you're not late with your payments."

"Don't worry, Mr. Hill. All of our payments will be on time. And when I receive a new contract, I'm hoping we can continue doing business. Mr. Evans and I are hoping to build a pool on our property, and we hope that Consumers will finance the loan."

"We'd love to do business with you. Just give me a call whenever you're ready."

"Thanks, Mr. Hill. Good-bye." I hang up the phone smiling. I knew a bank would give us an equity loan. I can't understand why Jett was so worried.

Now that I will have this loan to pay back, it's even more urgent for me to get a new book contract. I know I can do it, but I need to buy some time. I must keep Jett satisfied so he'll stop talking about selling our house. I decide to turn on the charm. I seduce Jett every day for a week and don't mention money or writing. I wake him up in the middle of the night and make him believe that making love is all his idea. By day eight he's worn out and ready to talk. Reluctantly, he agrees to give me a year. If my novel doesn't sell by then, I promise him that we'll sell the house.

7

"We need to send your novel to a book doctor," Arlene tells me when I finish it. It's the first week of December, cold as hell outside and inside of this house. I'm really not in the mood for bullshit. "If you don't, it's never going to sell. All of the editors are saying the same thing: the book needs doctoring. I've e-mailed you the names of three book doctors who I believe will do a good job. It's your choice."

Within days, I contact all three. I settle on the one who impresses me the most over the phone. Her name is Kate Connley. I tell her I'll get in touch with her again soon.

Even though I know better, I think about phoning Lynzee. We haven't spoken since June, when she dropped the bomb on me about Jett's daughter. I'm still afraid she'll tell Jett, and a little baffled that she hasn't done it yet. Maybe that's a good sign; maybe it means she doesn't intend to follow through with her threats.

And then there's the issue of the blacklisting. I hate to believe that she's so intimidated by my writing, but with Lynzee, anything is possible. Still, I'm desperate for a contract, and she knows the industry. Her advice could help put me over the top. I want to believe that her sisterly love for me will trump our other problems. Instincts warn me to be cautious, but I go with my heart and call her. She can't be guilty of the blacklisting, she just can't be.

"Lynzee, I could really use your help," I say humbly.

"Have you told Jett about April?"

"No."

"Why not?"

"Look. Stop bugging me," I say, finding my backbone. "I'll get to it when I get to it." It kills me to ask, but I say, "Have you met with her yet?" In my mind's eye, I can envision this girl: at least five-foot-ten, chocolate-colored skin tone, thin eyebrows and lashes, full lips, and Indian cheekbones.

"No, I haven't. She's been in the hospital with a bout of pneumonia. We plan on getting together when she's better."

Thank God. That gives me a little more time. "In the meantime, I still need your help."

"Oh." I can almost see the scowl on her face. Her tone is like a boss to his secretary. "Tell me what you need."

Here goes. "Can you recommend a good book doctor?"

"Why?"

I knew she was going to ask that question. Right then I know she wants to shout to the world that her little sister is an imposter, that I can't write to save my sons' life. She wants to tell the world that I don't deserve the millions of dollars that Mitchell and Montague paid me.

"Arlene submitted my book to my publisher and they turned it down." I don't want to tell her that my book is being shopped all over New York. It is really none of her damn business.

"Oh," is all she says. I could slap the bitch.

On average, book doctors in New York demand between five and fifty thousand dollars for their work. Two of my previous books needed book doctors. I shelled out more than thirty-five grand, but didn't need one for my last three books.

I give her Kate Connley's name. Lynzee says that she's heard of her. Of course she has. She knows everybody.

"She's white, Charity. Do you want your book to sound like a black person wrote it or a white person did?"

"You know that I want my work to sound like a sister wrote it," I challenge.

"I know the perfect editor," Lynzee says, her voice lifting.

"We've been friends for almost twenty years. I'll call her and see if she's busy. If she's not, I'll ask her to give you a call."

"You're not talking about Zedra, are you?" Zedra is Lynzee's best friend. She's a writer, too, but hasn't enjoyed the success that Lynzee has.

"No. Just be patient. This woman's work is top-notch and she's in high demand. It'll be a miracle if she's even available."

A warning bell should be going off, I suppose, but I decide to take her recommendation. When I tell him about it, Jett cautions me that I am making a mistake trusting Lynzee. I'm wondering if he's merely acting like he hates Lynzee. Maybe in truth he still wants her. After all, they had a child together.

"Why shouldn't I trust my sister, Jett? Do you know something that I don't?"

For a moment, he can't look me in the eye. "I'm just saying that Lynzee can't be trusted. She's always been jealous of you and you know it."

"What are you really trying to say?"

"Forget it. Don't let me be the one to come between you two."

I want to be blunt. I want to ask him about his sexual liaison with Lynzee. But I don't. I'm human. I'm also a coward, and time is running out. Sooner or later Lynzee and April will meet, and then who knows what will happen.

For the next week, Jett and I avoid each other. I feel that we both have more that we want to say, but neither wants to be the one to rock the boat. We used to be able to get over little arguments like this pretty quickly, but it seems like lately, neither one of us is willing to forgive the other. I know where my anger is coming from, but I wonder about Jett. Is his anger really about me trusting Lynzee, or is it something deeper pulling us apart? Each day, the tension between us builds.

By day six, Jett is apparently horny. That night, he doesn't speak, doesn't kiss me or hug me. He merely turns me over to my side and does his business. I'm so turned off, I'm stiff as an ironing board, but he manages to get off anyway. Afterward, he grumbles something inaudible and turns over to his side. Seconds later, he's asleep. I just stare at him. I'm hurt that he used me this way. I'm angry that he thinks that we don't need to talk this mess out. If he thinks the situation will work itself out, he's wrong. I'm not putting my career on the back burner for anything. If that means I have to deal with my sister, then so be it. He can accept it or go to hell.

When the editor calls, we hit it off immediately. Her name is Shirley Berry. I e-mail the book to her, and she reads it twice before she calls me back.

"I love the theme of your book, Charity. And I can really identify with the main character."

"Thanks, Shirley." She's probably just stroking me so that I'll give her the job.

But before I can get too euphoric, she hits me with the fee: $25,000. I am shocked shitless, but I have no options. I have only seven months left before the money runs out on our equity loan.

"Remember, Shirley, I don't need a ghost writer to totally rewrite my book. I only need an editor to make better transitions and line edit my writing."

"I'm following you, Charity,"

"Good. I want my book to sound like I wrote it."

"That's my goal."

"Good. And you say that you only need six weeks to finish the manuscript?"

"Yes. I flipped through it, and I don't foresee too many problems. Remember, I do this type of work all of the time. You'd be surprised how many big-name authors I've helped."

"I probably would. Just please give me the same quality of work that you gave them, and I'll be one happy writer."

"No problem. I'll call you in a few weeks." She hangs up.

I need money so bad right now I don't want to wait another day to sell my book.

Shirley ends up taking nine weeks. Before she mails the manuscript back to me, she tells me that she is confident that the book will sell.

As it turns out, the editing is horrendous. I nearly lose it when I see what she's done. There are so many grammatical errors, as well as misspellings and numerous inconsistencies. A five-year-old could have done a better job. On top of that, the ending makes no sense at all. The main character left her home twice in the same scene. I did not tell her to change the ending. How could a reputable editor do such an unprofessional job on my book? I am dumbstruck. I know that there is no way that I can turn the book in to my agent in its present state.

I have a deadline. Only three days remain before my agent is supposed to read the revised version. I wake up with the birds. I work nearly twenty hours a day until I revamp the manuscript.

Ultimately, it's a complete waste of time, and twenty-five thousand dollars. As much as I try to ignore what seems obvious, I can't. Has Lynzee done this to me on purpose? Did she know in advance that Shirley was going to sabotage my book and I wouldn't be able to sell it? Only the Lord knows.

Arlene calls me. "Hello, Charity,"

"Hey."

"I don't know how to say this, but the book was turned down by several editors."

"Why?"

"They feel that the characters aren't fleshed out well enough, and the ending seems rushed."

"Damn, Arlene, I did the best I could under the circumstances. I told you what happened."

"Yes. What a waste of money. I can try a couple more editors, but from the feedback I'm getting, it's really useless."

"Wow. I'm embarrassed and hurt. I shouldn't have trusted my sister to get me a good editor."

"I'm going to stay out of that one."

"I don't blame you. Just know that I haven't given up. I'm going to start on another book right away, and this time I won't need a book doctor."

After I call Lynzee and admit that my book is rejected, I tell her I want my money back from her friend. She quickly gets defensive.

"Charity, I spoke to Shirley while she was editing your book. It needed a ton of work. Your characters all sounded exactly alike."

"I told Shirley not to talk to anyone about my book."

"That didn't mean me."

"In my book it did."

"Nevertheless, you handed Shirley a book that she wasn't able to fix. It would have taken her three months to rewrite that novel."

"I didn't ask her to rewrite it, just edit it."

"You should just face the facts, Charity. You're not a very good writer. Shirley said as much."

"That bitch! How dare she discuss my writing abilities with you?"

"Like I said, we're friends. Maybe you should try going back to being a makeup artist. I hear that movie stars pay up to ten thou—"

"Fuck you, Lynzee. I'm not doing that shit again."

"Well, you were good at it."

"I'm a writer, Lynzee. If Shirley were that good, why hasn't she written a book herself?"

"She has."

"I've never heard of her."

"Like you, she wrote under her maiden name. The sales were good."

"Then why did she screw up my book?"

"Shirley didn't screw up your book. You did."

"You're going to take your friend's side over mine?" I feel my anger rising.

"I trust Shirley."

"Then fuck you and Shirley." I hang up.

It hurts me to know that my sister can be so cruel. It saddens me to believe that she is so resentful of me. Does she want me to lose my lifestyle? My home? My husband?

* * *

I receive a large envelope in the mail from Lynzee. I haven't spoken to her since our fight about the editor. What does this bitch want now?

I'm stunned when I open it and find that she's mailed me a picture of her and April. I guess it's her way of telling me they've finally met. Perhaps it's a warning that my time is running out to tell Jett what I know. Just like the picture from the private investigator, this one leaves no doubt in my mind. April looks more like my husband than Javed and Jamone do.

"Did you tell him yet?" Lynzee says when she follows up the picture with a call.

"Lynzee, I need more time."

"Why?"

"Because this could end my marriage. Is that what you want to happen?"

She hesitates for a moment. "No."

"Then . . ." I start crying. "Then give me some respect. I know my man, and I know when to talk to him about something like this."

"You're stalling."

"No, I'm not."

Every time I think about having a heart-to-heart with Jett, it seems to be bad timing. Since our money is running short, he had to start a new job. He hasn't worked in years, and he is exhausted every night. This is really the wrong time to talk about an illegitimate child. And again, I know my weakness. I really don't want to know the truth. I don't believe that I can stand the lurid details.

Tears sneak into my voice. "Jett's going to hate me for keeping this from him."

"That's not my fault." Her tone is curt.

"No? Then whose is it?"

"Ask your husband. He's the one who didn't wear a condom."

I clamp my hands over my ears. I don't need to hear this, nor do I need to visualize them being together. Right now, I hate both of them for creating this situation. "That's too much information, Lynzee."

"My bad." She sounds like she's about to laugh.

In my mind, I see Jett packing his bags. I see him calling me a bitch and then slamming the door in my face. My heart aches at the thought. "I need a little more time, Lynzee."

"How much time?"

I can't help it; I break down in tears. "I just need . . . I just need another . . . month. Then I'll tell him." My tears are flowing freely and my words are thick. "I promise."

"Fine, you've got a month. Then no more excuses." She disconnects the call without a good-bye.

I crumple over into a small heap on my desk and have a good old cry. I know that I can't take too much more of this. Telling Jett will mean that there will be an ultimatum. Will I be willing to file for a divorce if he insists on making this niece/ cousin/ daughter/she-devil a part of our family?

8

Up to this point, Jett hasn't bothered to tell me how much he hates his job as a car salesman. Now he decides to tell me about the politics of the business, the sales managers giving certain salespeople the house deals and so forth. I had no idea. I don't know diddly-squat about the inner workings of a car dealership.

"Those sons of bitches are giving me ulcers," Jett shouts one evening when he comes home from work. He removes his tie and stalks into our bedroom.

"What's wrong, Jett?"

"My sales manager cut my deal in half. The whole deal was mine." He walks into the closet and begins to remove his work clothes.

I don't know what to say. I know he's pissed. I'm waiting for him to put on his exercise clothes and rush downstairs, but he doesn't. He stands there in his skivvies and scowls at me.

"Charity, why can't you find a job?"

Honestly, I'd never thought about it. But what absolutely crucifies me is the look on his face when he says, "I knew this would happen." He means that I've gotten us into too much debt.

Do I have what it takes to fight back? To redeem myself in my husband's eyes? My ego won't admit that I'm on a roller coaster ride to hell and don't know how to push the stop button. Lord knows, I do not wish to see the devil anytime soon.

I ask myself the question that my deceased mother would ask me: "What are you made of?"

My answer would be, "Premium stock."

"Well, by God," she'd say, "show me."

Charity, why can't you get a job? Those seven words that Jett uttered are my call to action. They challenge me, give me a reality check. They force me to come to terms with my situation and realize since I had such a huge hand in creating this predicament, I need to play a part in resolving it.

The same night, I have a conference with my sons. I admit to them that I'm planning to look for a job. When they get over their shock, they say they have a friend who will be able to help me write a resume.

The friend turns out to be Jamone's girlfriend, Holly. She agrees to come over the following day. With Javed and Jamone's input, we work for six hours, until we feel we have it perfected. Thankfully, Holly won't accept any money, since I don't have any to give her anyway.

The following day, I log on to several online employment sites. Then I fax my resume and cover letters to more than seventy-five companies. Preferably, I hope to find a job as a writer at a newspaper or magazine. I can see Lynzee's finger wagging at me when I apply for a creative writing teacher's position.

"You've got some nerve," I can hear her criticizing. "If you didn't send your books to a book doctor, you wouldn't get published. You don't even have a degree in English, creative writing, or journalism. How in the hell do you expect to teach a class about the mechanics of writing when you don't even understand them yourself?"

With my maverick attitude, I would look at that efficacious heffa and say, "Fuck you, Lynzee. A published author doesn't need a degree to teach, and I do know good fiction when I read it. I also love people, and I know that with my enthusiasm, I'd make a great teacher."

My cockiness doesn't abate when I apply for jobs as a manager or an assistant. I don't qualify for a lot of the positions because I don't have a degree. Over the past twenty-five years, I have only taken English and literature classes and have about forty-seven credits. I can't stand math or science, so the likelihood of earning a bachelor's degree is slim to none.

While I wait to hear from employers, the twins and I begin to pack up the house. It is an endeavor that I never want to repeat. We're running out of cash and might be forced to sell the house. I pray on my knees nightly that I won't have to give up my home. It's been my dream since I was fourteen years old.

Jett's experience at the car dealership is getting better. His sales have improved from five cars a month to nine. He's even received a $1200 bonus for selling five F-150s in two weeks.

Jett decides to celebrate. He offers to take the twins and me out to dinner. This is a real treat for Jett because he doesn't think anyone can cook better than I can, and rarely wants to frequent a restaurant.

Back home in Detroit, where we lived for the first part of our marriage, Jett and I would on occasion dine out at Steve's Soul Food Restaurant. They served excellent food that even the mayor bragged about. In my opinion, finding that type of quality soul food in Memphis is an arduous task. I can't think of one that's as classy as Steve's. That said, we settle on Bonefish Grill, a very popular seafood restaurant.

"I have your table ready for you now," the waiter says after an hour.

The instant we are seated, I spot an acquaintance of mine, Elizabeth Spherion, three tables away. She owns a local magazine, *Queen*. While Jett and the twins are checking out the menu, Elizabeth and I chat. I want to hit her up for a job at her magazine, but I can't bring myself to ask. She's always been a bit of a gossip, and I don't want her broadcasting that I'm basically broke.

"When's your next book coming out, Charity? I'd love to do an article on you."

"Maybe next year," I say in a hopeful tone.

"Good. Say, have you forgotten about calling Lynzee for me?

You promised me that you'd ask her about attending the Women's Sisterhood Convention this fall."

I feel like a total hypocrite. "Excuse me, Elizabeth. Jett's waving me over. The waiter is there to take our order." I leave, telling her I'll call her soon.

"Mom?" Jamone asks. "Isn't that Ms. Spherion from *Queen Magazine*?"

"Yes," I say, taking a seat.

"Word. That's dope. Can't you ask her to do a feature about me and Javed? We could really use the publicity for our artwork."

"Yeah, Mom," Javed presses. "Getting a feature in her magazine could possibly get us some sponsors. Can you feel me?"

My smile is weak when I say, "Okay. I'll try."

Jett cocks an eyebrow at me and I immediately know that he knows what I am thinking. When you ask for favors, you have to return one. What do I have to offer Elizabeth? Maybe I can suggest a story about starving artists who've lost everything they owned. Or maybe she'd like to hear about a sister having a baby by her sister's husband. I'm sure that would sell a ton of copies.

It's the annual Memphis in May, and news of the barbecue contest has been splattered all over television, especially by Al Roker on the *Today Show*, who comes to Memphis every May. People come from all around the country to sample what is reputed to be the best barbecue in the nation. Unexpectedly, Lynzee flies to Memphis to devour the barbecue and visit for three days.

Her actions keep me guessing about her intentions, because in spite of the deadline she gave me, she let it pass without a peep. I don't know what to think now that she'll be in the same city as Jett. Part of me is nervous that this might be the beginning of the end of my marriage, but I choose to live in denial. Since she hasn't told him already, I choose to believe that she won't do it now.

I'm waiting at the curb in front of American Airlines when I spot Lynzee waving at me. I have mixed emotions. Aside from the issue about Jett and April, I'm also not sure if I want to confront Lynzee about the blacklisting issue. I worry that if I piss her off, she'll finally enforce her deadline and tell Jett about his daughter. I feel stuck, like I can't go forward and, at the same time, I can't go back to the rose-colored glasses I used to wear. I'm trapped, at the mercy of my jealous sister.

I pull up, get out, and open the trunk. We hug, tentatively at first.

Lynzee says, "You look good, bitch." When we haven't seen each other in a while, we always refer to one another as bitches. Her greeting me like this now helps me relax a little. Maybe this will be a peaceful visit, like none of the past year ever happened.

I tell her, "You look good too, for a rich bitch. Been to the plastic surgeon lately?"

She hugs and kisses me. "Fuck you, Charity."

"You too," I cut back.

Neither one of us mentions April. She's in the background like a bad seed. Right now we're loving each other again, and neither one of us wants to spoil the flow. Instead, Lynzee talks about the good news in her life. Her daughter, Tyler, is waiting to hear about her scholarship from Harvard any day now.

After we gorge ourselves on dozens of barbecue plates, we talk about old times, laugh, drink tea, and shop. She buys me several outfits. Scrabble and Boggle are the games that Lynzee and I have played for years. Both of us are very competitive. I kick Lynzee's ass in Boggle, and she does the same to me in Scrabble.

"I can see that the twins and Jett are doing well, but how about you? How are you feeling?"

"Defeated."

"Why? What's wrong?"

"I don't want to tell Jett, but we're almost out of money."

"Didn't you get an equity loan?"

"Yes, but it's been almost a year. I thought I would've had a new contract by now."

Lynzee opens up her purse and pulls out her checkbook.

"Here," she says while she's writing. "I hope this helps. It's all I can afford right now."

She hands me a check for $20,000. I hug her. "Thanks, Lynzee."

"You're welcome. Now I need something from you."

"Name it."

"Tell Jett about April. This has gone on long enough."

We both look up when we hear the shuffling of feet at the back door. It's Jett.

"Hello, ladies."

"Hey, Jett," Lynzee says and stands to give him a hug.

Inside, I'm cringing. He kisses my forehead and asks, "Why are you two looking so serious?"

Before I can open my mouth to tell a lie, Lynzee speaks up. "We were talking about Charity's writing contract."

Jett puts his hand on my shoulder. "Wow. So, you've got a contract, honey?"

"No," Lynzee interjects. "She just needs a few months to secure one. You've got faith in Charity's talents, don't you, Jett?"

"Of course I do."

"Then give her a little time. She deserves your support. After all, she's already proven that she can land a good contract." Lynzee winks at Jett. "Let her agent do her job. Charity should be getting that call anytime now. Will you give her a little time to prove herself?"

"Yes. Sure."

I cross my arms over my chest. I don't like this little scene one damn bit. How dare they speak about me as if I'm not even here? And Jett just caved in like a domesticated spouse. When Lynzee leaves, Jett and I are going to have a talk, and it's not going to be pretty.

"Why would you talk like I'm not present?" I demand as soon as Lynzee's plane lifts off the ground and we're sitting in our car at the airport.

"What are you talking about?" Jett says, looking all innocent.

"You know what I'm talking about. Don't play games with me." I know that my reaction to the scene with Lynzee has more to do with jealousy over their past relationship, but I can't tell him what I know, so instead I say, "Don't you ever pa-

tronize me again about my writing career. Do you understand?"

Jett shakes his head. "Hey, you're the one who didn't tell me
about your upcoming contract." He turns away. "That's your
dream. I've tried to be supportive."

Later that evening, I receive a call from Lynzee to let me
know she arrived home safely. "Don't forget," she says, "I still
expect you to tell Jett about his daughter."

A few days later, I call Lynzee. "I told Jett about April. He
doesn't believe it."

Lynzee believes me, even though I'm lying through my teeth.
I'll have to think of another lie when she asks me again.

When Lynzee calls one Saturday afternoon, Jett is off riding
his motorcycle and the twins are in their studio painting.

"Hey, Lynzee. It's good to hear from you. How's Tyler?" I try
to be friendly, and hope she hasn't called to start trouble.

"Giving me the blues. She and her boyfriend, Raymond, are
seeing too much of each other. The more I try to intervene, the
tighter they get."

"Oh, I'm so glad that I have boys."

"I'm calling about something else, though."

"Oh, what?" My knees are shaking. I can see Lynzee's face
glaring at me.

"I just received my royalty check from my movie. It's double
what I thought it'd be, so I put a check in the mail to you for
twenty grand."

I still can't understand her. One day she's giving me ultima-
tums that might destroy my marriage, and the next she's giving
me money. One thing about my sister: no one could ever call
her predictable.

"You didn't have to do that, Lynzee. I still have money left."

"Good. I don't want you to get broke."

"I'll pay you back."

"No need. Consider it an anniversary present."

"You remembered our anniversary?"

"Of course. It's the same day as Mom and Dad's. How could I
forget?"

It's moments like these when I regret that sometimes I talk about Lynzee behind her back. I feel like a two-faced traitor.

Lynzee even takes the time to read three of my chapters of my new book. She's never done that before. I'm confident that she's really trying to help me this time.

Then the old Lynzee resurfaces. One day, when she finishes reading the second draft of my third chapter, she says, "Charity, this chapter is horrible. There are so many mistakes, I've lost count."

"Maybe I sent you the wrong version," I offer weakly. "I'll e-mail it to you again." Before I send it, I carefully read over the pages. I find a few mistakes and resend it.

"Is this the best you can do?" she shouts in my ear after I say hello.

"What's wrong this time?" I'm starting to get angry. I'd bet my life that she hasn't found a mistake.

"You have no voice!"

"No voice?"

"You've read too many books. And by bad authors. Your writing sounds like a hodgepodge of all of them. You need your own voice."

You mean I need a voice that mirrors yours.

I'm so angry I could spit gasoline. Michael Crichton is a great author, and so are Patricia Cornwell, John Sanford, Scott Turow, and Dean Koontz. What in the hell is she talking about? Although these authors write thrillers, I feel that the pacing of their novels helps me when plotting my contemporary novels. I want my books to read like a movie reel.

I've finally had enough of her attacking my writing. I'm so sick of her sabotaging my career. I muster up the nerve to confront her. "Lynzee," I start, "I heard a rumor a while back . . ."

"Go on."

"I'm told that you and my old agent had me blacklisted. Is that true?" Tears wobble in my voice.

"How dare you ask me such a stupid question? Why would I do that?"

"Because you don't want to compete with me."

"Listen, Charity. I don't know how to break this to you, but you're not a good writer. You'll never enjoy the success that I have. I suggest you find a new career, because you'll never make it as a writer." She hangs up.

I know she's my sister, but with everything she's putting me through, I hate Lynzee. I'm going to hit that *New York Times* bestsellers list one day just to spite her. Let's let the public decide who the better author is then.

9

The twenty thousand dollars that Lynzee claimed she was going to send never arrives. We have run out of money from the first loan and desperately need another one.

"Mrs. Evans, I understand your reservations, but if I can't get your home equity loan approved, no one can."

That's exactly what the loan officer from Consumers Bank tells me. There are very few people that I dislike, and a few that I detest, mainly loan officers. I truly try not to hate people. Presently, I hate banks and bank tellers who try to smile at me when they handle my money—or lack of it. I hate broke tellers who look at my credit card being over the limit and kindly broadcast that fact loud enough so that two people behind me in line will hear.

This is so unfair.

I'm almost out of money, my marriage is a sham, and my self-esteem is lower than it has ever been in my life. I want a good marriage. I want fame. I want a seven-figure income. I want to take a vacation. Is that too much to ask for a woman who's willing to work twice as hard as anyone else to assure her success?

My heart says no, but life is telling me yes. A part of me wants to give up. I'm getting so frustrated, but the bitch in me keeps fighting. Something is warning me that if I give up, my life, my marriage, my family, and my career will be the laughing stock of the publishing industry.

I fight the urge to feel sorry for myself. I fight the urge to cry daily, and I forge ahead. I think about my late mother more and more and know that she wouldn't want me to give up.

That said, fuck Lynzee, and fuck Jett if he doesn't have my back. I deserve some respect around this camp. I pick up the phone book and get to work.

Consumers Bank is the same entity that swore they loved doing business with Jett and me. We haven't been late on a payment and still have equity in our home. So, what's the damn problem? Okay, I know we don't have a large stream of income coming in, but we can pay our bills out of the loan money. Why does it seem like no one else has faith that I'll get a new contract soon? Well, they can all go to hell, because I've paid my dues, and I know it's only a matter of time before things change and I'm on top of the publishing world again.

My forty-ninth birthday is next month, and it's going to be the first year that I won't be able to buy myself a present. Temporarily, I have put the matter of April and Jett out of my mind. We have more important issues to deal with. I've told Lynzee as much.

I told her, "He doesn't have the money for a lottery ticket, let alone an airline ticket to California to meet April."

I think I've finally figured out why Lynzee has been bugging me to tell Jett. She's always been the weak one in the family. She doesn't have the balls to tell Jett about his daughter. She wants me to do the dirty deed.

Now, Jett and I have once again applied at dozens of loan companies. Both of us have over sixty hits on our credit report. He walks around the house angry all the time, and I have to keep thinking of new and creative ways to keep him from bringing up the idea of selling the house. Some days it seems like our marriage is hanging on by a thread. I worry constantly that he's going to leave me, but then he surprises me one night.

Before we go to bed, Jett places my hands in his. "We need to talk." We sit on the bed.

"Why do you look so serious? Have I done something wrong?" I ask.

"No. It's me. I've been selfish. Charity, I don't want a divorce, now or ever. You mean the world to me. I don't care if you get a book deal. We'll work something out."

I breathe a sigh of relief. "My Lord, Jett. You had me worried. You know how stubborn you can be."

"You're right. But know this: nothing or no one will ever keep us apart. You're my soul mate, and we belong together."

"And you're my soul mate, too. I don't want or need anyone else." For a moment, I think once again about telling him about April, but something makes me hold back. I'm losing my house, I'm losing a book contract, and I'm losing my mind. I can't lose my husband, too.

He caresses my face. "Then show me."

Slowly, but deliberately, we make magical love. Afterward, we bathe and make love again in our oversized tub. By the time we make it to bed, we're both smiling and overjoyed with one another.

"I love you, Jett."

"And I love you, baby. I take one breath for me and another one for you." He wraps me in his arms and lulls me to sleep.

We finally accept the inevitable. No one will approve our loan. It doesn't matter that we have over a half a million dollars in equity. What hurt us the most are the three late payments on our mortgage that occurred twelve months earlier. I thought Jett would be furious, but he's merely perturbed.

Jett doesn't hesitate. He calls Crye-Leike Realty and puts our house on the market. "Charity," he says when I can't stop crying, "we don't have any choice. If we don't sell the house, we'll end up losing it. Is that what you want?"

"No." I keep silent as I watch him prepare to do something that I know that he hates to do: sell his Harley Davidson motorcycle so that we can pay the upcoming house notes. If we don't sell the house in six months, we'll be in foreclosure and completely out of cash.

Given our current financial straits, I find little consolation in the news reports that shout gloom and doom all over the States due to this national housing crisis. Apparently, we're not the only ones in this country facing financial shipwreck. In Memphis, people's homes are being foreclosed on, unemployment is almost thirteen percent, and the homeless rate is higher than ever.

Even so, when Jett suggests selling some of the twins' art work that we own, I refuse. I don't want to tell our sons we're in financial trouble. In truth, Jett doesn't want to sell any of their work either. He is as proud of them as I am.

One night, I find him sitting on the bed in the dark. I sit beside him and ask what's wrong. "I'm beginning to feel my age. I'm old as Chuck Berry without the guitar and dance moves."

"Hey, baby," I say, smiling and caressing his buttocks. "You still rock my world." He smiles because he's supposed to, and walks away.

I'm unable to muster the strength to put him in a better mood. The situation we're in is totally my fault. After Jett retired from Champion Motors, he hadn't worked in more than ten years. I know that he dislikes working at a car dealership at this stage of his life. It's killing him to work, and it's killing me to sell this house. I don't know which one of us is more depressed.

Our realtor, Elaine Faulkner, keeps in constant touch. Elaine is a Caucasian woman in her early sixties. She has the thickest dyed blonde hair that I've ever seen. A size ten, she's still gorgeous. She looks like she was the high school prom queen back in the day. Elaine is very spiritual and prays with Jett and me at least once a week.

Thus far, we don't have any appointments to show our home; however, Elaine informs us that she's received numerous calls inquiring about the property. Elaine explains to us that it's hard to sell a multi-million dollar home in Memphis, but with luck, we'll find a buyer, possibly one of the Memphis Grizzlies.

Even though we aren't speaking, I am tempted to call Lynzee and ask for her help again. She's got millions. Surely she can spare a few thousand. I dial the number over and over again, but keep hanging up. What if Jett and Herman are right? What if she wants me to lose everything? What if she brings up April again? How can I stall her this time?

Just like an ungrateful sister, I've forgotten about the money she gave me months earlier. I never told Jett about the money. Jett resents Lynzee as much as I do, and I don't want him to feel like he owes her anything.

Although we are nearly broke, I manage to send Tyler a birthday gift. She turned fifteen a week ago. I sent her some stationery with her name on it. I hope my small gesture will garner a call from Lynzee, but it doesn't.

My agent seems to have the perception of a tarot card reader. She seems to intuit when I'm depressed.

"I've got a suggestion," Arlene begins.

"Shoot."

"Why not write a thriller? There are very few black thriller writers."

"I love it, Arlene. Thanks."

I'm excited. I read books by Robin Cook, Steve Martini, John Sanford, and Catherine Coulter. In no time, I come up with a great concept: a female serial killer. I'm positive that this idea will work. It has to.

10

"Hello," Jett says, and then pauses as he balances the phone under his chin. "Why, hello, Lynzee."

Jett is always civil to people, no matter how he feels about them. I'm sitting in the living room watching *Nip/Tuck*. I hear Jett laugh. *What's so damn funny?* I turn the volume down so that I can hear his side of the conversation.

"Sure, the boys will love that." He pauses. "All right. I'll tell Charity. Thanks!"

My heart sinks lower than the grave. Is she finally going to tell him the truth about April?

Jett turns his back. The bastard. Are he and Lynzee having a discussion about April? My temperature rises fifteen degrees as I bide my time.

Before he hangs up, I'm standing in front of him, demanding a detailed report. My knees are shaking, but I'm trying valiantly to stand my ground. If it's over between us, it's over.

"Lynzee wants the boys to visit her and Tyler. I told her that it was fine with me." He challenges me with his eyes. "How do you feel about it?"

"It's okay I guess." I'm so relieved, I could kick my heels. "Who's paying for it?"

"She's going to overnight the tickets to them tomorrow."

I feel like I am going to suffocate. My instincts tell me that this isn't a casual visit. Lynzee has a motive, probably to find out exactly how bad our finances are, possibly to introduce the twins to their half-sister.

When we ask the boys if they want to go, they're thrilled. They chat with Tyler every month or so, and can't wait to see her in person. Tyler's IQ is over 160. She's been double promoted and will graduate before she turns sixteen. Though they rarely voice it, Javed and Jamone secretly admire people who are very intelligent. The twins, Zedra's daughter Naja, and Tyler, have vowed that they will go to Brazil once they are all enrolled in college. I wonder: Will this trip now include April?

On the morning the twins leave, I try to keep a straight face when we say good-bye to the boys at the airport. They seem so excited. I don't want to spoil their fun with my negative attitude.

While they're gone, I put in sixteen hours a day in my office, working on my thriller. It's going to be a series like John Sanford's *Prey* series, and have an ongoing main character like Sue Grafton's alphabet novels. I thank God that I have a very creative mind. In my desk there are at least twenty book ideas, some of them inspirational, some of them dramatic, and some sexy as hell. I admit I'm not good at editing, but I am a damn expert at plotting and thinking up themes.

I think of my mother constantly. She wouldn't want me to sell our home. She would want me to lie, beg, and steal to stay here. And I can feel, just like Halle Berry in *Gothika*, that because someone is dead doesn't mean they're gone. I know that she's right here watching over me and mine.

The following Monday we have our first house appointment with a couple that lives out of state. They both love the house, and keep complimenting us on the interior decorating. The husband wants to know if he can purchase more land. He owns horses and wants an additional five acres. There are nearly fifty unexcavated acres adjacent to our property. Elaine informs the couple that she is certain that buying more land is an option, and she'll have an answer for them in a couple of days.

"Jett and Charity," Elaine says after the couple leaves, "I'd like to talk to you two for a moment." After we're seated at the kitchen island she tells us, "The couple is pre-approved. They can well afford your house." She smiles. "And in this economy, that's a great thing."

"Thanks, Elaine," I say. "Jett and I really appreciate all of your help."

"It's my job to keep my customers happy and make your transition to your new home go well."

New home? Why'd she have to mention that? I'm not ready to deal with a new home right now. Elaine says a prayer, and she and I hug before she heads out.

"Baby," Jett says in an excited voice after Elaine leaves, "I want you to start looking for a house immediately."

I cringe. I am in such denial, I never thought about looking for another house. When Elaine calls the following day and tells us that the owner of the subdivision will indeed sell the five acres the buyer requests, I am downtrodden. I now have no excuse for not looking at potential homes.

The boys call us from Lynzee's house. I refused to dial her number. Undeniably, they are having a great time. Lynzee spent thousands buying them new clothes and gym shoes.

"Javed," I ask, "are you and Jamone having a good time?"

"Yeah. It's like 90210. It's live. Aunt Lynzee took Tyler and us to a Lil' Wayne concert. It was kronk. Everybody was there and we had front row seats."

"That's nice."

"We're going to see John Legend on Tuesday."

"Okay. Is there anyone else going with you guys?" I'm hoping that Lynzee isn't going to bring April out of the woodwork. All I need is her captivating my sons with all of her money and then making me look bad.

"Nope. Just Tyler, Jamone, and me. Oh, and Tyler's boyfriend is coming too. He's sleeping over that night 'cause we're not getting back until late. And, Mom, Aunt Lynzee hired a limo to drive us to the concert. Isn't that wild?"

"Yes," I mumble, but I don't think that he hears me.

I do my best to appear to be happy about their trip, but find it difficult to keep up the pretense, and hang up quicker than I normally do.

I keep myself as busy as I can while the twins are gone. I hope that they miss me as much as I miss them.

Since the two of us are rarely alone, I fuss over Jett like he's a little boy, and he loves every minute of it.

"I love you, Jett. Do you still love me?"

"You ain't never got to ask. I love you like my shadow. I need to be that close to you." He kisses me. "Bet on that."

When the twins come home, Jett and I watch as they model outfit after outfit. Neither one mentions April or any hint of an older sister. I'm assuming that Lynzee didn't tell them the truth—at least not yet.

That night, while we're watching the Detroit Tigers play the New York Yankees, Jett tries to console me. I'm crying like a three-year-old, and can't seem to stop. "Don't be upset, honey. Lynzee is just showing love to the boys that she can't show you."

I feel his words have merit. I also feel that there is an undertone in his voice. Since I've entered perimenopause, our sex life has changed drastically. Other than that week I spent convincing him that he needed to give me another chance, we only make love on the weekend. In our heydays, we made love three to four times a week, and back then that was also once or twice that same night. Sometimes waking up in the middle of the night and stealing a piece were some of the best moments of our marriage.

Since I turned forty-nine, I have tried to explain to Jett that my hormones are changing, and I don't get excited the way I used to. But how can you tell a man that you don't desire him anymore? I know I hurt his feelings, but he tries not to show it.

Tonight, my man seems nervous. After twenty-seven years together, I know what's on his mind. I have the foresight to apply the K-Y jelly that I never thought I'd need, before I get into bed. Lurking in the back of my mind is my need to prove to myself that I'm a better lover to Jett than Lynzee was.

Even though it's dark in our bedroom, I can still see his

handsome face. Jett reaches down, tips my chin up to his, and gazes tenderly into my eyes for a long moment. "I love you, Charity. I adore you." He kisses me the way a lover should. Then he says softly, "Passion lasts but a fleeting moment; compassion, a lifetime." He strokes my face. "A man needs a friend. Someone he can talk to, confide in." He kisses each cheek, and then brushes his lips swiftly across mine. "I am so grateful to have you. It's impossible for me to show you just how much I treasure our marriage."

"Maybe I can help you." I lower my hand to caress his essence.

"You don't have to do this, baby."

"I know, but I want to." I help him slide off his boxers. He reciprocates, removing my satin negligee. I taste the tingle of Listerine on his tongue. My senses are saturated with him, the calm, economical power with which he moves his hips. And his smell, steaming up at me, a musky animal fragrance, bringing images of Jett sitting on his Harley, his generous crotch bulging against the leather seat cushion. As I lay beneath him, our bodies a perfect fit, I feel guilty that I've neglected him for so long. At this moment, I want nothing more than to please my sweet man.

I don't realize that I'm moaning until I hear him say, "Moan to me, baby. I knew you were going to be good tonight."

"Hold me tight," I encourage. "Need me right now."

Jett kisses me once more, a kiss like those I dreamed of when I was a teenager. His touch is soft, tender, and loving. His skin is as soft as butterfly wings, satiny as port, but twice as intoxicating. I will gladly die tomorrow if my shroud can be so silk-like and snug as the feel of his skin against mine. He feels smooth and warm as he slides deeper and deeper into my flesh. I move with him as effortlessly as breathing. He makes it easy for me to forget my world and all its pressures. I notice for the first time on his face an expression so exquisite, so soft in its voluptuous delight, that *angelic* is the only term that I could apply to it.

Now, I am half hypnotized by the erotic grind of his hips. The molecules of earth mix with the molecules of flesh, and our skin shimmers like precious jewels. We pause at the same moment, in exquisite anticipation. When we begin again, our rhythm is synchronized. My hands feel like his hands; my shoulders feel like his shoulders; my breasts, his chest; my thighs, his thighs. He becomes me and I become him. Enraptured.

"I love you, Charity," Jett whispers. In the next breath, he withdraws, turns on his side, and, in seconds, falls into a deep and peaceful sleep. I listen to his soft snoring and watch the gentle rise and fall of his chest for a few moments, then turn on my side, tucking the sheet beneath my breasts.

I fall asleep that night more content than I have been in months. He can't have felt this way toward Lynzee. My body is glowing with love. My heart is full of hope. I believe that whatever challenges we face getting a new loan for this house, we will conquer and destroy them. Fuck the new buyers and their horses; they can find another dude ranch. Our home will no longer be for sale. It will forever be the Evans home.

And finally, fuck April. If she doesn't know her father by now, it isn't meant to be. Jett is quite happy being the father of his only blood sons, Javed and Jamone. April hasn't needed Jett's love to get to the point in life that she's at now, so why interfere in our lives? Lord, forgive me if I'm taking it out on this child who didn't ask to be born, but nobody wants an outsider trying to intrude into a family's private life. And by gosh, I'm going to make sure that April doesn't upset ours.

11

The twins have been back home for two weeks and are laughing and joking the way happy teenagers should be. I feel confident that Lynzee didn't introduce them to April. I've made their favorite meals, cleaned up their rooms, and cleaned up their studio. I'm feeling lovable and enjoy sharing my love with my two babies. None of us mention the possibility of moving in a couple of months. We're living for the moment. I told the real estate agent that we weren't going to sign the contract.

When I tiptoe upon my sons painting in their studio, planning to surprise them with oatmeal and raisin cookies, my ears start to burn.

Jamone begins: "That was some bold shit that Aunt Lynzee said about Mom."

"Word," Javed admits. "She shouldn't have talked that way about Mom's writing. Who the hell is she to criticize Mom's sex scenes?"

Momentarily, Jamone stops painting. "And to tell us that she was embarrassed about Mom writing such graphic fiction was totally uncalled for. That's some fucked up shit."

I gasp. How dare that bitch criticize my writing? I don't need to hear another word. I rush upstairs and dial Lynzee's number.

"Lynzee here," she chirps cheerily.

"You low-down bitch. How dare you talk about me in front of my sons?"

"Wait a minute. What the hell are you talking about, Charity?"

"Boy, you really had me suckered. I thought you invited my boys out there because you really wanted to see them. Apparently, that's not the case. You brought them out there to talk shit about their mother."

"Oh, I get it. Jamone told you."

"You damn right he told me," I lie, yelling into the receiver. "Did you think he wouldn't?"

"You don't have to scream in my ear. I hear you." She pauses. "Charity, I spoke out of turn. I'm sorry."

"No, you're not. You meant what you said."

"Give me a chance to explain, would you?"

"Hell no. You're just jealous. A hypocritical, envious bitch. I would think that since you're so filthy rich, you wouldn't be concerned about a lowly writer like me. Obviously you feel intimidated," I seethe.

"Not me, girl. I've got a huge fan base. You're the one who tried to capitalize on my last name."

"*Our* last name," I correct.

"Whatever. If you had an ounce of respect, you wouldn't write pornographic love scenes like you do."

"They're not pornographic. They're artistic."

"Bullshit. Zedra thinks they're foul, and so do most of my friends."

"Fuck you, Lynzee. I'll give you fair warning, cow. I'm coming back, and I'll be bigger than you ever were."

"I doubt it."

"What?" My voice begins to tremble. I can feel pitiful tears clouding my vision. "How dare you!" I hang up before my voice betrays my emotions.

I am overwhelmed with hatred. How have I been dealt such a selfish, self-absorbed sister? I think about my late parents. Where are you Mom? Dad?

I am too hurt to tell Jett what Lynzee said. He has enough on his mind. His test on the new Ford Edge is tomorrow, and I don't want to upset him unnecessarily.

Even though I feel like the biggest hypocrite this side of the Bible belt, I retreat to my bedroom and my Bible. I know that if I tell Herman what happened, he will tell me that God is testing my faith. He will go on to explain that faith is to believe, on the word of God, what we do not see, and its reward is to see and enjoy what we believe.

But I wonder if He is also testing the love that I have for my sister. The Bible speaks of a mysterious sin for which there is no forgiveness. This great unpardonable sin is the murder of the love-life in a human being. Right now, my heart is full of hatred, a hatred for my sister that is so deep I can taste it. I wonder, am I as guilty as my sister is of this treason?

12

Jett is in a foul mood. I have been stalling our real estate agent, so after I refused to sign the first contract, we've had no other offers on the house. On top of that, he's only sold two cars this month. His sales manager is riding his ass.

I'm not in a good mood either. I've continued to work with finance officers at local banks and mortgage companies. It's tedious as well as monotonous to keep faxing in three years' worth of income tax returns, my last publishing contract, and a letter explaining why we've been late on our mortgage payments.

It's truly killing me to think about moving. The hardest part is keeping up a front for Jett. I have to make him believe that I am actively looking for a new house. I actually do inquire about a few of them to Elaine. I even go so far as to view several houses. Jett accompanies Elaine and me on two occasions. Both times, he feels that the houses I'm looking at are too expensive. After all, the house that we buy has to be based on his retirement income. We can only afford a house that is a quarter of the cost of our own. That means looking at houses around 2500 square feet. I can't comprehend living in a house that small. Where will we put our exercise equipment? Family room furniture? Pool and game tables? Our twelve-seat dining room furniture? Artwork?

*   *   *

Jett nearly breaks my heart when he tries to get me to face reality. "Charity, we're going to have to sell the dining room set. The dining rooms in the houses we looked at are way too small."

We have just come home from looking at five houses. Each house was worse than the last. No house can compare to ours, but our choices seem like an insult. I feel like we're on welfare getting food stamps. The pickings are so slim. This is the first time in a while that I witness Jett's anger. He's not happy with our choices either.

"What? No. I can't, Jett."

He shakes his head, clearly irritated by me. "I suggest that you try to sell the furniture to the new owners when we finally do sell. You can sell this living room furniture, too. It's going to be too big for our new house."

I go into our bedroom. When Jett comes in, I'm sitting on the bed. The television is off and he knows that I'm pouting.

"Honey, I know you've been half-looking for houses. This has got to stop. I just received the fifth tax notice yesterday. We're a year past due. If we don't sell this house soon, the county can sell the house for back taxes. Do you want that to happen?"

I'd completely forgotten about the taxes. They're $14,000 every February. We also pay our home insurance, which is another $5,000. Momentarily, I can envision the headlines: LOCAL AUTHOR'S HOME FOR AUCTION DUE TO BACK TAXES.

I gulp awkwardly. "No, Jett, I don't want that to happen." I get up from the bed and hug him. "You've got to help me, honey. This is so damn hard for me. The thought of selling this house is killing me." Selfish tears fill my eyes. "I can't hardly stand it."

"Honey," he says, kissing the top of my head, "it's only a house. Just bricks, mortar, and wood. Stop making it so important."

"But it's my dream home."

He kisses my wet cheek and tries to sound encouraging. "You'll have more dreams. And who knows? We can always build another home."

I pull away. "No, we won't." In my heart, I know he doesn't mean it. What person in his right mind would consider building a house when they're over sixty? Not many. And not Jett.

Finally, we have more buyers, Arthur and June James. The husband is a surgeon at St. Jude Hospital. The wife is an attorney.

"They've offered one point one million," Elaine says.

Jett speaks up. "That won't cut it, Elaine. We'll counter at one point three-five."

The next day, Elaine says, "No go. They made a counter offer of one point two-five."

"That's bullshit," I say. "We'll counter at one point three-two."

Elaine comes back the next morning. "Their final offer is one point three million."

We were hoping to get what the house was appraised for: $1,450,000.

Jett and I say in unison, "We'll take it."

We sign the paperwork and June James comes over the following morning. June is a Caucasian female in her early forties. She's wearing a tan Christian Dior suit that I know set her back at least three grand. She has a six-carat emerald-cut diamond wedding ring on her left hand, and at least a three-carat pinky ring on her right.

"I want the light switches in the kitchen and foyer," June states.

"Uh, we'll have to discuss that later," I offer. Sometimes I can't stand rich people. They're so cheap; they want everything given to them. The two light switches she is referring to are the ones that a bookstore owner in Texas gave me at one of my book signings. The light switches are painted copies of two of my book covers with my name on them.

I can't resist asking, "Why do you want them? I don't get it."

"Because I want you to leave a living legacy to your body of work."

I am flattered. Jett isn't. He loves those light switches. I feel him kick my foot under the table.

"We'll have to get back with you on that request, Mrs. James," Jett says.

"All right." June heads for the kitchen. "I also want the cooking utensils beneath the range hood, and the cable cord for the television." There is a sixteen-inch Sony television on the end of the island that we watch while sitting on the sofa. Why she asked for the cord and not the television is beyond me. However, those stainless-steel cooking utensils are expensive. They're by Roscan and cost me more than three hundred dollars. I guess she isn't as stupid as I thought.

Is this woman in her right mind? I resent her thinking that we are so desperate to sell that we'll give in to all of her requests—even if we really are desperate at this point. We've run out of options and have applied at every possible bank. They have all turned us down.

"Mrs. James, my husband and I have no problem giving you these kitchen items as long as you allow us the time to locate a house. We're requesting ninety to one hundred twenty days to vacate the premises. How does that sound to you?"

"Fine. We have to sell our home in Germantown. That could take a month or two. Our fifteen-year-old daughter, April, is going to love this house."

Another April. I am again reminded of a nag that is killing my psyche. Just like that, my mind wanders to the love child of my sister and my husband. I am still trying to convince myself that she is nothing to worry about. So what if April looks like Jett? I'm told that we all have a twin in this world. That twin could have fathered Lynzee's child for all I know.

The only drawback about the James's offer is that they are requiring some repairs. Mrs. James hands me a list. It is fortunate for us that Jett is handy when it comes to doing work on the house.

He paints, caulks, and cleans the windows like a professional. We have to pay a cooling and heating company to repair one of the five air-conditioning zones and one of the heating zones. The garage company that we pay to get the electronic door openers up to code is yet another expense. Part of the stone on one of the chimneys needs to be torn down and rebricked. In total, the repairs cost us almost $6,900. That means that we have one less month's house note in the bank.

June comes to our house twelve times while we are making the repairs. She brings her kids, her mother, and her uncle to see the house. I am getting exceedingly tired of her visits. Like a fool, I give the woman our telephone number, and she calls nearly every day.

To be fair, I have begun to diligently look for a new house; however, when I actually do find a house that I like, Jett doesn't approve of the location or the size of the lot. He wants at least an acre. Since I'm not making progress quickly enough, Jett finds a house and asks me to look at it. When I check it out, I'm disappointed. The house is seventeen years old and the amount of dust inside looks as if it hasn't been cleaned since it was built. The saving grace is that they recently installed an in-ground pool. In my opinion, they should have spent the money updating and cleaning the house.

"I'm sorry, Jett," I say. "I wouldn't move in this house if they were giving it away."

Two weeks later, we finally agree on a house. It is five miles from our old home. The brick home sits on two acres of land. I'm not crazy about the architectural design of the front of the house, but I kind of like the inside. The only problem is that the price of the house is $40,000 more than we agreed upon, and because our credit is so challenged, Elaine informs us that we have to accept a higher interest rate and have to put down a bigger down payment. This means that our house notes are probably going to be two hundred dollars more a month than we budgeted for. It also means that we will have less than eight thousand dollars left in our savings account. The end result is this: if we buy the house, Jett will have to work until he's seventy-five unless I get a new contract. With all the zeal I can muster, I convince Jett that I am confident that I'll get a contract this year, possibly by the summer. He agrees, and Elaine finalizes the deal.

The flowers are blooming. We have hundreds of purple verbenas planted all around our property, as well as several flowering bushes: azaleas, magnolias, and Japanese ferns. The land-scaping is so pretty that we've won the house of the month award in our subdivision three times.

When Jett isn't at work, he and the twins work almost daily on the yard. He replaces several of the sprinkler heads on our underground sprinkling system, and puts black mulch around all of the trees. The yard has never looked so beautiful. In my mind, it's telling us good-bye.

One day when Jett is at work, I check out our bank account. It's lower than I remember. Completing those repairs for the Jameses killed us. But the repairs had to be made for our home to pass inspection. I finally realize it's time for me to deal with the reality of the situation. We are selling our dream house, we are selling our furniture, and we are moving into a smaller home. I try to cheer myself up by remembering that at least I still have my husband and my sons.

13

To my amazement, I receive a call from my agent. "Charity, Dutton's made an offer. Mind you, it isn't much, but it'll get your name back out there."

I don't hesitate. "That's great news, Arlene, but the bottom line is the money. Exactly how much is it?"

"Fifty thousand."

"Again? I can't believe it. I thought you were going to try to get me more money."

"Charity, the publishing industry has changed. No one is offering big contracts like they used to. By the way, the offer is for two books."

A fool could figure out the math: $25,000 apiece. I made more than that when I worked at the bakery.

"I'm sorry, Arlene. I can't accept it."

"I can try bumping it up a little, but I'm afraid that they won't offer too much more."

Tears sting my eyes and I feel my chin touch my chest. Has my talent as a writer sunk to such depths? Maybe Lynzee is right. Maybe I'm never going to be a *New York Times* bestseller.

"Let me know what happens, Arlene."

When I hang up, I feel a desperate need to talk to Lynzee. I guess it is just old habit. When anything having to do with publishing comes up, she is always the first person that comes to

mind. What would she think? And what would my mother suggest that I do? I miss having a family to talk to. I need to talk to
an unbiased person who can help me solve some of my problems.

I decide not to call Lynzee. Instead, I phone Herman two
days later.

"Charity, it's your decision. But it's been years since you've
been published. Getting your name back out there, in my opinion, should take precedence over the money."

I make the call back to Arlene. "Hey, I decided to take Dutton's offer."

Arlene is silent for a few seconds. "Charity, I'm sorry. Dutton
wouldn't consider a contract for a hundred thousand, and even
pulled back their original offer."

Flabbergasted is too mild a word for how I feel when I hang
up. Back to being blacklisted. Damn Lynzee. My career is now
shot to hell. What in the world am I going to do?

That night, a wave of hysteria hits me. My mind is reeling
and I'm feeling excruciatingly sorry for myself. I begin to cry,
and though I try my damndest, I can't stop the flow. While Jett
and I are in bed, I take the pillow and stuff it in my mouth. My
forehead is as hot as a blue flame. I'm still unable to stop the
tears, and the pain in my heart feels as if a cold dagger is
pierced inside it. A part of me wants to share my heartache
with Jett. I start to hiccup, and can hardly catch my breath. I
want to know when all of these trials will end.

14

I have finally come up with a book idea that I am certain will sell. It will also show Lynzee that she can't mess with me but for so long before I fight back. The book will be called *Revelations*. It's about two sisters who are both authors. One is very successful, and the other one isn't. The unsuccessful sister decides to tell the truth about her sibling's past that will ultimately change the way her fans view her. It's a classic case of sibling rivalry where the underdog is the victor.

I wake up at two in the morning and run to my computer. The book is so exciting that it's practically writing itself. I'm just the tool that is putting word to paper. I've got my swag turned on and I'm unstoppable.

I call Arlene and tell her about the book. "Charity, I know an editor who's very interested in buying books about famous siblings. How soon can you finish the book?"

Feeling optimistic, I say, "Eight weeks." My excitement is now bordering on the hysterical.

"Excellent. Keep me posted on your progress."

When I hang up, I run back upstairs to my office. I haven't told Jett about my new book. I want to surprise him when I have a check in hand. If I tell him now, he will probably be as negative as a botched Polaroid.

15

We are scheduled to go to closing on our house sale. Unfortunately, closing on the home we are purchasing is delayed. The closing isn't scheduled until the following Thursday. Thankfully, the buyers give us another week before we have to vacate.

Most women hate packing, and I am no exception. Over the past twenty years, we've moved four times. This time, I decide to take a different tactic. I intend to pack everything ahead of time and only leave out the clothes that we need to wear for five days.

On Wednesday of the next week, Elaine advises us that our closing on our new home is being pushed back again. The movers are scheduled for tomorrow morning. Mr. and Mrs. James refuse to give us another extension, so we are forced to move out before we have a place to go.

My mother used to say that I'm not a follower, I'm a leader, so I lead. I make reservations at the Homesuites Motel, just a mile away from our home. We put our furniture in storage. The twins are restless, being forced to stay at the hotel. They can hardly tolerate being so cramped up. The two of them are as spoiled as I am about having so much space.

"Listen, boys. I don't want to hear from any of your teachers that you haven't turned in your homework assignments on time." I stare them down. "Do I have your promise?"

"For sure, Moms," they say.

While we're at the hotel, I decide that it's time to get serious about looking for a job. I never want to be in this situation again, so until I get a new contract, I will work. I go on an interview. Ironically enough, it's for a car salesman's job. When I see the ad in the paper about how much a salesman can potentially make in a year, I am sold. Call me materialistic, but I like shopping at Neiman Marcus too. I am also a little perturbed. Jett has never shown me his check. I didn't have a clue about his salary until now.

The interview at Vector Mazda goes smoothly. The general manager is impressed by my energy, and offers me a job. I tell him I can't start for another week because of our move, but I take home educational materials to learn about the cars I will be selling.

After four days in the motel, it is finally time to move. We sign the closing papers at 9:30 a.m. at First Fidelity Bank and by ten have the movers ready to transfer our furniture to our new home.

I have to admit the twins are a great help, lifting, dragging, and hauling every item that the movers don't. It takes extra time to move all of the twins' various art supplies. The movers have to be careful not to break or tear any of the numerous jars or canvases. To make matters worse, the books from my office weigh a ton. The movers are sweating so profusely, I feel sorry for them. I offer them cold sodas and pastrami and cheese sandwiches. Ultimately, we don't finish until two in the morning.

For the first time in months, I'm not depressed. I am so excited about my new job that I can barely sleep that night.

The next morning, I jump up at five and begin to unpack. I estimate that it will take me three to four days to get everything in place. Thankfully, Herman comes over to pitch in, and Jett and the twins also help when they aren't at school or working.

Of course, everything doesn't fit. We overestimated some of the room dimensions. We end up calling the Salvation Army and giving away more furniture and boxes of books. It hurts my heart, but I have to do what I have to do. I'm starting a new chapter in my life.

By Sunday the house looks like a home. What really sets it off are the twins' beautiful paintings. In truth, they look even nicer in this home with the pillars and arched ceilings than they did in our old home.

The day before I am about to start my new job, Jett is in a terrible mood.

"Jett, do you have something to say to me?"

"You're not going to like selling cars."

As I wipe off the marble countertops in the kitchen, I ask, "Why not?"

"Because, like I said before, there's too many politics. The big wigs at the dealership treat the 'house mouses' like kings. It's not a job for a woman. Why do you think there aren't any females working in car sales in Memphis?"

I hadn't thought about that. When I bought my BMW four years earlier, I didn't give a thought to all of the male salespeople in the dealership. However, when I bought the Navigator back in Michigan, a woman sold me the SUV.

"I don't know, Jett. And I don't care." I carefully place the dishcloth across the sink divider and turn to look at him. "I'm going to be the best salesperson in this area, male or female." I can't help it if my mama raised me to have confidence. "Herman agrees that I'll be a good car salesman too."

Jett rolls his eyes at me.

I blow him off like a bottle of bubbles. I make up my mind that in order to be the best I have to be informed. Obviously Jett is not going to enlighten me about the car business. I am on my own. I retrieve my sourcebook. To avoid any foreseeable problems, I read and take notes until one in the morning. I don't have to be at work until 8:30, but can't sleep past six. After having coffee, reading the paper, and checking out the morning news on Channel 5, I dress with special care. When I check out my image in the mirror, I feel that I look sophisticated, just the look I want to achieve.

Day one is beyond my expectations. The other employees make me feel welcome, and the general manager is impressed by how quickly I've learned the information from the manual. I witness none of the politics and negativity that Jett warned me about, and I go home in a great mood. Unfortunately, Jett is still in a foul mood, so I don't even talk about work at dinner.

"I want you to quit," he demands when we get in bed later that night.

"Why?"

"Because I don't want my wife driving men around who could possibly assault her. You don't know a damn thing about these buyers. They could be drunks, rapists—"

"Wait a minute. We get a copy of everyone's driver's license and—"

"Fuck that! Do you know how many criminals have fake licenses?"

"Jett, you're being unreasonable. Nothing's going to happen to me."

"Not if I have anything to say about it." He jumps out of the bed and grabs a pillow. "You tell your boss that you're not coming back." The walls shake when he slams the door behind him.

I am furious. All the time he's been complaining about our financial problems, and now that I've gotten a job to contribute to our household, he doesn't want me to have it. I can't figure out what his problem is.

The next morning, we aren't speaking. I get myself ready for work and leave, severely disappointed in my mate. I can't wait until Jett confronts me about quitting my job again; then I can tell him to kiss my fat ass.

"Do you have something to tell me, Charity?" Jett asks after he takes a shower that evening.

"Yes. I'm keeping my job. I'm good at it and I love it. Besides, we need the money and you know that car salesmen bring in a good income. I can make over five thousand dollars on one deal. I can't ignore that kind of money."

Jett pounds the wall with his fist and storms off into our bedroom wet and naked. He doesn't sleep on the couch like he did the night before, but he stays on his side of the bed.

Sex is a no-no for the next two weeks. Jett says hello and

good-bye, but little else. I don't even get to tell him how excited I am when I sell my first car. The only thing I look forward to when I come home is receiving a warm hug from my sons and working on *Revelations.* Not only am I sure that this will be the book that gets me a new contract, but it will stick it to Lynzee after all the heartache she's put me through.

At night, I dream about the way my life used to be, when my books were being published and my marriage wasn't under so much strain. I long for those days. Will we ever get back to that place? With Jett's new unreasonable attitude, and the specter of Lynzee and April always hanging over my head, I don't know what will become of my marriage.

16

Revelations is finished, and Arlene has submitted it to editors at several publishing houses. She has received good feedback from a few, so I'm feeling hopeful this morning. I decide to take that positive energy and break the ice with Jett, who is still barely speaking to me.

I casually mention that a local radio host called and asked me to be on her morning program. I have been on twice before. "I told her that I don't have a new book out yet, but I can talk about my work at Mazda. Maybe my loyal readers will come down and buy a car from me while they wait for my next book."

I hope that this will get a laugh out of Jett, but he doesn't even look up from his newspaper. So much for breaking the ice.

Later that night, Jett finally decides to speak to me, but his tone is nasty when he says, "Charity, you don't get it, do you?"

"Get what?"

"How far you've fallen. You used to be a writer, and now you're a car salesman. That's sniggle material. Next to attorneys, car salesmen are the lowest people on the totem pole. No one trusts them."

I am ready to hit the roof. I also feel humiliated.

He isn't finished. "The buyers need you temporarily to get

their deal done. But secretly, they're calling you all kinds of greedy bitches behind your back."

"You're just jealous is all. Why don't you admit it? My commission check was bigger than yours and you can't stand it."

"That's bullshit."

"Car salesmen talk, and I heard all about the commission you made on that Shelby Mustang. And since I heard about you, you had to have heard about all the money I made on that Avalanche I sold. Kinda makes your check look like chicken scratch, doesn't it." I get all up in his face and put my hands on my hips. He frowns and pushes me out of the way.

His attitude is way out of line. Am I out selling pussy on the corner of Beale Street and Third Avenue? No. Am I consuming Hennessy by the fifth? No, not like I used to in the past. I haven't touched an ounce of liquor in three years. Then give me a damn break!

I still can't calm down enough to speak. Tears start in the back of my throat, hard tears that burn like nitro glycerin. How can he treat me this way? Hurt and embarrassment swell in my chest and shaky tears pollute my eyes. I get up on rubber band legs and walk away. I'll be damned if I let him see me cry. I will shit bricks before I let him see any evidence of my pain.

It's not long before I finally get the news I've been waiting so long to hear. My book has been accepted by Harold House Publishers! They offer me $150,000. Unlike previous offers where I've asked my agent to negotiate for more, I happily accept this offer. I believe in my heart that *Revelations* is going to be hugely successful and bring me royalties for years to come.

Until I get my first advance check, our funds will still be tight. Jett is finally talking to me again, but things are still a bit tense because I tell him I can't quit my job until the writing money starts flowing again. In a few months, I tell him, this job will be history. This seems to ease his mind a little. I know things will be fine; there is a light at the end of the long, dark tunnel we've been in.

17

When I return home from work one afternoon, I receive a letter from Lynzee. It's short and nasty:

I heard about your new book. I also know how much information that you revealed about my relationship with Heidi Armstrong. I could have told everyone about your suicide attempt in 1995, but I didn't. How could you be so heartless? I'll never forgive you for this. Not in ten lifetimes . . .

I wonder how she found out so quickly. Then I remember that her agent knows everyone in publishing. She has been in the business for twenty-seven years. She probably has a copy of the manuscript. By now, Lynzee probably has a copy too, even though it's not on bookshelves yet.

Nevertheless, I don't feel bad, because in the book, I only told the truth. When Lynzee was in her sophomore year at Chapel Hill University in North Carolina, she caught her boyfriend of eight months cheating on her. When she confronted him, he retaliated by giving her a black eye and breaking her left arm.

Lynzee was consoled by her friend, Heidi. Within a short period, they became lovers and continued their affair for over a year. Then Lynzee took a liking to Develle Ellis, a forward on the basketball team. Lynzee began dating both Develle and Heidi. Finally, Lynzee stopped seeing Heidi. Lynzee blew her off and continued her relationship with Develle. In the spring of 1976, Heidi killed herself. Lynzee didn't even go to the funeral.

Heidi's family was devastated. Heidi was on the dean's list and was considered a very religious young woman. Lynzee calls herself a Christian, but is only seen in church at a loved one's funeral. Lynzee told me once or twice that Heidi wanted them to get married. This was before gays getting married became fashionable. I always told Lynzee that she should have told Heidi the truth, that she always felt romantic and sexual feelings for men. Lynzee didn't agree. She felt that Heidi was just a fling, just a college experience that she'd eventually get over.

Heidi was the last woman that Lynzee had a relationship with, or so she says. In my opinion, I think that Tyler has guessed that her mother is bisexual. That's why she became sexually active at age fourteen. She doesn't want to be like her mother.

In *Revelations*, I also reveal that Lynzee didn't earn her B.S. degree at UCLA; she bought it. Her master's degree is a phony too. Finally, I tell about Lynzee's sexual misconduct with several bookstore owners who report to the *New York Times*. She screwed her way to the top—and it didn't matter if the bookstore owner was a man or a woman. She did what she needed to do to gain financial success.

Lynzee thinks she's worrying me by threatening to tell about my suicide attempt. Maybe she hasn't read the book after all, because if she had, she would know that I revealed that information in the book. It is a very moving and honest portrayal of a deeply depressed woman. I pray often for God to forgive my trespasses and not hold them against me. I know that I will have to pay for my sin, but I hope that God will be merciful and not make the punishment too harsh.

Lynzee's letter ends with a Bible quote: "*A gracious woman retaineth honour: and strong men retain riches. The merci-*

ful man doeth good to his own soul: but he that is cruel trou-
bleth his own flesh." Proverbs: 11:16-17.

This basically says that a woman who has cruel intentions troubles her own self. All I know is what Shakespeare once said: "The devil can cite Scripture for his purposes."

To hell with Lynzee. She needs to get down on her knees and pray for forgiveness. Maybe once they're raw and bleeding, she might feel redeemed.

18

After I receive Lynzee's letter, I don't hear from her, which surprises me. Usually her letters are a prelude to some really foul behavior. I expected this time to be even worse, since my book will soon be out there for the world to read.

I get a call from my cousin Kai, who tells me some shocking news.

"You're not going to believe this," she says.

"Come clean with it. What's up?"

"*What's Up* magazine is saying that Lynzee is hooked on Percocet and she just got out of rehab."

"Kai, please. You know that rag is just as bad as the *National Enquirer*. Most of the stuff they print in there is straight-up lies." I think Kai wants to believe it's true because she and Lynzee don't get along. Ever since Lynzee became famous, Kai feels that Lynzee abandoned her. Half the time, Lynzee won't even return Kai's calls.

"Yeah, but I think this one is true," Kai insists. "A friend of mine knows the personal trainer that works for Lynzee, and he's saying she really is hooked on drugs."

I am dumbfounded. I've heard all about Percocet, the drug of choice for some of Hollywood's biggest stars. It's habit-forming, and is easy to overdose because it makes you feel so good. Is that the reason why she's been so nasty to me lately?

In my heart, I am really only looking for any plausible excuse for her behavior, so that I can forgive her. Call me weak, or a fool, but I deeply love my sister. I don't want to see anything happen to her. I definitely don't want to entertain the idea that she's an addict. Is it just coincidence that this happened just as *Revelations* is about to go to print?

"Kai, I've gotta go."

"Why? I thought we'd gossip a little longer."

"I've got to call Zedra."

Zedra is Lynzee's best friend from junior high school. Zedra used to let me hang around her and Lynzee when we were younger, but we were never really close. Zedra lives in New York. She and Lynzee visit each other at least six times a year.

When I call Zedra, her voice mail picks up. I leave a message, but she doesn't call me back.

At work the next day, I can't get Lynzee out of my mind. I think back to the times when Lynzee was younger and she had to take care of me. Our mother worked as a cook at Big Boy Restaurant and our father was in and out of the tuberculosis sanitarium in Saginaw, Michigan. From the time Lynzee was in the fourth grade, she took over the household. Tall for her age, she could cook and clean better than a grown woman. Even though we were poor, our home was as spotless as the Rockefellers'.

She washed and ironed all of our clothes, cleaned the house, helped bathe me, and even cooked dinner. Even at age nine, when she issued an order or told me that "It's time for you to come home now," I scrambled as fast as I could. If I didn't, Lynzee would beat the shit out of me. I respected her as much as I did my mother, maybe even more. Lynzee didn't ask for this job. It was bequeathed to her by our mother, who worked long hours. My big sister took her job seriously. Out of respect, I rarely questioned Lynzee's commands,

Each night, she took her time to attend to my hair. Some mothers comb their kids' hair once a week, but Lynzee did mine every night. She would sit me between her legs and patiently work magic with her fingers. As I grew older, she would roll up my hair with paper curlers made out of grocery bags. Then I had to put a stocking cap over my head so it would look fresh in the morning.

I don't know how my mother and I would have made it without Lynzee. Unfortunately, Lynzee didn't have much of a childhood. She had too many responsibilities.

I grew up thinking Lynzee was Joan of Arc. I wanted to do everything like her. When she cut her hair, I wanted to cut mine. When Mama taught Lynzee how to sew, I learned from Lynzee. When Lynzee polished her nails, I copied. When she took typing classes, so did I. And when shorthand came later, my mother teased me about being Lynzee's shadow.

I couldn't help it. Lynzee could do just about everything exceptionally well. Why wouldn't I want to be just like her?

One of my fondest memories of Lynzee is when she taught me how to dance. I was incredibly stiff as a teenager, and didn't have an ounce of rhythm. I couldn't dance to save my life. Lynzee was patient with me. She wouldn't quit until I could dance as well as she could. My confidence grew and my best friend, Freddie Russell, and I, won numerous dance contests. We were the Fred Astaire and Ginger Rogers of our hometown. Thanks to my loving sister, I felt like I had wings.

And now my Joan of Arc is in trouble. How can I help her?

It doesn't dawn on me to call Lynzee's house. When I do, the recording comes on the first ring. I alternate calling Lynzee and Zedra over the next few days. Still nothing.

Finally, I receive a call from Zedra. She asks, "Have you heard from Lynzee?"

"Is this Zedra?"

"Who else would it be, heffa?" Her tone is terse. "Well, have you?"

"No."

"Look, I'm not going to say I'm sorry for not keeping in touch these past few years. It's not my style."

"You're so full of shit, Zedra, you must have a halo of flies above your head."

"I won't comment on that, cow."

My voice is firm. "Now, where is she? I called her house."

"She's supposed to be at a health spa in Arizona."

"Supposed to be? I heard about the Percocet."

"This isn't the first time," Zedra admits.

"You're kidding. No one ever told me."

"That's because you're so judgmental."

My free hand automatically brackets my hips. "Look, Zedra, I'm not in the mood to argue with you. Now, what's happening with Lynzee? Is she okay? And where's Tyler?"

"Whoa. One question at a time. Tyler is at Lynzee's neighbor's house. I'm not sure about Lynzee. I haven't heard from her in ten days. I called her editor. She claims that Lynzee hasn't contacted her either."

"Where could she be?" I'm getting as agitated as a termite in a cement castle. I have an eerie feeling that something ominous is going to happen.

"With her money, she could be anywhere."

Zedra is right. But there is one thing we know: if she is anywhere in the States, the place is expensive. Lynzee strictly goes first class or goes home.

"Charity . . . I . . ."

"What!"

"I might as well tell you." I can hear the trepidation in her voice. "Tyler told Lynzee that she thinks she's pregnant."

"You're lying. Not perfect Tyler?"

"I'm serious as death. She told Lynzee the day she checked in at the spa."

"How? When? How far along is she? Who's the father?"

"Her boyfriend Raymond."

"Lynzee should have seen this coming letting that boy stay overnight at her house."

"She claimed they slept in separate rooms."

"Bullshit. You and I both know that the moment Lynzee went to sleep they fucked like gerbils."

"I think that's why Lynzee made a quick exit. She doesn't want to deal with it. Think about all of the negative publicity: the Percocet, the teenage pregnancy, and more importantly, your book. What a bummer. The hate mail is already coming in from folks who read advance copies of your book. And to make matters worse, Tyler received a scholarship from Harvard Law School in January. If she's pregnant, she can kiss that opportunity good-bye."

"Who gives a fuck about a scholarship? What about Tyler? Is she thinking about having an abortion?"

"Hell no! Hell, I don't know. Like I said, she's not sure. Besides, have you forgotten about how many abortions Lynzee's had?"

"I only know about one," I offer weakly. I can't help but think, *And the one she should have had before that one— April.* I'm hurt that this is obviously another of the many secrets that they've kept from me. Then I know something for certain: Zedra doesn't know about April.

"She's had six. The last one in 1988. She almost died. We didn't tell you because you're so self-righteous. The doctors told Lynzee that it would be a miracle if she ever conceived a child. And then Tyler came along seven years later."

"So Tyler is Lynzee's miracle child?"

"Damn straight."

"I didn't know." *So, that's why she spoils Tyler so badly.* Who could blame her?

"Charity, what you don't know would make the world go 'round."

Momentarily, I don't have a comeback. That exact phrase was one that my mother used to say to me when I was younger.

Did Lynzee and Zedra plan on telling me the truth about Tyler, or were they going to keep yet another secret between them? It's common knowledge that secrets can tear families apart. My sister knows that as well as I do. Does she view me as being so sickeningly self-righteous that she, my own blood kin, has to keep things from me? But then again, who am I to talk? I still haven't found the nerve to tell Jett about his daughter. I don't know if I ever will.

19

As I'm getting ready for work one morning, I hear the door-bell ring. Jett and the twins have already left for work and school. I cover my slip with my housecoat and hurry to the front door, heels clicking against the ceramic tile. To my shock, I see Lynzee with a scowl on her face.

"Let me in, bitch," she snarls.

I open the door and say, "Did Zedra call you? I was worried about you and Tyler."

"And what about April? Were you concerned about her welfare too?"

I keep silent.

She stalks past me and goes into the kitchen. I follow. She slams her keys down on the island and turns to face me.

"I hate your fucking guts, bitch." She pushes her flat hand against my chest and continues, "I wanted to tell you face to face."

"Whoa, what happened to the twelve steps that they taught you in rehab?" I ask.

"Fuck rehab. Those fools don't have a clue about my real life. I told them a bunch of lies and they believed me." She snorts a laugh.

It kills me to ask, but I do anyway. "What about April? How is she?"

She snarls. "April is out of my life. I found out that she's an alcoholic and she's gay. Plus, she blames me for giving her up for adoption. In short, she hates my guts."

"Why?" I feel totally relieved.

"She's single and sterile, and did I say gay already? I have no tolerance for people who feel sorry for themselves and turn to their own sex for comfort."

Hot damn, she's homophobic! What an irony considering her past life. The hypocritical bitch! "You've got a lot of nerve, considering your indiscretions with Heidi." Oops. I should have kept my big mouth shut. I step back and she starts jamming her hand into my chest.

"Stop it, Lynzee." I feel my back press against the refrigerator.

Lynzee is wearing jeans and a sweatshirt, something she never wears. "You underestimate me, girl. It's time that I taught you a lesson." She quickly releases the belt around her waist. I grab her hand and she astonishes me with her strength.

"Stop it, Lynzee!" I try to fend her off, but it's getting difficult. "I'm not in the mood for your bullshi—" Before I can finish my sentence, she reels back and hits me on my shoulder with the belt. As I try to protect myself, the tie loosens on my housecoat. I tussle with her, but she continues to attack, and strikes me in the stomach with her knee.

"I'll show you, you soulless heffa." She spits in my face. "How dare you write about me in your book? I'll show you!"

I manage to grab the belt and push her back a few inches. She uses her shoulder to muscle her way forward, and pushes me until my back is against the oven door. I stomp on her feet with the heel of my shoe. She winces, but doesn't relent. In a matter of seconds, she grabs a handful of fabric. The shoulder of my housecoat rips. I crouch down, trying to ward off another blow from the belt. It's useless.

One slap of the belt hits my cheek and I can feel it swell. Another blow strikes my bare shoulder. It stings like hell. Now I'm mad. This bitch is going to get hers. I manage to grab the belt and sock her in the jaw with my left fist. I quickly follow it up with a solid blow to her chin. The skin splits and blood seeps out.

Lynzee is two sizes smaller than I am, but as agile as a snake and surprisingly tough for a woman in her fifties. As we struggle for leverage, I can smell her breath, foul with salami and cheese.

"You fat-ass motherfucker," Lynzee wheezes. "I'm going to kill your fat ass."

"The fuck you will," I say, putting force in my voice.

I don't see the next blow coming as she punches me in the eye. I'm wheezing, breathless with fatigue and filled with supreme hatred. A profound picture of April is lurking in my mind, and I can't dismiss the sinfully sweet smile on her face. We both lose our footing and slip to the floor. I can feel her fingernails digging into my wrists as she tries to pin me down.

My left eye is aching like a toothache, and I can feel that it, too, is swelling. She forces her narrow body on top of me and continues punching me in the face.

"Get off of me, you fool!" I scream.

I'm praying that Lynzee is getting as exhausted as I am, but she seems reinvigorated by my helplessness. As I try to arch my back and roll over to one side, I can't throw her off. I'm shaken by an involuntary muscle spasm as my body reacts to the growing interruption in my air supply and in the amount of blood to my brain.

"God, help me!" I plead.

I feel Lynzee's body relax for a fraction of a second. I manage to get a hold of my shoe and bring it up to my waist. I struggle to lift it up higher. When I do, I reach back, then forward, striking Lynzee on the back of the head. Momentarily, she appears to go limp in defeat.

As she slowly rises up on her knees, taking her weight off of me, I continue to attack her with my shoe. I back-pedal, trying to get into a better position.

In that brief moment, Lynzee regains her strength, raises her hands to my throat, and squeezes harder. I begin to gag and cough uncontrollably and drop my shoe. The other one has fallen off, and I can feel the heel of it close by. I have to hang on until I can take possession of it. Using all of my strength, I grab her hands and force them away from my throat.

I'm so exhausted, it hurts to breathe. As I grab my other shoe, we manage to get to our feet, both weary and out of breath. I don't expect it when Lynzee gives me a hard blow to the stomach. I stumble back a little, but manage to get my elbows up, almost simultaneously hitting Lynzee in the abdomen, back, and shoulder with my heel. She crumbles to her knees, the wind knocked out of her. I hate to do it, but I land one, then another blow to her jaw. I hear something crack, give.

Lynzee's two front teeth are nearly knocked out, and she's bleeding profusely from the mouth. As I move to grab her arm, Lynzee threatens, "I'm going to kill your ass. This isn't over."

Tears crowd my eyes as I grab her keys off of the island. I drag her beaten body to the front door. I open the door and push her outside. I throw they keys out into the yard. "Now, get away from me."

I wait with my back pressed against the door until I hear the motor start. Seconds later, I hear the screech of tires. I exhale and let my body relax.

I call into work and tell them I won't be coming in.

I should have expected it. Should have seen it coming. Still, her husky voice stuns me.

"You dirty, low-down bitch. You hurt my friend." The call comes in late at night.

It was Zedra. "Cut it, Zedra. Lynzee had it coming."

"You won't fare so good with me. I weigh two-eighty."

I hear Jett stirring beside me. He's pissed about my swollen face and all of the purple bruises on my body. "Let it go, Zedra. This is between Lynzee and me. It's none of your business."

Jett pokes me in the side and asks, "Who is it, Charity?"

I cover the mouthpiece. "Zedra."

Zedra's voice turns ominous. "Forget what I said. I'm going to pay someone to kick your ass. Someone professional. Just know that you won't know when or where. You better check over your shoulder every minute of your useless life." *Click.*

I can't help it; I tremble with fear.

"What's wrong, Charity?" Jett demands.

"Zedra threatened me."

He sits up in the bed and turns on the light. "Did you record the call?"

"I wish I had, but no. She hung up too quickly."

I tell him exactly what she said, and he insists that we can't take her threats lightly.

When we get up in the morning, Jett takes action. He gets all of the information I need to get a gun permit. Within two weeks, I attend an eight-hour seminar and take a written test.

I'll never forget the instructor's words: "When you shoot a gun, you're responsible for that bullet until it hits the ground."

Jett buys me a .25 semi-automatic Smith and Wesson with a pearl handle. Of course, I can't use it yet. It takes three months to get a gun permit. Even so, the next day Jett goes with me to the firing range. He's had his gun permit for seven years and is an expert shot. It hurts that he is so impatient with me. He wants me to shoot almost as well as he can. I can't. I try my best, but come up short. I believe that a human target is much larger than the one at the firing range, and when I need to, I won't miss. That's for damn sure. And permit or not, I'm going to be strapped day or night in case Zedra decides to make good on her threats. The po-po is just going to have to bust me red-handed for being in possession of an illegal gun.

After weeks of looking over my shoulder constantly, I decide that Zedra's threats weren't real. Maybe she has calmed down because it seems that Lynzee's career is not faltering due to the release of my book. The tabloids are in a feeding frenzy, trying to dig up people from the past to verify the details of Lynzee's past, but even so, the *New York Times* announces that Lynzee's publisher is going ahead with the release of her latest book, *Skull and Bones*. They are dropping a huge amount of money to promote the book.

Jett interprets it as a bad thing that they're spending so much to promote Lynzee's book. They printed 500,000 copies, and he thinks they're afraid that her reputation is damaged, and she will no longer be able to sell books on the strength of her name alone.

I don't know if I agree with Jett. In the past, Lynzee never had a problem selling hundreds of thousands of books, and I don't think her fans will turn against her now. After all, there are millions of people who are bisexual and homosexual. I also know that controversy sells books. *Skull and Bones* just might be her biggest novel yet, I think hopefully.

But just in case, I will stay strapped.

20

Now that my book is on store shelves, it's time to do a promotional blitz. I spend a large part of my advance on publicity. This is part of the reason I have kept my job, because I knew I would need money for my tour. My publisher is spending a lot also, but a rule I learned a long time ago is that an author must go above and beyond to really stand out. I am determined to be super successful, and I am willing to do whatever it takes.

I do a radio promo commercial and pay to have it aired in seventy-five cities. I line up interviews with radio hosts across the country who supported me during previous promotional tours. Herman takes a vacation day and helps me stay focused and organized during the interviews. I appear on *Good Morning America*, *Oprah*, and a host of local morning shows. My picture is on the cover of several magazines that cater to African American women.

Both *Oprah* and *Good Morning America* try to get Lynzee to appear on their show with me. She declines both offers. I'm not the least bit surprised.

I finally quit my job when it's time to go on the road and do book signings. I travel to thirty cities, where I am met by throngs of people who have read my book. My readers are back stronger than ever. The success of my book is almost better than I even imagined it would be.

I make the *New York Times* bestsellers list two weeks after my publication date. In no time, *Revelations* is in its tenth printing. The hardcover sales are in excess of 400,000 copies. My phone is ringing off the hook for speaking engagements. Since making the *Times*, Arlene has been able to lobby my speaking fees to $15,000. I am willing to do two engagements a month, but no more. Funny, not long ago I was broke as a sick dick dog; now I'm swimming in cash and offers.

Then I receive an e-mail from Lynzee and my euphoria comes to a screeching halt. It says: MY AGENT THINKS I SHOULD SUE YOU FOR A MILLION. I'M CONSIDERING IT. I wonder where in the hell she expects me to get that kind of money. I'm doing well now, but it's not like I have a million dollars lying around to hand over to her—not that she deserves a damn cent from me anyway.

Besides, from what I hear, her own book is doing okay. Maybe she's not selling as many books as she used to—and she damn sure ain't selling as many as I am, I think smugly—but she shouldn't be complaining. After all, I'm the one who went more than a year without a contract.

So, no matter what Lynzee says, I don't feel guilty. I feel cocky as hell. Is this what success feels like? I think I'll send Lynzee a T-shirt with a star on it and my picture in the center. Or maybe I'll send her a copy of my new book with a loving inscription on the title page in big, bold black letters: Sisters. Jealousy. Envy. Truce?

Maybe I'm more like Lynzee than I originally thought.

21

I've got money in the bank now, but have learned my lesson about spending. We put a large chunk of money in the bank before I allow myself to make any purchases. I pay off the mortgage on our home and then we make a few improvements. We build an additional two-car garage on our property. We splurge on an in-ground pool and deck, but decide against the tennis court. I give my close friends five hundred dollars apiece. Of course, Herman doesn't need it, but he appreciates the thought.

Things with Jett are getting back on track. To celebrate our good fortune and our love, we dance nude to old songs in our bedroom and have heated sex afterward. He surprises me with two dozen yellow roses, candy, a new gown, and a beautiful card.

I buy him silk boxers, a gold wrist chain, and take my time selecting the perfect card. Jett is so sentimental when it comes to cards. He gets all emotional, and reads the card at least three times. I love a man who appreciates the small things in life.

Though I'm trying not to spend like crazy these days, I take a trip to Atlanta to buy new clothes. I love Nieman Marcus, so I apply for a charge card. Twenty minutes later, I'm approved. I purchase several suits, shoes, and three Birkin purses. Trying to be fair to my husband and sons, I buy them each a casual suit, shirt, and shoes.

I can't wait to get my Neiman's catalogue in the mail so that I don't have to drive to Atlanta every time I need a new outfit. I love Memphis, but they don't have a Nieman's or a Nordstrom's. What's a woman to do?

I come home from my shopping trip feeling great, but Jamone is waiting for me in the kitchen looking concerned about something. He has just come back from a trip to New York, where he was selling his artwork at a large art show. Javed is at a similar event in Chicago. These two are great businessmen; they know how to divide and conquer to attend as many art shows as possible.

"Hey, Mom," he says, "I need to talk to you."

I sit my purse down on the kitchen island and take a seat on the sofa. "Talk to me, honey." I remove my navy pumps. My feet are killing me.

"I've got a lot to say, so please let me finish before you make any comments." He removes the band from his ponytail, combs his fingers through his hair, and then secures it back. His face looks like it's contorted with pain. I'm getting nervous wondering what could possibly be wrong. Has he gotten some young girl pregnant?

"I promise I'll wait until you're finished."

"Okay. So, you know that art show I went to in New York?"

I nod.

"Well, I'm packing up my stuff after the show is over, and next thing I know, this lady is all up in my face like the *Exorcist*."

I fear that I know where this is going, but I hold my tongue and let him continue.

"Mom, this chick was like a mirage. She looked just like dad."

Oh, hell no. Lynzee had to have been involved to let April know that her brothers were in town. I swallow my response and let my son finish.

"After she introduced herself, she asked me about Pops. Then she asked about Javed."

I couldn't resist. I interrupted him. "And what did you tell her?" I asked with my heart in my throat.

"Come on, Mom, I didn't tell her nothing. This chick could have just gotten out of the psycho ward for all I know."

I sighed with relief, but then he told me the news I had feared from the start of this conversation.

"Mom, this chick told me that Aunt Lynzee is her mother and our Pops is her natural father."

"Jamone . . ."

He holds up a finger for me to hush. "She told me all about the adoption and her quest to find her mother. She said that when Lynzee admitted who her father was, she was shocked that her birth father had married her aunt. You. To be blunt, she wants to establish a relationship with Dad and me and Javed."

"And what did you tell her?" I'm fuming. This whore has balls.

"I said that my pops would probably demand a paternity test. Knowing him, he wouldn't want to have anything to do with her. She was high as the neighborhood drunk, and drinking wine like it was a nickel a glass."

I get up and hug my son, then pat him on the back. My heart palpitates with fear. My worst moment has arrived. The very thing I didn't want to happen has happened. "I'm sorry that I didn't tell you and Javed the truth. I've known about April a few months. Lynzee told me."

His eyes get wide with surprise, but he doesn't seem angry. "Does Pops know?"

I shake my head and admit, "No, I've been keeping it from him."

Again, my son doesn't get mad at me. He looks at me with sympathy in his eyes. I think he understands that this has been hard for me too. "What are we going to do, Mom? I mean, should I tell Pops, or wait for April to contact him?"

"Let her make the first move. It's not your responsibility to tell your father about April."

Jamone goes to the refrigerator and pours himself a glass of orange juice. "So, I take it that Pops and Aunt Lynzee hooked up way back when?" He says it nonchalantly, as if he's talking about some teenage friends and not his own father. I decide not to make a big deal out of his seeming lack of emotion. Perhaps this is just his way of dealing with it.

"It was when Lynzee was a senior in high school, but they kept it quiet. I'm not even sure if my mother knew about it."

"Why didn't she have an abortion?"

"Jamone! Why would you say such a thing?" I scold him, but then realize I'm being hypocritical because I've asked myself the same question countless times already.

"Tyler told me and Javed that her mother has had several abortions."

"How does Tyler know this?"

"Aunt Lynzee told her about it when Tyler told her she thought she was pregnant."

"What do you mean, *thought* she was pregnant? Is Tyler pregnant or not?"

"No, she's not. It was just a scare."

"You know, Jamone, I hope you don't think I condone all of this discussion taking place in front of you boys. And I can't believe Lynzee discussed all her abortions with Tyler. Lynzee has always had a big mouth." I sit back down on the sofa. "But it doesn't matter now, Jamone. I'm just glad Tyler isn't pregnant."

"So is she," he says.

"And as for April, we just have to wait it out and hope that she doesn't bother us anymore."

Jamone puts his glass in the dishwasher. "Want me to tell Javed about April?"

"No. Let this be our secret." This just keeps getting worse. Now I'm asking my son to be complicit in this web of deception I've been weaving ever since I learned about April. I stare into the blackness outside. It's like I've got a black hole dead in the center of my heart and I'm powerless to fill it. "Go on to bed, Jamone. You've got school tomorrow."

My son kisses me goodnight and heads upstairs. After I'm sure he's out of earshot, I get out my cell phone and call Herman. I need someone to talk to.

"Herman, it's Charity. Can you come over my house tomorrow around noon?"

"Sure, I'll be there. Your voice sounds strained. Is something wrong?"

"Yes, but I'm helpless to fix it. Maybe you can give me some good advice."

"Sure, whatever you need."

"Tomorrow then."

The next day, after Jamone leaves for school and Jett goes out to run errands, I wait for Herman to arrive. Jamone seemed fine this morning, as if our conversation never happened. Still, my instincts tell me that he won't be able to keep a secret from Javed. I'm bracing myself for his numerous questions.

A few minutes later, Herman rings the doorbell. I open the door and hug him. "Hello." He kisses me on the cheek and makes his way to the kitchen.

Herman is the incarnation of the black McDreamy. He has clear chocolate coloring, a perfect oval face, high cheekbones, perfectly arched thick brows, and an aristocratic nose. His luscious lips looked as if they've just been kissed. He's wearing a tan Adolpho suit, white shirt, and a tan-and-orange tie. Handmade caramel-colored leather shoes adorn his feet.

"You look handsome, as usual," I tell him after he's taken a seat on the sofa. "Can I get you anything? Water? Juice? Coffee?"

He waves a hand and crosses his leg. "No, nothing. Now, let's get down to business. I barely slept last night worrying over you. I've known you too long to know when something is wrong. Now, tell me what the problem is, and we'll solve it."

I take a seat beside him on the couch and tell him the entire story about April, Lynzee, Jett, and Jamone. When I finish, I'm crying.

"Stop that, will you?" He gets up and hands me a tissue from the island. "Crying never solved anything. It merely gives you puffy red eyes that would look better on a teddy bear." He laughs. "Now, give me a smile."

I break out a smile. "There. Are you happy now?"

He nods. "I'm going to tell you my opinion. You can do with it what you please." He taps my hand and looks me in the eye. "First, you need to tell Jett the truth about April before he hears it from someone else. He's already going to be mad that you kept this secret from him for so long. So, get it over with and tell him everything."

"Oh, I'm not so sure about that. I mean, I don't want to lose Jett."

"To who? Lynzee?"

"I guess that type of thinking is stupid, isn't it?"

"Damn right. Jett loves you, and he expects you to be honest with him. So he's got a love child. This isn't the first or last time this will happen to a man. But let him know the truth and give him the option of deciding if he wants to have a relationship with her or not."

"So, it's that simple? Just tell him the truth."

"Works almost all the time." He smiles. "Besides, you could be just as mad at him that he didn't tell you about his relationship with Lynzee."

It's the *almost* that's killing me. What if telling Jett backfires and he ends up hating my guts? Still, I know my friend is right. I've waited far too long to tell Jett the truth, and now my secrecy is catching up to me. First April approached Jamone, and who knows what she's capable of doing next. I should take responsibility before things get even more out of hand. I'll just have to have faith that my marriage is strong enough to withstand this drama. Maybe now is the right time to do it, since our financial burdens have finally been lifted.

I pat Herman's exquisite hands. "Okay, I'll do it."

"When?"

"This weekend. The twins are going to be in Florida, so we'll have some privacy."

Herman rises. "That's the spirit." He checks his watch. "Now I've got to run. I've got two bodies waiting for me at the funeral home."

I cringe. "I know I've asked you this before, but doesn't it bother you to look at dead bodies all day long?"

"No. It makes me appreciate life. Let me make you smile. Listen up." He proceeds to tell me this joke: "A passenger in a taxi leans over to ask the driver a question and taps him on the shoulder. The driver screams like hell, loses control of the cab, hits a bus, drives up over a curb, and then stops just inches from a large plate window. For a few moments, everything is silent as a ghost inside the cab, and then still shaking, the driver says, 'I'm sorry, but you scared the beJesus out of me.' The frightened passenger apologizes to the driver and says that he didn't realize a mere tap on the shoulder could frighten him so much. The driver replies, 'No, no, I'm sorry. It's entirely my fault. Today is my first day driving a cab. I've been driving a hearse for the last twenty-five years.' " Herman laughs his ass off. I don't. His mortuary humor always creeps me out.

After Herman is gone, I walk to the bathroom and look in the mirror. I can envision the anger on Jett's face when I tell him the truth about his daughter, and I can almost feel the slap that I worry he'll respond with. In that instant, I know that I can't do it. I won't tell him. He's going to have to find out from Lynzee or April. Not me. Our anniversary is on November ninth, and I don't want anything to spoil it—especially if it means bringing an alcoholic daughter into the limelight.

Jett comes in later that afternoon. He says he's going to relax in his recliner and watch a movie. "Can you put me on a bag of microwave popcorn, baby?" he asks.

"Okay." I reach inside the cabinet and retrieve the package, unwrap it, and pop it into the microwave. While I'm waiting, I stare at my gorgeous, bald-headed husband. People tell me all the time that he looks like Louis Gossett, Jr. I think not. Mr. Gossett wishes he had the shit that Jett has. I love that man so much, sometimes it scares me. I'm guilty of loving that man more than I love myself. I know it's wrong, and my mother would kill me if she knew the truth, but I'm weak to love. Jett was my first, and I want him to be my last. I can't imagine being married to anyone else.

Popcorn done, I open it and hand it to Jett.

"Thanks, baby." He smiles. "You want to watch this Western with me? It's a new one."

"Not now, Jett. I've got some work to do in my office." Truthfully, I just don't know if I can handle being around him while I have so much on my mind. I turn to go, and then turn back. "Jett, I know that you were against us having children at first, but after the twins were born, you loved being a father."

He gives me a strange look, because to him, my words have come out of nowhere. But he knows how I operate; I won't budge until he speaks. So, he says, "Yes, I admit it. I was wrong. I love my sons. I wouldn't change a thing."

"Remember when I got my tubes tied?"

"Yes."

"You said, 'Baby, since we did so well on these boys, maybe we should have tried for a daughter.' Remember you said that?"

"Yes, but I wasn't serious. Two children are hard enough to raise these days, let alone three." He eats a few handfuls of popcorn before he says, "You know, if you'd gotten pregnant and we had a girl, I'd bet money that she'd be tall, articulate, love history, and look just like me."

"Jamone and Javed look just like you," I insist.

"Somewhat. They've got your nose, your forehead, and your hands. My daughter would look just like me in every area. I have no doubt about that."

I'm so hurt, I'm speechless. Does he already know about April and is keeping it from me?

Desperate, I ask him a question. "Jett, you didn't get anybody pregnant before you married me, did you?"

"Where are all these questions coming from anyway?"

"Just answer me, Jett."

"Hell no. I've used condoms since I was fifteen. I don't have any strays out there. I'm positive of that."

I fight back tears. *Then how did you get Lynzee pregnant? Are you telling me the truth?* As I consider the possibility that he is lying, I realize that if I don't tell him the truth about April, I'm guilty of being a liar too. Instead of doing what I promised Herman I would, I choose to bury my head in the sand again, and go upstairs without telling Jett about his daughter.

22

It's snowing cornflake size snowflakes in Memphis. The temperature is twenty-eight degrees. I hate cold weather. It's the main reason why we moved from Michigan. Now, we've had freezing cold for almost two weeks, and it doesn't look like we'll get a reprieve for another couple of weeks.

In spite of the bad road conditions, I hop in my car and head for the Olive Garden on Highway 64. I'm meeting Herman for lunch. Driving is brutal because there are splotches of ice on the road. I pass at least two accidents before I get to the restaurant. When I park my car and hurry inside, Herman is waiting.

We hug and say hello. "Can you believe this weather?" I ask.

"No. If it keeps snowing like this, we might have to cut our lunch short and head on back home. The streets are awfully slippery, and I don't want anyone hitting my car. I just bought it last month."

"Another new car? I guess the funeral business pays well," I comment.

He smirks. "You ain't kidding. I'm getting my flying license now, and if business is still booming, I should be able to buy my own small plane in a year or two—a new one, I mean. I'm already looking at some used ones."

That's why I love Herman. He's always trying something new and exciting.

After we're seated, we unwrap our coats, scarves, hats, and gloves. I drape my coat over the back of my shoulders. We accept the menus and scan the available choices.

"I'm going to have some hot soup," I say.

"Me, too. Soup sounds just right on a day like today."

We place our orders and hand back the menus. The waitress places a glass of ice water in front of each of us. I toy with the lemon slice.

"How are the twins doing?"

"Poorly. Jett found a blunt in Jamone's car. Jamone lied and said it was Javed's."

"Who did Jett believe?"

"Neither one of them. He beat the shit of out them with a hose. They're both grounded."

"A hose? Why not a belt?"

"Because it hurts more. Matter of fact, it stings like hell. Those boys were hollering like Jett was cutting off their balls."

Herman laughs. "My, Lord. I'm sure you don't have to worry about that anymore."

"I'm sure we won't."

Herman leans forward and whispers, "Did you hear the latest rumors about Lynzee?"

I lean forward too. "No. What have you heard?"

"Word on the street is that Lynzee and her friend Zedra have a lesbian relationship."

"What? I don't believe that," I say in an indignant tone.

"Girl, rumor is that they've been getting their groove on for thirty-eight years and it's the reason why neither one of them ever married."

"I don't know."

He adds more detail to his gossip. "Don't choke on this, but Lynzee is supposed to be the man, and Zedra is the woman."

I try to imagine the two of them embracing, and the image makes my stomach turn. I want to dismiss Herman's news as idle gossip, but then again, Lynzee just bought Zedra a 2010 BMW and gave her daughter, Naja, her assistant's old car, a 2004 Sequoia.

My cell phone rings. It's Jett. "Where are you?"

"At the Olive Garden. I'm having lunch with Herman."

"You need to get your butt home. Ice and sleet is forecast for the remainder of the day."

"I know how to drive in this weather."

"Charity, don't question me. I said get your butt home before I come and get you." He hangs up.

"Was that Jett?"

"Yes. He thinks I need to head on home."

"Are you going?"

I shake my head defiantly. "Nope. I'm going to enjoy my soup and leave when I'm damn well ready to leave."

Herman laughs. "You're a mess, Charity. Why's he in such a bad mood anyway? Did you two talk about his daughter the way you promised?"

I admit that I haven't told him. "I'm too scared to do it, Herman."

Rather than try to convince me, he merely says, "Okay, but when the shit hits the fan, don't say I didn't warn you."

After we eat and head outside, Herman sees the weather conditions and says, "Jett was right, you know. We should have left an hour ago."

"Be careful, Herman. Call me when you get home."

We go our separate ways. I start up my car and wait a few minutes for the heat to come on. I turn on the defroster, and then the wipers. Just as I'm about to put the car in reverse, someone slides into my back bumper. There is significant damage to my car, but by now, I just want to get home. I don't even exchange numbers with the other driver. I will just pay for the repairs myself.

When I make it home, Jett immediately comes into the garage. Rage is written all over his face. When he notices the large dent on the rear bumper, he walks around to examine it.

"What the hell is this?" he demands.

I don't like his attitude, so I answer with one of my own. "What the hell does it look like? Someone hit me in the parking lot. Aren't you going to ask me if I'm okay?"

He rolls his eyes at me. "Serves you right for going out in this weather anyway. You're going to need a whole new bumper. What insurance company does the other driver use?"

"I didn't get her information," I tell him as I step into the house.

"What?" Jett shouts as he slams the door. "You said she ran into you. She should pay for the damages."

"What are you worried about?" I ask. "It's not like I can't afford to pay for a bumper, Jett."

"There you go wasting money again."

"It's my money," I snap.

"Oh, it's *yours* now, huh?"

I don't know what's brought on this abusive attitude, but I've had enough of it. I tell him in a condescending voice, "Yes, it's *mine*. I don't see you out there writing any books. Hell, seems like you stopped working at the Ford dealership the second I cashed my advance check."

"You bitch!" he yells.

I try to talk some sense into him before this gets any more out of control. "Look, Jett, I don't know what your problem is. I promised you that we wouldn't get broke again, and I think I've kept that promise."

He's not backing down. "Yeah, and then you go and let the other driver off scot-free. If you keep making stupid decisions like this one, we'll be broke before you know it."

I turn to face him. "Are you calling me stupid?"

"I call it like I see it." He pushes past me.

"Don't piss me off, Jett. I can separate this money any time I get ready."

"I knew this would happen," he says bitterly. "You've been looking for an excuse to cut me out, and now you've found it. Fuck it. Take all of your money. I don't need it."

Now I feel stupid. It shouldn't have to come to this.

"I'm sorry, Jett."

"I'm sorry, too. I should have never quit my job." He walks off. I'm left with the shocking realization that my marriage is not nearly as close to being back to normal as I thought. Where is his underlying hostility coming from?

A knock on the front door interrupts my thoughts.

A Caucasian man, wearing a baseball cap, sneakers and jeans is standing on the top step.

"Can I help you?" I ask when I open the door.

"Are you Charity Evans?"

"Yes."

He hands me an envelope. "You've been served." He hurries down the steps that Jett had the foresight to salt.

I shut the door and go into the kitchen. Standing in front of the island, I open the envelope. I read the contents, getting angrier by the minute.

It's a court summons. Lynzee has filed a civil suit against me. She's claiming one million dollars in damages. I grit my teeth and march into our bedroom. Jett is at the sink dying his mustache.

"You won't believe what I just got."

He turns to look at me, anger still in his eyes.

"A summons. Lynzee has filed a civil suit against me."

"For how much?"

"One million dollars." I try to show him the summons, but he refuses to look at it. There is a long, uncomfortable silence. Finally, I ask, "Aren't you going to say anything? This could ruin us."

"You mean ruin you. You're the one with all of the money, remember?" Jett goes into his closet and picks out a pair of dress pants and shirt. He selects a tie and loops it around his neck. He then removes a nice pair of loafers from his shoe rack.

"Jett, I said I was sorry. You know you'll be pissed off if something happens to this money."

"I'm sorry too—for trusting you with the money." He rinses the dye out of his mustache and then dries his hands.

"That's not fair."

He begins to get dressed.

"Where are you going?" I ask.

"Back to the Ford dealership to see if I can get my old job back."

"You're kidding, right?"

He slides a belt through his pant loops and sneers at me. "Do I look like I'm kidding?" He trudges past me.

"I know you're not going out in this weather."

"If you can drive in it, so can I."

I grab his arm. "Please stop this, Jett. I'll give you money to put in an account in your own name."

"No, thank you. I'm a man. I can handle my own business." He walks toward the kitchen and grabs his coat and gloves.

"Jett, I'm begging you. Don't do this. How many times do I have to say I'm sorry?"

"None."

"Then don't go." I block the doorway. He pushes me aside. "Jett . . ."

"Go upstairs to your office and write, Charity, and leave me the hell alone."

He leaves and slams the door.

I feel like black mud that someone has stepped in and the suction is pulling it in deeper. I feel like slapping the shit out of Lynzee. That ghetto rich bitch has got a fight on her hands. If she thinks that I'm going to let her railroad me and take my money, she's sadly mistaken.

23

For days, Jett and I keep up a pretense in front of our sons, but when we're in our bedroom at night, he retreats to his side of the bed and stops all communication. We watch television without saying a word to each other.

I'm hurt that I can't talk to him about the lawsuit Lynzee has filed. It's weighing heavily on my mind. I speak to a few friends and my cousin Kai about the lawsuit. Kai tells me I should settle out of court. I'm incredulous. I haven't done anything wrong. Why should I settle? I'm determined to defend myself against her ridiculous claims of slander. I only wrote the truth. In the meantime, I hope I can keep my family together through all this stress I'm dealing with.

I'm upstairs in my office working on a speech when Javed comes in. It's after three and he just returned home from school. He looks angry. "Mom, I need to talk to you 'bout somethin' important. You got a few minutes?" Javed is wearing oversized jeans and a silver Sean John sweatshirt. As usual, his cornrows are neatly braided and his mustache has been trimmed recently. He has an iPod in his pocket and earphones in his right ear. He is nodding to the beat as we speak.

"Always. Have a seat." My office is not very big, but I've got enough room for a blue recliner, television set ensconced in an armoire, and bookshelves that hold about seven hundred books. My mahogany desk is U-shaped, and is usually packed with papers and reference materials. My old office was four times bigger with a kitchenette and bathroom. With the money I've made lately, I feel like adding on to our home and making my office larger, but I'm obligated to Jett to not to spend too much money. It's killing me to keep that promise. A girl needs things.

"Jamone and I been talkin'."

"Yes?"

"Jamone told me about April."

"Oh." I don't know how else to respond. So much time has passed that I almost thought Jamone really was going to keep April a secret between me and him.

"Have you told Pops about her yet?"

"No."

"Why not?"

"The timing just isn't right." I can't look him in the face, I'm so ashamed.

"Pops is going to be real angry when he finds out. Me and Jamone think all three of us should tell him together. You know, make a united front."

"That's an option. I'll think about it. Give me until the weekend." I don't want to tell him that their father is so angry at me right now that there's no way we could add news of April to the mix.

An awkward silence fills the room. Javed is about to leave, but then he turns back around. "I thought we had money now. Why is Pops back working at the Ford dealership?"

I'm thoroughly embarrassed. I admit, "Because he's angry at me. He doesn't have to work. He's making a point and I don't like it."

"Then tell him to quit."

"I've tried. He won't listen to me." I lower my head.

"I hate it when y'all fight," he says.

"So do I, son, but sometimes these things happen. Don't worry, though. We'll get through it."

"You know, Mom, Jamone and I appreciate y'all's marriage. Both of us want the two of you to stay married forever."

I wink my eye at him. "Don't worry. Jett doesn't want a new

partner, and neither do I." Even though they are practically adults, it kills me to think of how it will hurt my boys if Jett and I can't repair our marriage. I have to find a way to apologize for insulting him the other day and telling him it's my money.

A great idea comes to me.

"Hey, Javed, you know your father has been wanting a new Harley ever since he had to sell the other one to pay bills, right?"

"Uh-huh."

"Well, I'm going to buy him a new one. I want you to see if you can pick his brain and find out what color he'd like."

"That's easy. I already know. He's always telling us he wants to get a red Harley."

Armed with this new information and inspired to improve my marriage, I finish up the speech I was working on, jump in my car, and head to a Harley-Davidson dealership. In no time, I have picked out the bike, specifying that it should be red, and arranged a delivery date.

On the drive back home, I'm bubbling with joy. I know that Jett is going to be happy. But I'm not finished. I plan on getting up in the morning and going to the bank. I'm going to put half of the money in Jett's name. I know the manager at the bank, and I'm sure that she'll let me open an account in his name.

Herman calls me before I get home.

"I finished my training and now I have my pilot's license. I want you to come flying with me to celebrate."

"Unh-uh. No way are you getting me up in no small plane."

"Why not? It's completely safe. What, you don't trust me?"

"Sure don't," I joke. "You might be trying to take me up there to drum up new business."

"What the hell are you talking about?"

"Uh, you're a funeral director. What better way to get more dead bodies than to take all your friends flying in some rattling old plane?"

He laughs, but insists again that it's safe and I should come flying with him. He's begging so much that I begin to wonder what's going on. He has been calling a lot lately, asking me to do things with him. Maybe my friend is going through a dry spell and he's lonely.

I can't ask him about it, though, because he just keeps talking about that darn plane. He talks so much I don't even get a chance to tell him about the new motorcycle I just bought. It's probably better anyway. If I mention Jett's name, Herman will just ask about April again, and I don't want to hear it. I am in a hopeful mood, and I don't want anything to ruin that.

I get off the phone because I'm tired of hearing him beg. The best he gets out of me is "I'll think about it." I park in the driveway and head into the kitchen. I'll make a nice dinner, and maybe Jett and I will enjoy a peaceful family meal with our boys.

24

Jett ends up being his usual moody self during dinner, but I don't let it bother me. I know I'll have the husband I know and love back as soon as I hand him his bank book and the keys to his new motorcycle. I head up to my office to begin working on ideas for my next book.

I gather my notes and scan the pages. I've got at least five book ideas, but not one of them, I feel, is a bestseller. I know that I'm going to have to dig in and come up with something within the next few weeks so that I can keep my editor happy. Because *Revelations* made the *Times* list, Arlene was able to negotiate a much better contract. They will be paying me almost ten times more than what I got for *Revelations*, so I have to make sure this book is even better than the last.

Music always relaxes me. I pop in an Everette Harp CD, and enjoy the beat. Minutes later, I'm popping my fingers and feeling like I'm making strides. I try to write about subjects that are hot topics on the news and in the newspapers. The hottest topic is the Afghan war, but I don't want to write about that. Then there's the Swine Flu virus. That doesn't interest me either. What about the sex-trafficking industry? Yeah, that could be big if the children have been brought to the States. No, that won't work. I'm back to square one: the Afghan war. What if I write a story about a female vet who was injured in Afghanistan and comes home to an unsympathetic home life? She could be suffering physically with her lost limb, and mentally with Post Traumatic Stress Syndrome. I could go up to the Veterans' Administration hospital and interview the female vets. And what if she . . .

The phone rings, interrupting my flow. "Hello?"

"Hello, it's me."

Fucking, Lynzee. She's got some nerve calling me. "Yes. What do you want?"

"Revenge."

"Revenge? What have I done to you?"

"You ruined my career. You slandered my name. You're going to pay for that."

"Lynzee, I only told the truth."

"And some of those truths were private. The public didn't need to know about Heidi."

"I may have gone a little too far on that. I'm sorry. I didn't know that—"

"That you would fuck up my life?"

"Lynzee, what are you talking about? You and I both know that your sales were already sliding before I published *Revelation*. It's not like your publisher dumped you or something."

She hesitates for a minute before delivering a comeback. "No, well, uh, it's hurt my lecturing jobs. The colleges view me as some trashy has-been now that I've been splattered all over the gossip pages. Even the late-night talk show hosts have turned me into a joke in their monologues. You fucked me real good. I'm never going to forget this. I would never do you like this. Never in a million years. I thought you loved me."

"I do. I do, Lynzee. I'm really sorry that things turned out like this. Tell you what, I've got some money. What would you think about making a settlement? I'll be fair."

"How much?"

"Let's say two hundred thousand."

"That's chump change. I know you can do better than that."

The CD stops and I put another one on. "How about two hundred fifty-thousand?"

"No. No amount of money can reduce the shame you've brought to my name." I can hear her taking a long drag on a cigarette. "You could say publicly that the book was a bunch of lies."

"Then what would that do to my credibility? No, I told the truth and you know it."

"Then I guess we're back to the lawsuit." She exhales. "And you've forced me to take further action."

"What do you mean?"

"I'm going to have a press conference and reveal to the public that all of your books have been written by book doctors."

"You wouldn't." My lips curl in anger.

"Why shouldn't I? Then again, I could keep silent for five million."

"How in the world do you expect me to come up with five million dollars?"

"I don't care. My attorney says that I've got a good case and he's sure we can win."

Now I'm fuming. She never intended to settle the lawsuit. She just wants me to beg her. "I've got a good attorney, too, Lynzee, who assures me that we can win."

"I doubt it. The public is going to find out that you're nothing more than an opportunist." She takes another long drag, and I realize that her smoking session with me is soon coming to an end.

"That's not true."

"The hell it's not. The only reason you made the *Times* is because you defamed my name. The writing was pitiful. But I'm not surprised. You never could write."

"Fuck you, Lynzee. I'm a good writer, and it's about time that you acknowledged that."

"You couldn't write an article for a magazine without an editor."

"That's not true."

"I heard that you paid a book doctor fifty thousand for your last book. If you could write, you wouldn't need one. I have never needed one."

"For your information, I didn't use a book doctor on my last book. I wrote it all by myself. I will agree that I was given a senior editor this time, something that hasn't happened in the past. But you know all about that, don't you?"

"I don't know what you're talking about." She chokes on the smoke and expends a bout of coughing. Her doctor told her years ago to ditch the cigarettes. She wouldn't listen.

"You and your agent had me blacklisted. You made sure that I didn't get a good editor. You felt so threatened by my work that you would go to any means necessary to stop my success. That's really pitiful. A part of me feels sorry for you."

"You bitch. I'll see you in court. And by the way, have a box of tissues with you. You're going to be crying like a baby by the time my attorney finishes with your fat ass."

I hear her coughing again as she hangs up.

My head falls into my cupped hands. I never thought that Lynzee and I would fight like this. I wish Mama was here to help fix things between us.

I'm worried about the lawsuit. What if she wins? What if I have to go back to work selling cars?

I check my watch. It's nine-fifteen. I shut down my computer and organize my notes. I'll work on my book when I'm in a better mood. I turn off the lights to my office and go downstairs to my bedroom.

I take a shower and change into one of my prettiest gowns. I need to feel the arms of my man tonight. I need to know that he's got my back.

I find the remote on Jett's nightstand. To get him in a good mood, I turn on the Western channel. Then I get into the bed and wait.

Jett doesn't make an entrance until ten forty-five. I want to ask him why he's so late, but I let it slide. I don't need to start another argument right now. I wait patiently for Jett to take off his clothes, shower, and get into the bed.

Like he has for the past few weeks, he gets on his side of the bed as far from me as possible. He picks up the remote and changes the channel to the eleven o'clock news.

"Jett?" I say, turning to face him. "Lynzee called."

To my relief, he answers me. "Oh yeah?"

"I offered to settle the lawsuit, but she wouldn't."

"I don't know why you're surprised. She wants to take everything you have. She wants to sabotage your career and bring you back down to the struggling writer that you used to be."

I casually slip my arm across his waist. He doesn't pull back. "Do you think it's my fault that Lynzee's fans have lost respect for her?"

"No. If you didn't tell her story, someone else was bound to. The truth can be a hard pill to swallow."

"Thanks for your support, honey." I learn over and kiss him on the lips. He kisses me back. The kiss deepens, and I feel his hands pushing open my thighs. I'm in heaven. I wasn't expecting all of this. He inserts two fingers in my vagina, and then strokes me until I'm wet. Sensing that I'm ready, he removes my gown. I remove his boxers and exhale. I reach over and massage his organ, creating a smooth rhythm that I know he enjoys. In less than a minute, his tip is moist. I hear him groan, and I know he's ready.

I casually push him onto his back and get on top and straddle him. He loves for me to take control, and I don't mind it a bit. I reach down and kiss him, and continue to massage him down there. He moans again, and this time, I moan with him.

I feel him reaching over for the remote. Seconds later, the television set is off. I push his love muscle inside me and start a slow pelvic gyration. His hips lift up against mine and match my hypnotic rhythm. I suck in air and begin to speed up the pace. He's riding high along with me, and I hear him sucking in air, too.

I release his lips and shift into third gear. We're entering the point of no return and are powerless to stop. Then I feel him arch his back and raise his hips higher. We ride each other at a racehorse pace until I feel him stiffen, and then relax.

I try to keep it going, because I'm not finished. I need another minute and I'll share the pleasure with him. He's up for the challenge and gives me more of him. My heart is beating like bass drums. I'm close, so close . . . and then I'm there. I feel impassioned. I feel loved.

As we clean ourselves with tissue, Jett kisses me again. Finished, I turn over to my left side. Seconds later, I feel his arm wrap around my waist. I feel like singing. I'm so happy.

In less than a minute, I hear the soft murmur of Jett snoring. I smile and snuggle deeper into him. Right now I know I can conquer anything. I know that I can beat Lynzee at her own game and come out swinging. I close my eyes and imagine the judge rendering her verdict.

"I find the defendant not guilty," the judge says. I smile, and in seconds, fall asleep knowing everything is going to be just fine in the Evans household. Just fine.

25

Jett waves bye and heads back to work with a smile on his face. Things have been steadily improving between us, especially since I gave Jett his new Harley and his bank book. He loves his motorcycle even more than the one he had to sell.

The moment I step into the kitchen, my cell phone is ringing. I pick it up. There are five missed calls from Herman. It's Herman calling now.

"Hello, Herman. What's with all the calls?"

His voice sounds bubbly. "I bought a small used plane! I want you to go for a ride with me, and I won't take no for an answer."

"I told you that I'm scared."

"Of what? Airplanes are safer than cars. And I'm a damned good pilot. C'mon. Just go with me on a short jaunt. I'll have you back home in ninety minutes."

I check my watch. It's almost one. If he gets here in thirty minutes and we go for the ride, I've still got time to have dinner ready by five. Things are improving with Jett, and I don't want to rock the boat by having dinner late.

"Okay, I know you're never going to stop asking until I say yes, so I'll go. But I have to be back home by three-thirty."

While I wait for Herman to come over, I climb the stairs to my office and jot down a few notes. I've got three chapters completed on my new book, and I must say that it's coming along pretty well. The speech that I gave last week was well received. My agent told me to start expecting more calls. Things are getting better all around. The only dark cloud lurking is Lynzee's lawsuit.

I meet with my attorney Teddy Bell once a week to discuss Lynzee's witnesses as well as my witnesses. He prepares me for the questions that the prosecution is going to ask me. We go over and over my answers until he feels that my rebuttal will weaken their case. Sometimes he comes out to our home, or I stop by his office. He's gathering more information on Lynzee's background to prove that everything I said in my book is true. He is even more confident now that we'll win.

I'm jotting down a few more notes when I hear Herman's Mercedes pulling up in the driveway. I hurry downstairs and answer the front door.

"Hello there," I say, giving him a hug.

"Hey." He smiles. "You about ready to get going?"

I pat my pockets down, feeling for my keys. "Just a minute." I retrieve my keys from the laundry room hook and leave the twins a note, then lock up the house and follow Herman to his car.

Even when he's casual, Herman is dressed to the nines. Violet silk slacks and a matching windowpane top are draped on his body like a mannequin. I compliment him as usual. For a man who doesn't own a pair of jeans, I expect to see him always looking his best. He never disappoints me.

We buckle our seat belts after we're seated in his car, and head out of the driveway. The music is turned on to 103.5 FM.

He pats my leg. "So, tell me. How did Jett enjoy his gift?"

"He absolutely loved it. I couldn't have made him happier."

"Not even with sex?"

I tap him on the shoulder. "You're not going to get X-rated on me and start talking about sex, are you?"

"Possibly." His smile is wicked.

"Well, I'm not telling you a thing. You're always trying to get me to share details, but you never tell me a thing about you.

I'm beginning to believe that you're lying about being gay."
Even though I'm joking, I realize as I say it that the idea is not
so far-fetched. I have never met one of Herman's dates.

"Why would I lie about that? Matter of fact, I just got back
from a weekend tryst with my significant other."

"Oh, yeah?"

"Yes. I've got plans for next month, too." He winks at me.
"Do you believe me now?"

"No."

"Like I said, why would I lie?"

"I haven't figured out that part yet."

As he turns onto the freeway and heads toward Memphis International Airport, Herman changes the subject. We talk
about the twins. Herman wants to see their latest artwork. He
needs a new piece for his foyer. Herman owns a home on Mud
Island. Only people with money live where he lives. Harold
Ford Jr., the ex-congressman, used to be one of his neighbors.

I've come to expect Herman's jokes about the funeral business, and he doesn't disappoint me.

"A funeral is being held in a church. At the end of the service, the pall bearers are carrying the casket out when they accidentally bump into a wall, jarring the casket. They hear a
faint moan, open the casket, and find out that the woman is actually still alive. She lives for ten more years and dies. A ceremony is again held at the same church. At the end of the
ceremony, the pall bearers are again carrying out the casket.
As they walk by the husband, he cries out, 'Watch that wall!'"

Herman's jokes always make me laugh.

"Jamone told me something funny the other day. Would you
like to hear it?" I ask coyly.

"Shoot."

"A man walks into a bar and sees a little old man dressed in
plaid pants, a striped shirt, and a black beret. I mean, he looks
ancient. The old man is sitting alone, crying into his drink. The
young guy stops and asks the old man what's wrong.

"The old man says, 'I have a twenty-two-year-old lover at
home. She makes love to me every morning, then she makes
me blueberry pancakes and sausage. For lunch she makes me

homemade soup and my favorite cherry crisp for dessert.' He's crying even louder now as he says, 'Then she makes love to me all afternoon. For dinner she makes me a gourmet meal with wine and then makes love to me until three a.m.'

"So the young guy says, 'She sounds perfect. Why the hell are you crying?'

"The old guy wipes his red eyes and says, 'I can't remember where I live!'"

Herman laughs his ass off. "That was tight, Charity. You got any more?"

I laugh too. "Not right now. I've got to hit up Jamone again. He's the jokester in the family."

We pull up to the private hanger and Herman parks. When he shows me his small single-engine plane, I see that it's even smaller than I expected. It doesn't look like there's any way to survive a crash in a plane this size. I feel my heart start galloping in my chest.

Herman is ecstatic. "Isn't she a beauty?"

"Uh huh," I say, feeling a bit faint. I want to back out, but don't want to disappoint my friend.

He helps me into the plane and I fasten my seat belt while I say a quick prayer. I've got goose-bumps on my arms, I'm so scared. What have I gotten myself into?

Herman closes the glass top and steers the plane onto the runway. He hollers over to me. "It's okay to be a little scared. I was, too, the first time I went up. In a few minutes you'll feel differently, though. Bet on it."

I'm strapped in, but I grip the arm rests for dear life. We whisk off down the long runway and then get in line for take-off. I'm so nervous I feel like asking Herman to let me out. I think about my sons. I think about Jett. I think about Lynzee and Tyler. What would they do without me? I do know that Jett would want to kill me if he knew that I was going up in a plane with Herman. I've learned not to tell him all of my business, especially when it comes to spending time with Herman. I'm sure that he does the same thing. We love each other, but we know how to avoid rocking the boat most of the time.

Before I know it, Herman and I are speeding down the runway in preparation for take-off. The engine sounds so loud. I start praying harder than I've ever prayed before.

Herman looks over at me. "You okay?"

I nod yes, but I'm lying through my teeth. I hear Herman speaking to the tower. The next thing I know, the tiny plane is lifting up and up and up. I close my eyes and hold my breath. My fingernails are digging into the armrests as I brace myself for whatever might happen.

"Relax," Herman says in a soothing voice.

"That's easy for you to say." My eyes are still closed. I slowly open one and glance at my surroundings. I can see clouds and nothing but blue, blue sky. I open both of my eyes in total awe. We are inside one of the clouds, and in these close surroundings, I feel like I can almost touch them. Fear leaves me. I'm beginning to understand what Herman was talking about. Nothing but natural beauty is all around me. I turn my head from left to right, observing and enjoying what I'm seeing.

"You okay now?"

I smile. "I'm just fine. It's beautiful up here, and so serene."

Herman smiles back. "See, I told you. Riding in a plane like this one is a unique experience. It's wild. Like stupid wild. You following me?"

"Yes." I look down below and see the ground layout of Memphis. All of the plots look so well designed. And Interstate 40, which makes a circle around the city, looks like a postcard.

"Thanks, Herman. I'll never forget this."

"It ain't no thang. And we can do this again sometime. I'd like to fly you down to the Bahamas. If your schedule permits, we can go in June or July. We can rent a car and drive down to the Grand Bahamas, do a little gambling, and come on back home."

"That would be fun." I'll have to start thinking of ways to get away for a few days without angering Jett. Speaking of Jett, I remember I have to get home and prepare his dinner. I check my watch. Damn, it's getting late. "Herman, it's almost two-fifteen. Remember I told you that I had to be home at three-thirty."

"I'm right on it. We'll land in a few minutes. Just let me get clearance from the tower."

I listen as Herman makes contact with the air traffic controller. He gives us the okay to land ten minutes later. I'm surprising myself with my chutzpah. I never felt that I could make such bold moves, but I'm proud of myself for getting beyond my fear. The man above is letting me know in his own way that the sky is the limit for me. It's time I listen.

Once on the ground, my legs feel light. Herman salutes a fellow pilot as we pass by, and we walk to his car. The drive home goes quickly, and we arrive at twelve minutes past three. I kiss Herman good-bye and hurry inside the house.

I clean my hands and face and start dinner, chicken and sausage jambalaya. Soon, the twins are in the kitchen, checking out what's in the pot.

"Mmm, Mom. Something sure smells good," Jamone states.

Javed says, "I saw Herman's car leave. Where'd you two go?"

I smile. "We went for a ride in his plane." I set the table. "One of you should call him. He needs a new piece for his foyer."

"I'll call him tomorrow," Javed says. "Business is slow right now." He taps my shoulder. "I think that Herman is really feelin' you, Mom."

"Word," says Jamone.

"Herman is gay. I've told you guys that over and over again. He's my friend. Nothing more."

"Then why don't Pops like him?"

Just then Jett comes in through the kitchen door. "Did someone mention my name?"

I rush to my man and hug him tightly. "Yes. I was just telling our sons how much I love my husband."

Jett looks at Javed, then Jamone. They all bust out laughing. "Your mom has always been a terrible liar." He taps me on the butt. "Now, Mrs. Evans, fix my plate. I'm starved."

26

Jett rides his bike almost every day and loves it. He still insists that he's going to keep his job at King Ford, but I don't believe it. He rarely stays until nine the way he used to. And to my pleasure, we've been loving each other so much, it's like we're living in *The Best Little Whorehouse in Texas*.

The trial is coming up in July, but I'm not worried. I haven't heard from Lynzee again and don't expect to. What surprises me is that Tyler has cut off all contact with Javed and Jamone. I know their feelings are hurt. They used to be close. I'm positive that Lynzee is responsible for Tyler's actions. It's a shame that she had to get the kids involved in our business.

My cousin Kai, who told me to settle the lawsuit with Lynzee, is as shocked as I am over Lynzee's greed. Being an attorney, she gives me every piece of advice that she can about when and how to state my objection to the lawsuit. She also wants to make sure that I make it clear that Lynzee was involved in having me blacklisted. Thankfully, my attorney has found concrete evidence that concludes that Lynzee is guilty as hell. He has a witness that is willing to testify at the trial. A part of me can't wait to get the trial started, and another part of me hates to think that I'll be in the position once again to ruin Lynzee's career.

Speaking of careers, mine is still going well—better than ever, actually. It takes me two to three hours a day to answer all of my fan mail on the Internet. Along with fame comes responsibility. I can afford to hire an assistant like Lynzee has, but I'm too cheap. And I can just hear Jett complaining about wasting money.

While reading the newspaper with Jett early one morning, I come across an article about a black woman who enrolled at the Memphis Culinary Academy, graduated, and went on to open her own catering business. She's known as the black Martha Stewart around town. She's booked six months in advance, and is making more money than she ever has in her life.

"Do you think I'm a good cook?" I ask Jett.

"One of the best I know." He continues reading the sports section.

"What about my baking?"

"You know that nobody can compare to your sweet potato pies and cobblers." He glances up over the paper. "Why do you ask?"

"I'm thinking about enrolling in college." I sip my coffee. "A culinary college. I think I'd like to open up a French bakery."

Jett laughs. "Whoever heard of a black woman running a French bakery?"

"That's the kick. It hasn't been done. Of course, I'd hire two workers that are actually from France to work with me." My mind is racing like a ticker tape at the stock market. I can go to school for two years, take a couple of seminars in France, and open up my bakery within a three-year period.

"What about your writing career?"

"I can still do that. I can finish this next book, then enroll in classes for the fall semester. I just think it would be a good idea to have a plan B, you know." The one thing I don't admit to him is that some of my zeal for writing is gone ever since the publication of *Revelations*. I love my success, but hate the drama that has come along with it.

He looks confused. "Charity, for years you wouldn't get another job. You said all you wanted was to be a *New York Times* bestseller."

"Yes, and now I've done that." I smile proudly. "But I've been

giving it some thought lately. The publishing industry is changing, especially for black authors. I've been in this business for
almost twenty years, and I know the future. It doesn't look
good for writers like me. When I first started in the nineties,
the publishers were actively seeking black authors, handing
out huge contracts. Now the market is gutted with black authors. Besides, they're coming up with e-books, Kindles, and
books online. It's only a matter of time before publishers start
paying out much smaller contracts. And then where will we
be?"

Jett gets up. "Well, thank God we paid this house off."

"I know, but we still have other obligations, namely the
twins' tuitions for college. That's going to cost a pretty penny."

"And now your tuition. Any chance that I can talk you out of
it?"

"No, not a chance." I get up and take Jett's and my cups to
the sink. "The more I think about this, the better I like it. I'd
like to leave a family business for our grandchildren to run one
day."

Jett kisses my cheek. "Time for me to go. I might be late
tonight, so don't wait dinner."

I walk him to the back door, give him another kiss, and wave
him off. I stack the dishwasher and then head upstairs to my
office. After consulting the Yellow Pages, I find the school,
call, and ask for an admissions application to be sent to my
house. It turns out that many people have been calling because
of the article in the paper. This just feels right. I can't wait for
the brochures and application to come in the mail. I know I
can be a success.

Later in the afternoon, the twins come home. Jamone brings
Holly with him. Javed is alone, as usual. I say hello to Holly and
wait for them to go upstairs to Jamone's room. I signal Javed
that I have something to talk to him about.

"What's up, Mom?" he asks, chomping down on a pretzel.

"Your love life. Jamone has been dating Holly for two years.
I've never seen you bring a female home. Why is that?" I take
one of his pretzels.

"I'm straight. I've been dating someone for over a year."

I'm surprised. "Then why haven't we met her?"

"Because she's African and a Muslim. Pops wouldn't approve."

I shake my head. "Her religion would be a problem."

"I know. That's why I never bring her around."

"Sooner or later your dad is going to find out."

"That won't be until I move out and move into my own place."

"You're not thinking about reneging on college, are you?"

"Yes. I'm not college material. And with my grades being so low, I won't be able to get into a good college, so why waste the money?"

"You're going to break your dad's heart. He wanted both of you to go to college and get a degree like he did. He also wants grandkids soon. He's not getting any younger you know."

"Then maybe April will give him some."

My mouth drops open. I'm speechless.

"I know you haven't told him yet. Mom, if you don't hurry up and tell him the truth, I can't say much about the future of y'all's marriage." He puts his hand on my shoulder. "I know if my wife knew a secret about my life and didn't tell me, I'd never trust her again."

He leaves me with my eyes as wide as an owl's.

27

I've been working very hard to finish my next book, and I'm dead tired: tired of writing, tired of giving speeches, and tired of having to lie to Jett. I'm glad for the diversion when the phone rings and I see that it's Kai.

We've been talking a lot lately. I guess she likes having someone to talk to since Lynzee no longer takes her calls. In fact, I know she has hard feelings about Lynzee, because half the time when she calls, it's to offer advice on beating Lynzee at trial. This time, she calls with gossip.

Kai always hears the news about Lynzee before I do. She spends hours every day reading blogs on the Internet. Sometimes I wonder how she ever gets any work done.

"So, do you want to hear the latest on your sister?" she asks.

I balance the cordless phone and say, "Hell yes," as I decide to whip up a batch of brownies for the twins.

"First off, Lynzee's got a job."

"A job? Where?" I get out the pan for the brownies and coat the surface with Crisco.

"At UCLA. She's teaching creative writing."

"That's good news," I say.

"Um, you realize that this is a step down for her, don't you? She hates teaching."

"I know, but she told me colleges had stopped calling her for speaking engagements. This is better than nothing."

Kai laughs. "Stop trying to sugar-coat this. You know Lynzee must be miserable in the classroom. I'm sure she only took the job because no one was offering anything better."

Of course, Kai is right. My mind is envisioning Lynzee speaking in front of a classroom of horny, disrespectful teens. It doesn't fit. Lynzee's ego is too big to teach.

Then I remember that UCLA is in Los Angeles. "What about her house in Oakland?"

"Her house is on the market. Right now she's renting a home in L.A."

"How'd you find this out?"

"Girl, you know I have my sources." She sneezes. "Trust me, lady. This information is right on point."

I pour the thick mixture into the pan and place it in the hot oven. "I'm sorry, Kai, I don't like this. Sure, I want fame and fortune, but not at the expense of Lynzee losing her livelihood."

"It's too late to think about that now."

I take a seat on one of the bar stools and glance at the clock on the microwave. It's two o'clock, noon in California. "Maybe I should call her."

"For what? You can't change her situation—unless you're willing to give her that five million that she's asking for."

I bite my bottom lip. "I don't have that kind of money."

"And what if you did? You'd be broke and doing the same thing that Lynzee is doing, teaching. I'm sorry, Charity. I know that you love your sister, but she stabbed you in the back when she had you blacklisted. Look how long you suffered without any money."

"I know. I'll never forget it."

"Then stop being a mamsy-pamsy and buck up. Lynzee deserves exactly what she's getting."

I'm a little surprised. I didn't know that Kai's feelings about Lynzee run so deep.

"I know Lynzee is getting payback, but when you see someone you love suffering, it hurts."

"Bullshit. Get yourself together, lady. I betcha Jett won't be hurt about it. He had to go back to work, remember? And you had to prostitute yourself as a car salesman too. Don't tell me that job wasn't humbling."

"Yeah, it was."

"Then teaching school won't kill Lynzee. At least she's working in her field. She might learn something. You know that all of her books sound alike. She gets on a soap box and can't stop preaching." Kai laughs.

I laugh too. "You're right. All of Lynzee's books do have the same scenario. She thinks that she knows everything."

"As far as I'm concerned, she's in the right place. You know how much it hurt me to see you working at that Mazda dealership. I don't have any respect for someone who purposely harms you or your family. I love Lynzee because she's my cousin, but I don't like her. Don't you know how much I love you, lady?"

I smile. "Yes, I know, Kai. And I love you, too. Why couldn't the gods have made you my sister?"

"We're just like sisters," she says and sneezes again.

"Are you getting a cold? What's the temperature there?"

"Yes, I'm coming down with something. It's about fifty degrees here, cold for this time of year. I've been outside too much tending to my roses."

"Girl, you and those roses. But I can't blame you. I tried to get Jett to plant a rose garden but he won't do it. He says that he doesn't want to cut out another section in the yard."

"Damn. Don't y'all have two acres?"

"Yes, we do, but with the garden and the pool and pond, all of the extra space is taken up. As it stands, all three of our flower beds are full with annuals and bushes."

"Not to worry, lady. I know your yard is pretty."

"Thanks to Jett, it is." I pause. "You know that Lynzee had a rose garden. It was right next to her pool."

"So, we're back to her."

"Yeah. I still feel bad. Call me gullible, but I can't help it." I turn on the oven light and check on the brownies.

"Well, I might as well tell you the rest of the news. You might change your mind about Lynzee after you hear what she's done."

I brace myself. "Tell me, Kai. What's happened?"

"Did you know that Tyler is pregnant?"

"No, she's not. Jamone told me it was just a scare."

"That was the first time. This time it's for real."

"What! How could Lynzee let this happen? Didn't she know enough to keep Tyler away from that boy after the first scare?"

"Keep her away from him?" Kai says with a laugh. "Are you kidding? Lynzee signed for Tyler and her baby's daddy to get married."

"What! Tyler is practically a baby herself! What could she know about a husband and baby?"

"I feel the same way. If it were my daughter, she would have aborted the fetus. Then again, if Tyler were my daughter, I would have had her on birth control."

No wonder Tyler hasn't called the twins. "When did Tyler get married?"

"On Valentine's Day."

"How cute."

"How ironic," Kai states. "Especially since the reason they got married in the first place is so that Raymond wouldn't go to jail for statutory rape. Such a shame. But the worst thing I can say about the scumbag is that he's a republican."

"First it was Colin Powell, now we have one in our own family? What is this country coming to?" I check on the brownies. The kitchen is alive with the chocolaty fragrance of fresh baked goodness. "I hate to say it, but Lynzee isn't a very good mother. She's thinking more about her son-in-law's legal problems than her daughter's future. Tyler could be divorced by the time she's seventeen."

"The fact that Lynzee never married might have something to do with it."

"Yes, I hadn't factored that into the equation." I pause for a long time. "You know, Kai, speaking of mothers, I've been meaning to tell you something about Lynzee."

"You mean her daughter, April? I've been waiting for you to tell me." She sneezes again and blows her nose.

"When did you find out about April and how come you never

told me you knew?" I wasn't expecting to hear that she already knew about all of this.

"You should know by now that I have my ways of finding stuff out. It took you long enough to talk to me about it."

"I'm sorry. I was just so embarrassed about the entire ordeal."

"I know. Don't worry about it. Does Jett know yet?"

"No, I haven't told Jett."

I hear footsteps. I turn around and see Jett enter the kitchen. He says, "Haven't told Jett what?"

28

Sweat breaks out on my forehead as I scramble for a plausible answer. Then I think, what the hell? I'm too tired to keep up the charade any longer.

"Jett, I've got something important to talk to you about." I tell Kai that I'll call her back later.

Jett removes his tie and stands before me. I'm quaking in my boots, hoping that he won't be too mad. "I'm really tired, Charity. Can we talk later?"

"No. This has been going on for far too long." My heart is beating so fast, I can barely control it. "Why didn't you tell me that you had an affair with Lynzee years ago?"

He's deathly silent. It takes him quite a while to answer. I wonder if he's trying to come up with a lie, but he doesn't deny it. "Because it didn't mean anything."

"Fuck that, Jett. You screwed my sister. That's something that I should have known before I married you."

"Would it have made a difference?"

"Yes."

"Well, it's too late now." I notice that he's sweating. He takes a seat at the kitchen table. "I never loved Lynzee, if that's what you're thinking. We were both young. It was just sex."

"Maybe for you, but not for her."

"Why are we talking about this now?"

I take a seat across from him. "Because you got Lynzee pregnant."

"No fucking way!"

"Yes, you did. And she had a girl child. And she put it up for—"

He jumps up from the table. "What the hell are you talking about? A baby?"

My body is so tense it feels like steel. I grab hold of the side of the chair and plow on. "She gave her daughter up for adoption. Her name is April. She'll be thirty-four years old soon."

"Stop bullshitting with me, Charity. I used condoms."

"Apparently, it busted or had a hole in it." I stare him dead in the face. "I've seen a picture of April. There's no denying it. She's your female twin." Now the tears come. They roll down my cheeks like molasses.

He stands in front of me with his hands on his hips. "You've seen a picture of her? How long have you known about this?"

My bottom lip quivers. "Since last summer." More tears fall as I brace myself for his upcoming anger.

"And you're just now telling me?"

"Yes. I was afraid of what you might do. You've always wanted—"

"A daughter." I can see his temples jumping. "So, you're a liar. And you're not trustworthy."

"Jett, I—" I stand up, hoping to feel his arms wrap around me. Instead, he slaps me.

"You lying bitch. I could kill you for this." He slaps me again. "You're not fit to be called my wife."

I feel my fury rising. How dare he try to put all of this on me!

"This is as much your fault as it is mine! You lied, Jett. You weren't honest."

"You shouldn't have lied about my daughter. That's unforgivable. It should have been my decision whether I wanted to make contact with her or not. Not yours." His nose flares open. "I can't stand the sight of you." He turns to walk away.

"Jett. Please let me explain."

He keeps walking. I crumble back down on a chair. My face falls to the table and I cover my head with my hands. My shoulders heave up and down, wracked with sobs. It's over. I know it's over. He hates my fucking guts. I should have told him long ago. I should have listened to Herman, Jamone, Javed, and Kai. I feel like the biggest fool in the world. What have I done? What's to become of my marriage? Will Jett leave, or will he give me a second chance to be the kind of wife I know he wants and needs?

I don't know how long I sit there crying my eyes out. The sound of quickly approaching steps makes me lift my head. It's Jett. He has two suitcases in his hands.

"Where are you going?" I demand. I get up and move beside him. I try to touch his arm.

He yanks his body from mine. "That's none of your business." He begins to walk toward the back door.

"Jett, please don't go. We can work this—"

"You and I have nothing. Nothing. You disgust me." He opens the door. "I'll be back in a few days for the rest of my things. Don't bother trying to call me. I have nothing to say to you."

"Jett," I plead, "I only withheld the truth because I love you."

He spits in my face. "If you loved me, you would have told me about my daughter." He leaves.

I fall to my knees crying. *What in the world have I done?*

29

My phone rings. It's Herman. I'm so relieved, because I really need a shoulder to cry on after what just happened.

"Oh, Herman, I just told Jett and—"

"Charity . . . stop," he croaks.

"Herman, what's wrong? You sound terrible."

"I'm in the hospital."

"What for?"

"Someone beat me up and . . . raped me."

"When did this happen?" I ask.

"Last night. I was coming home from the gym when two guys attacked me."

"Look. Which hospital are you in?"

"Saint Francis in Germantown."

"I'll be right there."

I leave a note for the twins and rush out to the hospital. I'll tell them about their father later.

I arrive twenty-five minutes later and stop at the information desk to find out where Herman is. The receptionist directs me toward a block of elevators that will take me to the fifth floor. I have no idea what kind of advice I can give Herman. I just pray that his injuries aren't too serious and he can get back on his feet soon.

With trepidation, I enter the semi-darkened room. A few steps in, I spot Herman. He's turned away from me, facing the window. I know the back of his hairline as well as I know Jett's. I can't tell if he's sleeping.

"Herman?"

He turns over and faces me. My hand immediately goes up to my mouth. Herman's handsome face is nearly double its normal size. He has a bandage on his head and a cast on his left leg. I see cards, flowers, and a large teddy bear sitting on the side table. Herman tries to muster a smile, but I can tell that it hurts him to do so.

I pull up a chair and take his hands in mine. "Damn, I hadn't expected this. Did they give you painkillers? I know you must be in a lot of pain."

"Yes. They've got me doped up pretty good." He turns his head from side to side and swallows hard. "I'm kinda tired, though. I've had a lot of visitors today. First Doug, my neighbor stopped by; then Larry from the flight training school; my brother Seymour; Senita, the secretary from the funeral home; and now you. So, if I fall asleep on you, don't take it personal."

I grip his hands tighter. "Can you tell me what happened?"

"I'll tell you what I remember." He swallows hard again.

"Can I get you some water?"

"Please."

I move to the rollaway cart and pour Herman a glass of ice water from the gold plastic pitcher. I bring the glass and straw to his lips and wait for him to take a few swallows. He shakes his head, signaling that he's finished. "Thanks."

I put the pitcher and glass back and once again take Herman's hands in mine. "Take your time."

"I was walking outside Celebrity Fitness Gym on Park Avenue, carrying my bag and heading toward my car. There was a van and an SUV parked on either side of me. I didn't think anything of it until I pushed my unlock button. Then everything moved fast. A man jumped out of the van and another man hopped out of the SUV. The short guy grabbed me and started beating me in the head with a baseball bat. Then I felt the taller dude kicking me in my abdomen and buttocks. I begged them to stop, but they kept right on."

"Did you recognize either of them?"

"Yeah. They live in Hickory Hill. Their sister just died, and the family wanted the body cremated. The sister's two brothers, the ones who attacked me, didn't want her cremated. They wanted a regular funeral. They tried to bribe me with money to embalm her. They said when their mother saw how pretty she looked, she wouldn't want her cremated. I told them that I couldn't do it. They threatened to take me down, but I didn't believe them." He closes his eyes for a few seconds.

"And the rape?"

"I don't really remember it. I was passed out from the beatings. When I woke up, my pants were down to my ankles and I was bleeding from my rear end. I managed to get to my cell phone and call the police."

"So, it's only a matter of time before they're behind bars?"

"No. I'm not going to press charges."

"Why not?"

"Because they'll get out on bail, find me, and kick my ass again. Not filing charges will end it."

"How do you know? Did the girl get cremated?"

"Yes."

"Damn."

"It's okay, Charity. I decided to sign up for karate lessons. As soon as my leg heals, I'm going to get started."

"Karate classes? What are you going to do if they have a gun?" I stand up and start pacing the floor.

"That won't happen."

"I think you need to buy a gun."

"I'm scared of guns. Besides, I could never shoot anyone."

"Well, you're nothing like Jett. He's got an arsenal at the house. He'll shoot anybody that attempts to come on our property without permission."

"I'm not like Jett. Sorry." He closes his eyes again. "Speaking of Jett, have you told him yet?"

I fight back tears. "Yes."

"From the look on your face, I take it it didn't go too well."

"He left." Now I can't stop the tears from falling.

Herman reaches out and wipes the tears from my cheeks.

"I'm sorry. But don't worry. I'm here for you. Everything's going to be all right."

We sit quietly together for another hour. Each of us is hurting badly, him physically and me emotionally, so we don't talk much. We hold each other's hands and murmur soothing words. I thank God for a friend like Herman.

Outside in my car after I say good-bye to Herman, I lay my head against the steering wheel and cry until there are no more tears. A year ago, I might not have had a book contract, but at least my husband and I were together. Now I'm a bestseller, but Jett is gone and my sister is suing me. My life is in shambles, and I don't know who's to blame more, me or my hateful sister. If she'd never told me about April, none of this would have happened.

30

Even though Jett told me not to call, I call him anyway. He won't answer. I think about calling and calling until he finally answers, but figure that I'll probably be making a fool out of myself.

I check my watch. It's fifteen before eleven and the twins aren't home yet. I fix myself a cup of tea and wait in the family room. Around 11:45, I hear the garage door go up. A few minutes later, I hear the twins coming through the back door.

I call out, "Javed? Jamone? Come here. I need to talk with you two." The television is off and I've got jazz playing on the radio.

"What up, Mom?" Javed says. He's dressed in baggy jeans and a white T. Jamone has on black jeans and a black Sean Jean shirt. "Where's Pops? I didn't see his car in the garage."

"You two sit down. I've got something to tell you." I stand up and without thinking begin to pace. "First off, your dad left." Jamone starts to say something. I stop him with a wave of my hand. "We had a big argument about April. I finally told him the truth. He was furious at me for knowing about her so long and not telling him the moment I found out."

Jamone spoke to Javed from the side of his mouth like Bogart. "I'm not surprised."

I keep on pacing. "I tried to stop him from leaving and reason with him, but he wouldn't listen." Tears flood my eyes. "I know this is all my fault. I'm sorry, you guys. I know I let you two down."

Jamone comes to my rescue. "Javed and I will talk to Pops. Don't you worry about nothin'. Pops will be back home before you know it."

Javed puts his arm around my shoulder. "Jamone is right. We'll get everything straightened out with Pops. He's not perfect and he shouldn't expect you to be." Javed turns off the radio. "Now, it's way past your bedtime. You need to get some rest."

I thank God for my sons' maturity. They both know that this is my fault, but love me too much to tell me the truth. Tears wobble down my cheeks. I'm so embarrassed I feel like crawling into a corner and crying for my mother.

"Boys, I'm sorry." I feel my heart punching against my chest.

"We know. We know. Now, let's get you to bed," Javed says. The twins walk me to my bedroom door. They give me a kiss on the cheek.

"You know, Jett and I could go to California together and meet April." I smile to myself. The more I think about the idea, the more I like it. Yes, that's what's going to happen. Jett and I will meet April together.

For the next few days, I alternate visiting Herman in the hospital with working on my novel, only getting two to three hours of sleep each night. I need to keep my mind trained on something other than Jett. Otherwise, I'll lose my mind. The twins were unsuccessful in getting their dad to come back home. I no longer fantasize about us going together to visit April. I now understand that this won't be fixed easily, if at all.

31

Jamone and Javed talk to their father every day. Weeks have passed and still we've had no communication. Sure, I've cried myself to sleep on several occasions, but I try not to cry. Crying makes me feel weak. I need to be strong.

The twins' upcoming graduation gives me a reason to smile. I didn't think that I would have to go to the festivities alone, but I try to put on a cheerful front for my sons. They know I'm hurting, but there's not much that they can do.

The twins and I shop at The New York Suit Exchange for suits to wear to their graduation. The salesman does his best to try to get the twins to buy matching suits. They flat out tell him no. It takes some time, but they settle on two tailored suits, one charcoal gray and the other one olive green. That done, we go to the tuxedo rental store and they both try on tuxedos. It takes nearly two hours before both of them are satisfied. The prom is this weekend, and the graduation is in two weeks.

I want to host a graduation party for the twins, but they refuse. They tell me that there are already too many parties going on, and I should save my money to help decorate their apartment.

They found an apartment five blocks from the University of Memphis, where they'll be attending school this fall. I'm so glad that Javed changed his mind about not going to college. They're so excited about getting their own place that they're moving in the first of June instead of waiting until August.

It took the twins two hard-fought days to convince Jett to let them stay out all night for their prom. Jamone broke up with Holly and Javed has put things on hold with his African girlfriend, so both of the boys are going out solo. Each is driving their own cars and not renting Bentleys and BMWs like some of their friends are.

On the night of the prom, I take their pictures and give them a hundred dollars apiece. That night, I don't sleep well. I kept waking up, checking the garage to see what time the boys arrive home.

Jamone comes home around ten-thirty, and Javed doesn't lumber through the back door until noon.

I finally see Jett when the twins graduate. Jett cries when I do. We're both so proud of them. I tell myself that April hasn't done anything in her life to make Jett proud. Oh, so badly I want to talk to Jett, to start all over and explain the situation again, but he won't give me the opportunity. He barely speaks to me that day.

He still won't answer my calls. I feel like stopping by his job, but fear that he'll embarrass me and I'll end up crying all night.

The only bright spot in my life is my visit with Kai. She comes to Memphis for the annual barbecue contest. I wanted to look like she remembered me, so I started a diet and exercise routine at the beginning of April. I've already lost fifteen pounds. Kai is a size two, and has been for most of her life. She's developing a little pouch in front like her deceased mother did, but otherwise, she looks the same. I want to lose eight or nine more pounds so that Jett will see me and remember the woman that I was when he first married me.

I have shopped for all of the foods that Kai likes, and filled the wine rack with white and red wine. Sometimes the urge to take a drink surfaces, but I refuse to give in. I used to have a drinking problem back in the day. Ten years ago, I was writing in my office and drinking Christian Brothers like it was Gatorade. One day Jett was up on the roof of our home. Mind you, we were in our four-story house back then. He had a panic attack and kept screaming my name. I was upstairs loaded and didn't hear him. After about an hour passed, he found the nerve to get down. He came up in my office, and finding me high as a kite, cussed me out. I felt like a total failure. My husband could have died if he fell off of our house. I was in such denial about my alcoholism that Jett threatened to leave me. That woke me up. There was no way that alcohol meant more to me than my husband did. So, no, I wasn't going to start drinking again now, when my goal was to win my husband back.

So now, Kai can enjoy the wine and apple martinis. I'll play it safe and refrain. Besides, my sons are old enough to know if I imbibe. Back then, they were too young to fully understand how I was killing myself.

Kai comes downstairs. "Hey, lady. You ready to get out and about?"

"Definitely. Would you like a glass of wine first?"

"No. Maybe later."

"Then get your purse and let's get downtown. Maxwell is going to be singing on the rotunda soon, and I'd like to get good seats."

It takes a lot of navigating, but I manage to locate a parking space six blocks from the rotunda. As expected, it's jam packed, and men and women of all ethnicities and shapes and sizes are enjoying the melee and mayhem of the last week of Memphis in May festivities.

Kai and I push through the crowd and manage to get two of the last seats on the bleachers. She tells me to watch the people to our left. They look like drug addicts. I clutch my purse tighter.

It's almost eight-thirty. It's dark out, but the stage is lit up like a movie set. A local band is playing, warming the crowd up until Maxwell makes his appearance.

Kai elects to get a beer and I purchase a soda. We wait patiently and sip on our drinks until Maxwell comes on. Like the children inside of us, both Kai and I scream when Maxwell comes on stage. For the next ninety minutes, he puts on a helluva performance, singing his new and old songs. When it's over, Kai and I are bubbling with cheer and ready to go home.

The next day, Herman comes over to accompany Kai and me downtown. We go to BB King's place and enjoy hearing Ruby Wilson sing her ass off. Next, we go down to Riverside Drive and join the crowd in the continuous celebrations.

As expected, Kai gets a crush on Herman. He flirts with her too. I'm so glad he's feeling better since his attack. I'm still on him about pressing charges, but he still refuses.

For the next four hours, the three of us sample dry rub and regular barbecue. Kai imbibes three beers and gets pretty tipsy before we manage to call it a night and mosey on back home.

Herman opens the door for me and Kai. "Good night, Charity. Kai, it was a pleasure meeting you."

"Thanks, Herman. It was special meeting you, too."

Herman waits for us to enter the house before he drives off. It's about ten-thirty. The twins could be anywhere.

"You sure you're okay, Kai? You really socked that beer away."

"I'm floating, lady. Just steer me in the direction of my bedroom and I'll be just fine." I take her arm and help her up the steps to her room. We hug good night.

I go back downstairs, clean up the mess in the kitchen, and then head to my bedroom. I'm feeling great after a fun night with my cousin and my friend. Just the kind of stress-relief I needed.

The phone on the nightstand rings. It's Jett. So much for my lowered stress level.

"I need to say something to you."

I sit down on the bed, holding my breath. Maybe he's decided to come back home.

"My daughter called me."

"You don't know if she's your daughter."

"I'd bet my life on it. April told me that she met Jamone months ago in New York."

"Uh-huh." I don't know what else to say.

"So you knew that my son met my daughter and you still didn't say a damn thing?"

"Jett, put yourself in my position. I didn't know what to do."

He shows me no sympathy. "I'll never forgive you for that. I never knew that you could be so low down and dirty. I have a total disrespect for you as a woman and as my wife. I would never have done anything like this to you. I thought married people were supposed to be honest with one another. Trust and honesty are the cornerstones of a good marriage. Without it, you ain't got shit. This marriage is a farce."

"Jett, I'm sorry. We can work this out." Tears stream down my face and my bottom lip trembles. "I didn't want to upset you. We were going through so much with the house and all. You know your pressure was up. It just never felt like the right time."

"That's no excuse. I can't believe you'd stoop this low."

"Well, why didn't you tell me that you slept with my sister? Better yet, why didn't you use a condom?"

"I did use a condom. But that's neither here nor there. April is here now. I have a child in the world, and you kept her from me. I'll never forgive you as long as I live." That's when I broke down blubbering. "I'll call April. I'll invite her over to our house. I'll do anything you want me to do, Jett."

"No. I've made arrangements to see my daughter. I don't need you to do anything for me except stay the hell out of my life."

"Jett! Please. I'm so sorry."

"I'll never trust you again. You make me ill."

Doesn't he realize how much I love him? How much I've sacrificed for him? I fall down on the bed crying. "I'm sorry. Please give me another chance." For some reason, I can't feel my face. It's numb with pain.

"For what? To tell me more lies? Fuck you, Charity. You'll be hearing from my attorney." He hangs up.

I sit there like a fool with the phone in my hand, hoping and praying that everything that just happened was a bad dream. Then I feel the tears on my face. They're still warm. They're still flowing. I hang up the phone and I know that this isn't a dream. It's the worst day of my miserable life.

32

I can't stop crying. I can't go to sleep. I can't think. My hurt is too deep to make any kind of responsible decision. I just know that it feels as if my heart has been cut out of my chest with an ice pick.

When I look in the mirror at my swollen eyes, I'm disgusted with myself. Why didn't I listen to Kai, the twins, and Herman?

I wash my face with cold water and go into the kitchen. It's 5:15 A.M. I prepare a pot of coffee and take a seat at the table. Kai is planning on driving back to Nashville around two this afternoon.

Jamone comes into the kitchen when I am preparing a cup of coffee. "Hi, son. Did you sleep well?"

"No." He walks up to me and gives me a hug. "I heard you and dad arguing last night on the telephone. I started to come in your room later, but I didn't know what to say."

"Oh. I'm sorry that I was so loud. And I'm sorry for being so bullheaded and not listening to the good advice that you gave me about April. I should have known that Jett would react this way." Tears cloud my eyes. I wipe them away with my sleeve and go to sit at the table.

Jamone gets a glass of apple juice out of the refrigerator. "I'll talk to him. I'm sure this can all be resolved in a few days."

I shake my head no. "No, son. I think that Jett is through

with me. You should have heard the hatred in his voice when he was arguing with me. He's never spoken to me like that before." I feel that ice pick chipping at the remainder of my heart. This time I don't wipe away the tears. It's useless.

Jamone takes a seat opposite me. "I told Javed about Dad's call. He's going to go with me to talk to him later. We know that he's staying at a motel near Highway 64."

"Oh my God, Jamone. How did I let it come to this? I didn't want Jett to leave me. I don't want a divorce. I love that man."

"I know, Mom. I know how you're feeling. You should try to get some rest."

"Look, son. Your mom will be okay." I try to pull myself together and assume my role as the parent again. "You guys are going to be fine too. We come from strong stock."

"Don't worry. I'll fill Kai's tank up with gas. What time is she leaving?"

"At two. Thanks, Jamone."

Just then, Kai comes traipsing down the steps. "Good morning, everybody. Why are y'all up so early?" She stretches, and then goes to pour herself a cup of coffee.

Kai walks up to me and stares. "Have you been crying?"

I nod yes. "Jett called last night." My voice is hoarse and my hands are trembling. "I don't know if he's ever coming back." I drop my arms on the table and place my head on top of them. My shoulders shake while tears rack my body.

Kai comes over and pats me on the back. "Don't worry, honey. We'll get things worked out. Jett will be back. He just needs a little time alone to think about things. You and I know how much he loves you."

I raise my head. "You mean used to love me."

"Mom," Jamone says, "I'm going to let you two talk." He turns his attention to Kai. "I got the keys to your Jaguar off the key rack. I'm going to fill it up for you." He smiles and leaves.

"I don't have to go home, Charity. Maybe I should stay until Jett comes back. I can—"

"No, this is all my fault." I pat her hand. "Don't change your plans. The boys and me will set things straight with Jett. I appreciate your offering to stay with me, but I've got to pay for my own mistakes. Can you understand that I need to fix this on my own?"

For the next five hours, Kai and I go over Jett's and my entire argument last night. We've dissected every plausible scenario and realize that there was nothing I could have done last night to make Jett see my point. It's apparent that he's not ready for a reconciliation yet.

Kai takes a shower and packs her things. When she comes back downstairs, she hugs me so hard I can hardly breathe. She promises to call me when she gets home.

Unfortunately, the twins aren't able to talk Jett into coming back home. In fact, he tells them that he is filing for a divorce. I have dialed his number at least sixty times, but only get voice mail. I leave him pleading messages, telling him how sorry I am. I beg him to give me another chance.

Days go by and I hear nothing back from him. I'm thinking seriously about going to see a therapist. Even going alone would help my state of mind and help me to put my marriage into perspective. I make a mental note to call one today.

Herman comes over to support me. He's healed physically, but not mentally. He's sorry about the separation, but knew it was coming. He doesn't have to say, 'I told you so.' That is already obvious. He wants to take me back up in his plane so that I can relax. I'm thankful, but ask for a rain check.

When Jett's birthday arrives on June ninth, I don't hear a peep from Jett. I'm so brokenhearted I feel numb. At this point, I have no more tears left. Only regrets.

By the seventh week, I still am unable to eat or sleep. Dark circles form under my eyes, and new worry lines are beginning to etch my face, but I couldn't care less.

I've seen a female psychologist several times. She wants to put me on Xanax for my depression, but I refuse. I want to get through this on my own mettle. I don't want to numb my emotions. I want to feel every ache and pain. That way, I'm constantly reminded that I'm not dreaming. The divorce action that Jett's taken is real. I need to be strong and keep all my wits about me.

Then Kai calls. She has some disturbing news. Lynzee's at it again.

"You're not going to believe this," Kai says, "so brace yourself."

"Tell me. Nothing can shock me now."

"This might. Lynzee has taken out a half page ad in the *New York Post* and blogged on Twitter and Facebook. She's acknowledging the discovery of her long lost daughter, April Tempest. She's having a party at her home on July third to welcome her daughter into the Lavender family." She takes a breath. "But the kicker is that she announces that April's father is Jett Evans. There's a photo of April and Jett holding hands."

"What! Did he get a paternity test already? Or is he taking Lynzee's word for it?"

"I'm not sure. All I know is that, in my opinion, Lynzee is trying to embarrass you."

"No shit. Last time I talked to her about April she said that she wanted nothing to do with April because she's an alcoholic and she's gay. I guess she's back in touch with her—or at least pretending to be, just to hurt me."

"What are you planning to do?"

"What can I do?" I rub my temples with my palm. I'm hurt beyond belief.

"Take out an ad. Blog on the Internet, too."

"To say what?"

"That you'll support Jett's daughter and make sure that she has a relationship with his sons."

"But I'd be lying."

"So? At least it will exonerate you."

I rest my right hand on my right hip and cock my left leg. "I've done enough lying already. I refuse to get caught up in another lie. If Jett wants to have a relationship with his daughter, let him. I've given him thirty good years. I've been a good wife, help-mate and mother. I've also been a more than a decent sister to Lynzee. I don't need to prove anything to anybody."

"Maybe you should think about this before you make a rash decision."

"No, I've had enough. I'm getting real mad now about this whole thing. It's not my fault that April was born. Jett swore that he used a condom when he dated Lynzee. Then how could she get pregnant? One of them is lying. I believe it's Jett. He hates using condoms."

"Most black men do."

"And he's no different. I tried dozens of times to make him use condoms in the beginning of our marriage. We had agreed that we didn't want children, but the birth control pills that I was on were constantly making me sick. Plus, I started getting blood clots. It didn't matter. Jett still wouldn't agree to use the condoms."

"What'd you do?"

"I talked my doctor into fitting me with an IUD. You weren't supposed to get those put in unless you'd already had a baby, so it was a tough sell to my doctor. After ten years, I decided that I wanted kids and had it taken out. I got pregnant eight months later. You know the rest."

"What do the twins make of all this?"

"They don't want to have anything to do with April. The sad thing is, they're so mad at their dad right now, they don't have too much to say to him either."

"Yeah, Javed and Jamone have always been mama's boys."

"You're damned right." For a brief instant, I feel relief. I decide right then and there that I'm going to stop feeling sorry for myself. I've still got my sons, my health, and my career.

"Kai, thanks for keeping me updated, but it's time that I got my shit together. I'm getting ready to go upstairs to my office and get to work. My agent has been calling me, but I haven't returned her calls. It's time that I did."

"Okay, then. I'm proud of your new attitude. You do your thang, lady."

"Thanks. Bye."

I force a smile, make myself a pastrami and cheese sandwich, grab a Sprite, and head upstairs. Suddenly, I'm ravenous.

I turn on Maxwell's CD and let the music soothe my soul as I eat my sandwich and quench my thirst. When I'm finished, I dial Arlene's number. I'm feeling stronger as each minute passes by.

"Hello, Arlene. It's Charity Lavender. I'm returning your call."

"Why, hello, Charity. I was just thinking about you. I've got some good news."

Just what I need. "Tell me. Did you hear from my editor?"

"Yes. They've agreed to accept *A Woman's War* as your next book. They want you to change the title, though. They want the word 'Afghanistan' in it."

"That's not a problem."

"There's more. Twentieth Century Fox is thinking about buying the movie rights." Her voice is excited. "Isn't that great?"

"Yes, I couldn't be more pleased." I pause. "Arlene, did you read the blog that Lynzee put on the Internet and in the *New York Post*?"

"Yes, I did, and so did your publisher."

"And what do you or they conclude from this tactic to sabotage my career?"

"I'm shocked. This ad had to have cost a pretty penny. Lynzee always does things big, no matter what the cost. I guess that's the privilege of the rich and famous."

"I agree." I put the receiver closer to my mouth. "Do you think I should make any kind of response?"

"I didn't, but your publisher does. Since you've got a new book coming out, they don't want anything affecting the sales. They asked me to ask you to come up with an article that tells your side of the story. It doesn't have to be long. Just let the public know that you support your husband's daughter."

The hairs rise on the back of my neck. "I can't do that, Arlene. I wouldn't be telling the truth. I don't support that heffa. She's responsible for ending my marriage. Why should I lie?"

"Good point."

"I'm tired of being the scapegoat. I haven't done anything wrong."

"I'll convey your thoughts to Gail. After all, she's been married for about thirty-three years and is now getting a divorce, too. I'm sure she'll understand."

"Good. I'll talk to you soon, Arlene." I hang up.

I stand up and stretch. I walk to the windows and look outside. I've got to think of something to counter Lynzee's act of defiance.

I stare out of that window for nearly thirty minutes before I come up with an answer. Hot damn, I'll have a party.

I call the twins. They moved into their new apartment last week. Jamone answers the phone.

"Son, I need you and Javed to help me with something."

"You know we've got your back, Mom. Shoot."

"Could you two help me gather up the vegetables in the garden? I need to blanche the greens and beans and can the tomatoes. Ordinarily, I can do it by myself, but I'm in a hurry. I've got something planned."

Jamone asks, "What's up, Mom?"

"I'm going to have a party on July third."

"Why July third?"

"It's the same day that Lynzee is having her party. I'm going to invite the same people that she's inviting."

"What kind of party, Mom? What's the occasion?"

"My publisher just bought my new book and I'm getting a big advance. Can you think of a better reason to celebrate?" I force a sincere smile.

"Gosh, no. Javed and I will do whatever it takes to help you."

"Thanks, son. I knew that I could count on you guys."

That Friday, I sign up for classes at the Culinary Academy. Nothing works better to clear my mind than to have it challenged.

On Monday, I call the *New York Times*. I take an ad out about my Garden Book Party on July third. I'm sure that this ad will really piss off Lynzee. I pay for the ad, hang up, and smile to myself. I haven't felt this good in a long time.

Next, I call Hilton Party Planners. "Hello, this is Charity

Lavender. I'm planning on having an outdoor party in three weeks. I'll need a large tent, table, chairs . . ."

Javed comes to the house two days later. He looks like he's got a lot on his mind.

"What's wrong, honey?" I say after he comes in the back door.

"It's Dad. He wants Jamone and me to meet with him and April. He says that April is our blood sister, and it's time that we accept it. We both told him no. We don't want to have anything to do with her."

"Good for you, son."

"Did you know that he's thinking about getting her an apartment in Memphis and getting her a new Ford Mustang?"

"No." My mind clicks like an adding machine. Where is he getting all of this money from?

"Oh, hell no." I hug Javed. "Thanks for keeping me informed, son. I've got to go to the bank." *He hasn't even spent that much money on our sons. I'm not putting up with this bullshit.*

I get my purse and keys and rush to the bank. I speak with the manager, who I've known for over ten years. I explain my problem about Jett's account and him not signing it. In less than an hour, she transfers the money back out of his account and into mine. My smile is wicked.

I get back into my car and start the ignition. I look in the mirror and smile again. I envision Jett's face looking at me. "You don't know who you're fucking with, dude. You'll never use a dime of my money to pay for your love child. If April gets a new apartment and car, by God, your King Ford check better be long enough to pay for it."

33

The house is buzzing with caterers and the party planner's crew. They brought some of the prettiest flowering plants that I've ever seen. There are pink and purple chrysanthemums, pink kalanchoes, African violets, blue hydrangeas, bronze cushion mums, pink azaleas, and exotic bromeliads.

It's nine o'clock in the morning and the party starts at three. Javed and Jamone are helping the party planners with setting up the huge tent. I've gotten more than two hundred RSVPs, and the party looks like it's going to be a hit.

Of course Jett called me when he found out about the money in the bank. It was the second time we've spoken since he left.

"I didn't think you would stoop this low. I thought you said that the money in the bank was mine."

"Listen, like Richard Pryor told one of his ex-wives, 'You ain't told 'nare joke,' you, my man, ain't wrote 'nare word.'"

"You're a greedy bitch."

"Oh, yeah? Well, that bitch you call your daughter will never spend a dime of my money."

"Oh, so it's like that. You're not only greedy; you're a selfish bitch, too."

"Fuck you, Jett. I don't owe you a dime."

"No, fuck you. I hope Lynzee sues you for ten million. And when you're broke, don't come crying to me."

"I'd eat dirt before I'd ask you for a penny."

"All right then." His voice is filled with venom when he says, "Eat dirt and go to hell, bitch." He hangs up.

Any other time, it would have hurt me that he called me so many bitches. But under the circumstances, maybe I have earned the title.

I learned from the twins that Jett found a one-bedroom apartment in mid-town. The twins reluctantly brought the rest of his clothes and belongings from our house to his place. Not wanting to see me in person, he had the Harley towed to his apartment.

Without him saying so, I know that his next move will be filing for a divorce. Of course, I don't want one, but if he insists, I know that I'm strong enough to move on. In my heart I know I'll never love another man the way I still love Jett, but if the Lord allows the divorce to go through, then who am I to question His reasons?

Throughout the day, the telephone rings non-stop. I answer some of the calls, and then turn phone duty over to the twins. It seems that friends and relatives can't understand the map that I included in their invitation. To my delight, nearly sixty of Lynzee's friends have elected to come to my party instead of hers. I know she's pissed off, but won't let it stop her shenanigans.

By noon, I walk around the house and yard and check to make sure everything is in place. I have five caterers who have really done an exceptional job. Instead of having an ice sculpture made, I had one of the chefs make a three-tiered sculpture out of watermelons. It's a work of art and even the twins are impressed.

At twelve-forty five, I'm in my bedroom getting dressed. I ordered a silver-and-gold two-piece beaded caftan from Neiman Marcus. The silver-and-gold sandals look like they were handmade for a princess. I purchased the matching oversized rhinestone jewelry at Joseph's. I take my time applying my makeup and immediately feel youthful as I apply a final coat of lip gloss.

The band starts playing at two sharp, and some guests arrive early, eager to get the party started.

Kai surprises me and comes down for support. Herman arrives at two-thirty dressed for success in an off-white Adolpho suit and cream-colored alligator shoes. He's giving Kai all of his attention.

When I enter the tent with Kai and Herman at three, the place is packed with smiling guests. I walk around, mingle, and hand out compliments. By three-fifteen, I stand up in front and deliver a prepared speech.

"Thank you, friends and relatives for coming to my party this afternoon. We're here today to celebrate my new contract and the success of my book, *Revelations*. This is the first time that I've made the *New York Times* bestsellers list." There is a loud applause. "Thank you. I consider everyone here tonight very special people that I care deeply about."

"You've probably heard about the problems that Lynzee and I are having and her upcoming lawsuit. I assure you that my attorneys have the matter under control. It's unfortunate that something like this had to happen between two sisters, but sometimes life is stranger than fiction. Sibling rivalry has been going on for ages and will continue to be a contention between family members long after I'm gone. Just know that I wish my sister well. I wish her all of the success in the world. But know that she's met her match. I will not rest until I'm victorious in this civil suit. My attorneys have assured me as much, because everything I wrote in *Revelations* is true, and the truth will vindicate me."

I turn to Kai. She hands me a flute of champagne. "Here's to victory. May the best woman win." I smile and take a long sip of the bubbly liquid. There's another round of applause.

"Now, let's get this party started!" I turn the event back over to the band.

A wet bar is set up in the far left corner and there's a line three feet deep.

The party is costing me almost a hundred thousand dollars, but it doesn't bother me. It's lifted my spirits and helped me put Jett's and my relationship into perspective. If Jett won't listen to reason and go to see a marriage counselor with me, then I'll accept the divorce and move forward with my life as a single woman. I'm still attractive. I'm still marriage material. Maybe I'll be like Javed and find me a rich African man. Who knows?

The band is set up in the front, off to the left. They're a group of six and their name is Strike Force Three. Javed and Jamone found them for me. I love the fact that they have a female lead singer, Ashley Hill. She sounds like a songbird.

Thankfully, my guests aren't shy, and the dance floor fills up quickly. Even Javed and Jamone are on the dance floor doing their thing. Since Jett isn't here, Javed brings his African girl-friend, Misty, to the event. It doesn't bother me one bit. I just want him to be happy.

At six-thirty, the outside torches are lit, and a line forms for dinner. Trash cans are strategically placed around the tent, and the partygoers don't make too much of a mess.

I dance with Herman three times, and notice that Kai has danced with him at least five.

By ten-thirty, the guests come over to thank me and head home. By eleven-fifteen, the tent is nearly empty. Kai and Herman are on the dance floor, slow dancing to the last song of the evening.

"Mrs. Evans," the supervisor from Hilton's says, "we'll have everything cleaned up in just over an hour."

"Thank you."

"Jimmy," I call out to the senior chef, "could you make sure that the food is taken to the food kitchen downtown? I'm sure that the homeless people would be happy to have this food."

He agrees and starts to seal up the food. In no time, he's got the food in aluminum trays to transfer to the shelter. I pay him and give him a two hundred dollar tip. He thanks me and asks me to contact him again if I ever need a chef.

I kiss Kai and Herman goodnight. Both say they had a great time.

"We have to do this again," Kai says.

"I agree. And soon."

"I concur," Herman adds, smiling. "I'm going to say my good

nights to you two. Good night, Kai. You were wonderful." He kisses her hand and turns to me. "I'll call you tomorrow, Charity. I've got something to talk to you about." He kisses me on the cheek and leaves.

Kai shakes her head. She looks gorgeous in a black beaded mini-dress. "I'm sorry, Charity. That man is not gay."

I watch Herman as he walks to his car. "I'm beginning to wonder myself."

I wave good-bye to Kai in the morning. We hug and promise to keep up our weekly Sunday conversations. Seeing her leave, I feel nostalgic. Kai has really been there for me since Jett left. I only hope that I can be as supportive for her if she ever needs a shoulder to cry on.

It hurts me to know that Kai is almost too old to bear children. She'll turn forty-one in August. After she divorced her husband in 1996, she planned on getting married again and having at least two children. I wish she hadn't moved to Nashville, because the shortage of men is not a secret. She's had a few serious relationships, but nothing solid. Kai is a super aunt to her niece and nephew, Juhrissa and Jahvel. They're both grown now, but Kai continues to support them financially, academically, and spiritually. Without question, Kai would have been an excellent mother. I pray every day that a miracle will happen and Kai is able to find a husband and birth a child.

34

Hey, Bitch. You think you slick, but I just want you to know you a low-life, conniving heifer with what you did, having that party. My so-called friends that attended aren't really my friends. My true friends were here with me, partying and hating your fucking guts. . . .

The following Monday, I'm greeted with a nasty e-mail from Lynzee. Apparently having my party on the same day as hers really hit a nerve. She didn't mention how many people showed, but I know that it was much lower than she expected. She ended her message by saying that April and Jett are getting along famously. And, she asks, did I know that Jett was in the process of moving April to Memphis?

That last tidbit cuts a hole in my heart. If Jett and I ever get back together, April is definitely going to be a problem. I can't understand why he wants her to move here. Fortunately, I'm told, she is still able to keep her job as a flight attendant at Northwest Airlines. Jett knows that he can't afford this kind of expense right now. I heard that sales are down at King Ford. Only the big wigs are making money.

It's getting easier for me to go to sleep at night without Jett. Sure, I miss him. I miss his smell. I miss his soft feet caressing mine. I miss his arm thrown casually over my waist. I miss his light snoring. I miss watching the late night news with him. I miss my old husband, not this conniving character who's taken his place.

35

The trial is set to start next Monday. My attorney, Teddy Bell, states that he's more than ready to take on the infamous Lynzee Lavender. We're in his office downtown on Main Street. He has three other partners, and two of them are working on this case with him.

"Just so you know, Mrs. Evans, your sister has amended her suit to ten million dollars."

"That bitch," I mumble under my breath.

"Her attorney states that since you just received a new contract, you can well afford it."

"I don't believe it. Can she really amend the amount of her suit?"

"Yes, as long as she does it before the trial begins."

I'm angrier than a mouse caught in a trap. That heffa wants to take me for every dime I've got, and every dollar I'll make in the future. Right now, I can't stand that cow.

"How long do you think the trial will last?"

"When she first filed and her attorney listed her witnesses, I figured the trial would be over in two to three weeks." He sighed. "But now she's tripled the amount of witnesses that she plans to use to testify. It seems that quite a few of her old college friends are coming to her rescue. That means we're looking at six to eight weeks."

"Damn. That time frame doesn't work well with my schedule."

"Oh, I thought you worked at home."

"I do, but I'm supposed to start classes next month. There's no way that I can go to class and be at this trial." *Damn that bitch.*

"Would you like me to ask the judge for a postponement?"

I get up from the chair. "No. Let's just get this over with. I'm ready to go on with my life the way it used to be."

The following Monday, the trial starts. Javed and Jamone accompany me to Circuit Court at 201 Poplar Avenue. I want them to see how scandalous their aunt can be. I spot Lynzee in a yellow shirt dress, getting a drink of water at the water fountain.

I look around to see if she brought April with her, but I don't see her. I train my eyes on Lynzee's form and slow down my steps. Jamone notices Lynzee and grips my arm. "C'mon, Mom, let's get into the courtroom. Your attorney is waiting for you."

Just then, Lynzee looks toward us and waves. The look on her face is one of pity. Javed says, "Ignore her, Mom."

Lynzee is mouthing, "Look at me. Look at what you made me do."

I want to tell her, "Look at me, bitch. I'm you're fucking sister, not your enemy. Don't fuck with me now."

I turn my head away and walk into the courtroom. Teddy is waiting at the defense table along with two of his partners, James Anderson and Ashton Woods. I shake their hands and take a seat. The boys sit directly behind me.

I hear chairs shuffling across from me. I sneak a glance to my right. Lynzee is sitting at the plaintiff's table with her two attorneys. Teddy told me that their names are Arthur Dinkins and William Walker. Dinkins and Walter are prominent attorneys from California. Ordinarily the trial would have been held in California, but Teddy managed to get a change of venue because of Lynzee's popularity, so that the trial could be held here in Tennessee. He claimed that we wouldn't be able to find an impartial jury in Lynzee's home state.

Less than ten minutes later the bailiff reads the complaint. "Lynzee Lavender versus Charity Lavender Evans." Then he says, "All stand. The honorable Judge Cathy Fudge is presiding."

The judge pounds her gavel. She makes it clear that she won't tolerate any outbursts in her courtroom, and that this is going to be a fair trial for both sides. She acknowledges the jury then nods to Mr. Bell to begin his opening arguments.

Teddy stands up and unbuttons his jacket. He slowly walks toward the jury and then stops. He's wearing a double breasted houndstooth Calvin Klein suit, and has on black tasseled loafers. He complemented his look with a red power tie. He looks like a winner. I feel proud that he's my attorney.

"Ladies and gentlemen of the jury, we are here today to prove that my client, Charity Lavender Evans, is not guilty of maliciously slandering her accuser, Lynzee Lavender." He begins to pace back and forth in front of the jury box. "Through a series of highly respected witnesses, we will show that not only is my client not guilty, but Lynzee Lavender is guilty of sabotaging my client's career. Let the records show that my client and I are countersuing for ten million dollars."

He clears his throat. "I realize that some of you might be aware of the infamous Lynzee Lavender. You may know that she is one of the best-selling African American writers in modern history. I applaud her for that. My client, Ms. Lavender Evans, is also a *New York Times* bestselling author and is famous in her own right."

Lynzee glances at me and rolls her eyes. I roll mine back and turn away from her and her team.

Mr. Bell continues. "Yet we are not here this morning to acknowledge who is the better writer. We're here to determine if my client deliberately tried to defame Ms. Lavender's career and name. I will show that my client's book, *Revelations*, did not reveal anything about Ms. Lavender's personal life that was not already known in the public sector. . . ."

I turn around and look at my boys. They're both wearing suits and look like collegiate gentlemen. I'm so proud of them.

Teddy finishes his summation and the judge turns the floor

over to Arthur Dinkins. He stands, unbuttoning his jacket as he does so. He has on a navy blue single-breasted suit, also with a red tie, and black square-toe shoes. He briskly walks over to the jury. He paces back and forth for a few minutes, seemingly to get his thoughts together.

"Mr. Dinkins, are you prepared to give your opening statement?" the judge asks.

"I am, Your Honor." He walks back to his table and extends his arm toward Lynzee. "This is my client, Ms. Lynzee Lavender. As Mr. Bell stated, she's a successful African American science fiction writer. She has a total of fourteen million books in print. She is highly respected in the publishing industry and commands twenty-five thousand dollars per speaking engagement. Before Ms. Lavender Evans wrote *Revelations*, Ms. Lavender's first printings of her science fiction novels were at least five hundred thousand. After Ms. Lavender Evans' book was published and my client's personal business was made public, my client's book sales remained stable, but her speaking engagements ended.

"Because of Ms. Evans' revelation about my client's bachelor and masters degrees, she was subjected to unprecedented humiliation, as the college boards went through her background with a fine-toothed comb. They concluded that Ms. Evans' allegations were false and unfounded, but the damage is done. Now my client's ethics are in question.

"You may ask: how is that possible?" He turns and points at me. "I will show through a series of testimonies by men and women of integrity and character that Ms. Lavender Evans is the culprit behind my client's defamation of character. I will show that with malice and sheer envy . . ."

They eyes of the people of the jury are boring into me. Some look bewildered and some actually look mad. I glance at Teddy, who pats my hand. I feel the twins patting my back. I fight back tears. The truth is finally going to come out, and I'm not sure that I'll be the victor.

My God, where is my husband when I need him the most? I need him here beside me to support me and let me know that everything is going to be all right. I need him to give me that winning smile that lets me know that his love for me and my love for him is all that matters in life. I need him to tell me that April couldn't possibly mean as much to him as our sons do. I need him to tell me that he understands why I kept April's birth a secret for so long. I need him to tell me that he forgives me for not being perfect, for making a mistake in judgment. I need him to tell me that nothing will ever stop him from loving me and our sons. I need him to hold me. Lord, God, I need him now.

36

As each day of the trial progresses, my hatred toward Lynzee grows. The plaintiff's attorney presents their case first, and their witnesses are doing a helluva job making me look like an opportunist.

Mr. Dinkins' first witness is Danielle Robeson. She owns the African Heritage Bookstore in Chicago. When she gets sworn in and then takes her seat, my heart sinks. When I notice that she's rolling her eyes at me, my heart sinks even deeper. Why did I have to open my big mouth? Especially to her. I thought she liked me. Why would she turn against me? When I was at her bookstore for a book signing for *New Collar Blues*, she told me that she loved my writing. She also told me that she thought I was a better writer than Lynzee. She told me that a lot of her customers felt the same way. That's when stupid me let my guard down and boldly said that I wanted to be the first African American author to sell a million hardcover books. Danielle told me that if I kept writing the way I was, it was only a matter of time before I could claim that title. I believed the bitch.

Teddy asks Ms. Robeson, "What was the tone of voice that Charity Lavender used when she spoke with you at your store?"

Ms. Robeson Shrugs. "I don't know what you mean?"

"Did you think she was joking?"

"No. I don't think—"

"Or was it just a casual comment?" Teddy asks.

Ms. Robeson thinks for a moment. "She wasn't joking. I think she was dead serious."

"Have you ever seen Charity Lavender socially?"

"No."

"Have you ever had conversations with her on the telephone?"

"No." Ms. Robeson looks annoyed. She glances at Lynzee.

Teddy has a stern look on his face. "So, you don't really know my client?"

"I didn't say that I did. I only know what she said."

"How my client said what she said is what's important here today. I believe that my client was joking about being the first African American female to sell a million hardcover copies."

"No, she was dead serious." Ms. Robeson crosses her arms across her bosom.

"By your own account, you don't really know my client. So there was no way that you would know if she was serious or joking."

"I know what I heard. And I know that she's jealous of her sister's success."

Teddy scratches his head. "I intend to prove otherwise, Ms. Robeson. Thank you for your enlightening testimony. You may step down."

When Teddy takes a seat at our table, he winks at me. I smile back. He may have gained ground on Ms. Robeson's testimony, but I fear things will only get worse. I chastise myself silently for having such a big mouth.

My crucifixion continues. Witness after witness makes me out to be a woman who would do anything to outdo her sister, a writer who would lie and cheat to make the *New York Times*. One witness even accuses me of plagiarism in *New Collar Blues*. She says that I stole lines from Harold Robbins' book, *The Betsy*. That was a bold-faced lie.

By Friday, I am exhausted. My hope of winning the case

seems futile. When I have a conference at Teddy's office Friday evening, he tries to lift my spirits.

"Listen, Charity. We talked about this. It's the attorney's job to paint a negative picture of you. No one on my staff is surprised by any of their witnesses or what the witnesses revealed."

I'm sitting in a navy leather chair opposite him. "I know what you said, Teddy, but I wasn't expecting that these witnesses would stare at me with such hatred in their eyes. I feel like a gnat that's about to be crushed when their eyes meet mine. It takes all the chutzpah I can muster to not look away from them."

"And I'm proud of you for doing that. You should continue to look those witnesses right in the eye. Half of them are lying anyway."

"I know. By the way, James, Ashton, and you are doing a great job of refuting the witnesses' testimony."

"Thanks. I think we know what we're doing." He smiles.

"I wish I did." I finger a plant nearby and cross my legs. "You know, I wish Lynzee would have taken the settlement I offered her. This trial could ruin both of our careers." I shake my head.

Teddy comes around his desk and rests his buttocks on the edge. "I'm going to make damn sure that that doesn't happen, especially to your career. You're going to come out of this trial looking like a hero."

I look at him with hope in my eyes. "You think you can do that?"

"Absolutely." He takes my hand and lifts me up. "Now, it's time for you to go home and get some rest. Let us worry about the trial. All we want you to do is come to trial looking as pretty as you can and wearing a big smile on your face. Can you do that for me?"

I stand, smiling. "I think I can manage that. Thank you, Teddy."

He walks me to the door. "Good night, Charity."

"Good night, Teddy. I'll see you on Monday."

On the drive home, my confidence is waning. Lynzee has

thirty-one more witnesses to testify. I only have eighteen. There's something wrong with that picture.

The twins will start classes soon and they won't be in court to support me. I'm already missing their loving faces smiling back at me.

37

When I pull into the garage, I immediately turn to where Jett used to park his truck. It still surprises me to see the empty space. I wish that I could snap my fingers and change things back to the way they used to be.

I put my key in the door and open it. The telephone is ringing. I rush to the desk. "Hello?" I set down my purse and keys and take a seat on the desk chair.

"Hi, lady, it's Kai. How did the trial go today?"

"As well as expected. I'm not looking forward to going back on Monday, though."

"I know it can't be that bad. Lynzee is a real bitch to go through with the suit. I could've sworn that she would drop it."

"No way. That chick is out for blood and she won't be satisfied until I'm broke and disgraced."

"Don't get mad, but I e-mailed your attorney. We went to law school in Detroit."

"Oh, I didn't know." I put on a pot of tea and grab a can of corn chowder out of the pantry.

"By law, he's sworn not to disclose any of your business. However, he told me that the trial was going just the way he thought it would and he can't wait until it's his turn to put his witnesses on the stand. He also said that he has a surprise witness that even you don't know about."

"I'm still scared, Kai." I reach for a cup from the cabinet.

"What are you scared for? Teddy is one of the best attorneys in Memphis. Stop worrying so much. You're in good hands."

I pour the soup in a bowl and pop it in the microwave. "Thanks for your support, Kai. Your friendship is priceless. Especially now."

"I value your friendship, too. You know how much I love you, lady." I can hear the smile in her voice.

"And I love you, too, Kai."

"Alrighty now, back to business. I've got some dirt on Lynzee."

The whistle blows on the tea kettle. "Tell me quick." I prepare the tea.

"Lynzee is hooked on Percocet again."

"You're lying."

"No, siree. She must be worried about the suit, or is on a heavy guilt trip for putting you through this mess. In my opinion, her guilt is killing her. She needs that Percocet to cope with looking herself in the mirror every morning."

"Damn, I hate that."

"I know you don't want to see her hooked on that shit again, but I'm told it's too late. Her habit is worse than last time. She's getting weekly shipments into Memphis from an old doctor in L.A. Sooner or later she's going to have to go back to rehab."

"If Mama was alive she would slap the shit out of Lynzee." I remove my bowl of soup and get a spoon out of the drawer.

"If Aunt Katherine was alive, Lynzee would have never filed this suit."

"You're right." I swallow a tablespoon of soup. "Have you heard anything about Tyler? Her baby should be due in a couple of months."

"No. I don't hear too much about her. I know that she's still planning to go to school."

"Good for her."

"I believe her husband has gotten a job at a Jiffy Lube. He's working full time and will also be going to school full time. It appears they're trying to make it."

"Odds are against it," I say and take another swallow. I sit back and sip on my tea. "Still, I wish them the best." Lynzee's apparent hatred of me is not going to change how I feel about Tyler. She's family.

I finish my soup, rinse out the bowl and stack it in the dishwasher.

"Is April still working for the airlines?"

"As far as I know." I make a second cup of tea. "I know that Jett can't afford to take care of her."

"Ouch."

"My ass. Things didn't have to turn out like this. You know, I used to feel bad about the whole thing. Now I'm angry. I'm angry at Jett for giving up on us. I sensed that something like this would happen. That's why I didn't want to tell him. Secretly, he's always wanted a daughter."

"My, my. Do you think he knows that she's gay?"

"I doubt it. Jett is homophobic. He can't stand gays and lesbians. When he finds out, I feel sorry for April. He's going to turn his back on her like he did me."

"Payback is hell, and Lynzee's got it coming too."

"That's too bad. May God have mercy on our souls."

The next morning, a knock at the front door wakes me up from a deep sleep. I put on my housecoat and hurry to answer it. When I open the door, I see a man standing there with a piece of paper in his hand. *Oh, no. Not this shit again.*

"Mrs. Charity Evans?" he says all businesslike.

"Yes."

He hands me the paperwork. "You've been served. Have a good day." He skips down the steps to his awaiting car.

I shut the door and go to the kitchen to put on a pot of coffee. I have no idea what this petition is. Then, before I can fill up the tank with water, it hits me. Jett. He's filing for a divorce. I slam down the coffee pot and open up the papers. I read quickly.

It's all there in black and white. Jett wants a divorce. I cup my hand over my mouth to stifle a scream. How could he?

I sit down at the table and read the entire contents. He's leaving me the house, furniture, and artwork. His only request is money—half of the money from my last two contracts.

"That greedy son of a bitch," I say to myself. "How dare he?"

I make up my mind to call Jett. If he doesn't answer, I'm going to keep calling until he does.

I dial his number and as expected, get his voice mail. I keep dialing every thirty minutes. By noon, I'm pissed and ready to stop by his job. He's going to talk to me either by phone or face to face. A confrontation between us is long overdue.

I've taken a shower, dressed and cleaned up my bedroom. Since Jett's been gone, I started a bad habit of laying my clothes on the chaise lounge. The room looks a hot mess before I clean up behind myself.

Finally, I get a call on my cell. "Hello."

"It's me."

"I got the papers today. I think we should talk." *Lord knows I got the blues.*

Jett's voice is firm. "There's nothing to talk about. This farce of a marriage is over."

"Tell me to my face. Either you come over here, or I'll come to your job. Which will it be?"

38

"I don't know why you insisted on a meeting, Charity. I don't respect you anymore. It's that simple." Jett extends his long legs and crosses them at the ankle. He looks at me with disgust on his face.

We're sitting out on the lower level patio of our home. Twenty huge pots of variegated flowers are spaced along the sixty-foot edge. I prepared a pitcher of iced tea. Jett's is halfway gone. I've barely touched mine.

"Let's talk about respect. You've disrespected me more times than I can count. Namely, you had sex with Lynzee without protection. You might as well stop lying about it. I know the truth. You hate wearing condoms."

"I may have slipped up a time or two when Lynzee and I were intimate, but—"

"You should have told me about you and Lynzee before we were married." I'm getting mad now.

"Nobody knew. Not even your mother. I thought it was best to keep it that way. When you and I got together, Lynzee had moved to North Carolina. Thinking about her and my relationship was the last thing on my mind."

"That's some bullshit, Jett. I should have been told the truth. The people you've been intimate with before you strike up a relationship with someone is important. Especially if that person was your new lover's sister. If I had known, I wouldn't have dated you, let alone married you."

He straightens and takes a gulp of tea. "I realized how you would feel. That's why I kept silent about it. You meant everything to me back then."

"Oh, back then."

"Yes. I don't feel the same way about you anymore. I never knew that you would keep a secret from me that could possibly change my life."

"Your life! You mean *my* life." I glare at him. "Your love child that you claimed you didn't want in the first place has ruined our marriage."

"No, you ruined our marriage by lying to me."

I stand up and move in front of him with my hands on my hips. "No, you're the one who lied first. Why don't you admit the truth?"

"It doesn't matter now. What's done is done. I've got a daughter that I'm proud of. I only wish that I could have been involved in her life sooner."

How dare he act like he deserves the Father of the Year award? I move away from him. Maybe trying to salvage this marriage is a mistake. I turn my back to him.

"If that's all you want, I've gotta get back to work." He stands.

The bitch in me comes out. "Did you know that April is gay?"

He looks like someone slapped him. "How would you know that?"

"Lynzee told me."

"I don't believe it." The look on his face is pure fury.

I knew I hit a hot spot. Then thoughts about the divorce decree surface. "About the divorce—"

"What about it?"

"I'm not giving you a dime. You and your daughter can live off of your salary. I don't owe either of you nothing."

"You're not being fair. I read all of your books and even helped you edit them."

"That was years ago. You stopped, remember?" My smile is

coy. "You haven't helped me on my last three books. You lost faith in my writing abilities. You thought my career was over."

"That's not true."

"Bullshit. You wrote me off just like Lynzee did. Hell, for all I know you two could have been comparing notes behind my back." My head aches. I rub my face with my right hand and take a deep breath. "You're right, Jett. This was a bad idea. I don't know why I would want a man who's clearly got his priorities mixed up. I think you better go."

He walks toward the steps and then turns back around. "You're wrong about the money. I've been married to you for almost thirty years. I deserve to leave this marriage with something other than my clothes."

"The only thing you deserve is the frozen vegetables in the freezer." I open the sliding door to the patio. "I'll see you in court."

After Jett leaves, I go into my room and lay on the bed. I have a long cry. Jett never mentioned love not one time. Has he stopped loving me so quickly? Do his feelings for April trump our love for each other, and his love for his sons? Was I wrong not to tell him about April for so long? I know that I'm feeling sorry for myself, but I can't help it. I'm feeling lonely and sex deprived. For a woman my age, that isn't a good mix. I should be sitting on an exotic island drinking non-alcoholic margaritas.

I fall asleep and see Jett's snarling face in my nightmares. I awaken with sweat beads on my forehead. I go into the bathroom and wash my face and hands with cold water.

I hate to admit it, but seeing Jett depressed me. I wanted him to take me in his arms and tell me that everything is going to be okay. I wanted him to tell me that he wants to stay married and keep our family together. I wanted him to assure me that April would never come between us. I wanted him to act like the caring and mature man that I fell in love with.

I dry my face and go upstairs to my office. I'm irritated as hell. I can't seem to find my speaking engagement notebook.

I'm supposed to speak at Lemoyne-Owen College on a Sunday, but I'm not sure if it's this week or next week.

For the next thirty minutes, I tear up my desk and file cabinets looking for my notebook. It's nowhere to be found. For some reason, I can't seem to find the Rolodex with my booking agent's number on it. By now, I'm fuming. Has somebody been going through my things? I haven't changed the locks since Jett left. Maybe I should do so now.

I pick up the Yellow Pages and scan the advertisements. I find a couple that will change locks twenty-four hours a day. I call the one closest to my home.

Within an hour, EZ Locksmiths are doing their thing on six doors that keep my home safe. When they finish, I pay the technician $228. I feel a little more comfortable knowing that Jett can't walk in and scare the shit out of me. I should have done it when he first left, but I always believed that he would only be gone for a few days and come back home.

I'm feeling cocky now. Fuck Jett. If he wants a divorce, then so be it. Who's to say that I can't find a better mate? A better lover? A more attentive man? A better provider?

Immediately, I think of Herman. Like I've been suspecting and Kai agreed, maybe Herman isn't really gay. I decide to call him. I need a distraction before the trial starts again on Monday.

Sitting at my desk, I dial his number on the home phone. "Herman, it's Charity."

"Hi. I was expecting a call from my neighbor, Josh. The flood lights are out in our subdivision."

"Oh. Maybe I should call back later."

"No, Josh can get it handled. I'll call him when you and I finish talking. Now, tell me what's happening with you. I don't want to hear about the trial. I've already read about it in the papers."

"Good, 'cause I don't want to talk about the trial either. It only makes me angry." I smile to myself, feeling like a naughty girl. "What are you doing tonight? Would you like to come over for dinner?"

"Sure. What time?"

"Around six. And Herman, bring a bottle of champagne."

"You sure? I thought you didn't drink anymore?"

"I didn't. But I did that to keep Jett happy. Now I'm on my own and I can do what I want." I'm lying. I stopped drinking for my self-respect. But now, I'm discovering a new me, and this one doesn't want to believe that alcohol can control her life.

"I don't know, Charity. I think you had to stop to keep from killing yourself. I don't want to be responsible for getting you started drinking again."

I play with the telephone cord. "Tell you what: I've got some wine downstairs. I'm going to pour me a glass when you hang up. So, consider yourself not guilty, okay?"

"What's with you?"

I smile. "Jett was here today. We talked about the divorce. It's over. Now I want to celebrate. Is that cool with you?"

"Yes. Okay then. I'll be there at six."

I hang up the phone and traipse downstairs to the wine rack. I get out a wine glass and select a bottle of Bordeaux. I'm rusty, so it takes me a few minutes to get the bottle open. Having success, I pour half a glass and take a seat in the living room. I turn on the CD and listen to Beyoncé. In minutes, the wine slices through my body like fire. I relish my newfound feeling of freedom and finish my glass.

With the music still playing, I pour another glass of wine. This time I start to dance. I've been asking Jett to take me dancing for years. He says that saved people aren't supposed to dance and go to parties. I beg to differ with that. Saved people can enjoy some of life's pleasures too.

Funny, I don't feel like I'm getting inebriated. I feel like I'm freeing my soul of unwanted baggage.

Then I think: dinner. What am I going to cook? I haven't gotten groceries since the twins left. I go into the kitchen and check the freezer. There are a few packages of chicken wings and a box of frozen fish sticks.

"That won't do." I need to go to the store. I go into my room and retrieve my purse. I collect my keys and head out to my car. Minutes later, I'm at Schnucks supermarket selecting two large lobsters. That done, I stop by the butcher's counter and pick out two porterhouse steaks. I drop a bag of salad mix in my basket, select a bunch of fresh flowers, and head for the checkout.

While I prepare dinner, I finish the remainder of the wine. By now, I'm floating and feeling kinda sexy. I can't wait for Herman to get here. I finish dinner and go into my bedroom to select an outfit to wear.

I choose a raisin-colored mini-dress, with large silver hoops and silver sandals. I take a shower, put on my makeup and get dressed.

I go into the kitchen and fill up two bowls with the salad mixture and place it on the table along with the flowers. I set out plates, glasses, silverware, and napkins.

I step back and assess everything. Perfect. I think about lighting candles, but feel that will be overkill.

Herman arrives promptly at six. He hands me a bottle of Cristal. I put it in the refrigerator and lead him into the living room. I put on the *Dreamgirls* soundtrack. Jennifer Hudson's version of "And I am Telling You I'm Not Going" is playing, and I ask Herman if he wants to dance.

"Dance?" he asks. "I didn't know you still danced, Charity."

I grab his hands and put them around my waist. "There's a lot about me that you don't know." I smile seductively.

I let Herman dance me around the over-sized living room. When the record is over, I kiss Herman on the cheek. I'm feeling so bold, I'm shocking myself.

Herman touches his cheek, looking a little shocked.

I don't know what I'm doing, but I'm ad-libbing nicely. "C'mon," I say, grabbing Herman by the arm, "let's have some champagne before dinner."

I go into the kitchen and select two champagne glasses that Lynzee bought me. The frosted flutes have three-dimensional metal leaves wrapped around the stem and end with a pink ceramic rose on the cusp.

With the lobsters needing only minutes to boil, I rinse off the ugly creatures and toss them into the seasoned boiling water.

While I fill up the glasses, my hands shake. I have a bout of guilt, and wonder to myself what the hell am I doing. I shrug it off and bring the glasses into the living room.

"How are the twins handling the divorce?" Herman asks as we sip our drinks.

"They're bright kids and chose not to take sides."

Herman looks contemplative. "You know I always wanted twins. But I wanted a girl and boy twin. You know, get it all over with at once."

I get a quick flash of April's face and nearly spill my drink. "Sorry." I jump up from the sofa. "Dinner's ready. C'mon, let's eat."

I prepare the plates in a colorful and professional manner the way my mother taught me, and fill the glasses with ice water.

For the next twenty-five minutes, we eat and chat, and laugh about the fun times we've had together.

"I'm stuffed," Herman says, wiping his lips with the napkin.

"Me, too." I rise and take the plates to the sink. "Ready for more champagne?"

"Do ducks quack?" He smiles.

I haven't felt this good in years. I feel so light on my feet, I feel as if I'm floating. Once we're back in the living room, I turn back on Beyoncé's CD. I refill our glasses. We sip and smile at each other.

"Halo" comes on and Herman extends his hand. I get up and we dance. Though I know I shouldn't, I snuggle up to Herman. His response is to kiss me on my neck.

"Mmm, that's good," I murmur. *He can't be gay. He just can't.*

The next thing I know, Herman is kissing me on the mouth. I kiss him back. Then I freeze. What in the hell is going on?

I step out of his arms. "Herman," I say licking my lips, "I thought you were gay."

He smiles seductively. "I'm not gay. I've just been waiting on you to give me a chance to show you what kind of man you really need."

I drop my head back. "Lordy, Lordy, how did I get into this?"

Herman guides me back to the sofa. He looks into my eyes

and says, "I love you, Charity. I always have. I don't want any woman other than you."

I drink my champagne and nearly choke on it. "Herman, you must know—"

"That you still love Jett. I know. But once you see the kind of husband I can be to you, I think you'll give me a chance."

I pick up my glass again and bring it to my lips. I gulp hard. It seems that I can't get high enough tonight to offset this odd feeling that's stirring in my loins.

"Herman, I—"

There's a loud knocking on the kitchen door. "Excuse me." I pick up my glass nervously and head for the door. I forgot to turn on the back porch light, so I can't see who's out there. I turn on the light with my right hand, and balance my glass with my left.

It's Jett. He screams through the glass, "Charity, what the hell are you doing?"

39

I'm so embarrassed I could sink right through the floor. The angry look on Jett's face terrifies me. I'm stone cold busted.

"Let me in!" he hollers.

"What do you want?" I'm not going to let him bully me.

"This is still my house. I said let me in before I call the police."

Hesitantly, I open the door. "Why are you here?"

"Is that Herman's car in the driveway?" He glares at me. "Don't lie." He pushes past me and heads for the kitchen. I follow him. "What the hell is going on in here?"

Herman gets up from the sofa. "Charity and I were having dinner."

"If I were you, I'd get the fuck out of my house before you get your ass kicked."

"There's no need to get angry, Jett. Charity and I—"

"Are good friends, Jett. You know that. Why are you making a big deal out of this?" My hands are shaking.

"Do I smell alcohol on your breath?" he says, turning back to me.

"I had some champagne." I look defiant. "So what?"

"Oh, so the moment I'm out of the picture, you forget all about church. You forgot about your promise to me to never drink again."

I pick up the champagne glasses off of the cocktail table.

"You've got a lot of nerve talking about promises." I head toward the kitchen. Jett grabs my shoulder.

"Don't fuck with me, Charity. You're still my damned wife."

I push away from him. "Not for long."

Herman gets up. "I think it's time for me to head on home. Good night, Charity. Jett. I'll see myself out."

After Herman leaves, I pick up around the house, throwing away empty bottles and putting the champagne glasses in the sink to wash out by hand. "I thought we finished our conversation this afternoon," I tell him. "What did you come back for?"

Jett takes a seat at the table. "Don't try to change the subject. What was Herman doing here so late?"

"I told you. We had dinner."

"And what else? And why are you wearing that mini-dress?"

"Nothing. This dress happens to be one of my favorite outfits. You picked it out for my forty-fifth birthday, remember?"

Jett's mouth bunches up. "That dress was for my eyes only."

I finish wiping off the counters. "Why don't you go home, Jett? It's late and I'm tired."

He gets up. "I don't appreciate your drinking. And when the twins find out, they're going to be disappointed too."

"I'm a grown woman. I do what I want to do. Now, are you going home, or do I have to call the police?"

"I'll leave." He makes it to the hallway and turns around. "Why did you change the locks?"

"Because you don't live here anymore."

"What if I moved back? What if I said I wanted to work things out between us?"

"Are you asking?"

"Yes, I'm asking. I had second thoughts about getting a divorce. So what if I moved back?"

It hurts my soul to say these words, but they have to be said: "You're not welcome. You walked out on me. As far as I'm concerned, you can keep right on walking."

When I wake up Sunday morning, I have a splitting headache. It has to be the alcohol. My body is not responding well to this unhealthy invasion.

I turn on the water and sit on the bench in the shower for thirty minutes. By then, I feel refreshed and ready for anything.

I reflect on last night, and I'm a little embarrassed. I practically threw myself at Herman, who now says he's not gay. I still can't believe I never figured it out. I'd never seen him with a man, but since I'd never seen him with a woman either, I just took him at his word. After all, who would believe a straight man would claim to be gay?

I go upstairs to my office and whip out my horoscope book. Herman is a Leo. I'm an Aries. As I read the text, I'm stunned to find that we're compatible. I sit back and think about my emotions. Could I really care for Herman? No, I tell myself, it's way too soon to begin a new relationship. Therapists say that you should wait at least a year after your divorce before you date. I assume they know what they're talking about. I close the book and shut down my emotions. Not now.

I decide to go by the twins' apartment. I grab my things, leave out of the back door and get into my car. When I try to start my car, it won't turn over. I try again and again. Still nothing. I go over to Jett's tool cabinet and remove the battery charger. Within minutes, I've got the red and black cable handles connected to the right source. I get back inside my car and crank it up. It starts. I put the charger back and get back in my car.

Then a thought hits me: my 550 BMW is five years old and paid for. Why shouldn't I buy a new one? I can damn well afford it.

"Yeah, why not?" I say to myself.

So, instead of going to the twins' apartment, I drive down Germantown Parkway to the Ambassador BMW dealership. Car salesmen give me time to check out the inventory before they approach me.

"Hello, I'm Seymour. And you are?"

"Mrs. Evans."

"Welcome to Ambassador BMW. Can I help you with anything? Answer any questions you may have?"

"I see a car I like. I'm here to get a good deal. If the numbers work out, you've got a sale. If not, I'm outta here." There are approximately two to three hundred cars, shining like diamonds on all four sides of the lot. I'm interested in the 760 Li.

He extends his arm. "Follow me inside, Mrs. Evans."

The glass-and-silver building is impressive. It's only been open for two years. When I bought my old BMW, I had to drive to Atlanta to purchase it.

I trail him to his small cubicle. He offers me coffee or water. I decline both. I want a new car, but I don't want to be too rash. What if I lose the lawsuit? How am I going to pay for it? My inner voice says that I'll find a way. Nothing makes a woman feel better than a new baby, a new house, or a new car.

While sitting at his desk I say, "Here's the vehicle identification number. I'll tell you right now, I used to be a car salesman, and I don't plan to pay more than five hundred dollars over cost. Are we clear?"

The vehicle I selected is a silver 760 Li Sedan. It has 535 horsepower, 20-way power seats, keyless start and stop, a hard drive–based navigation with voice activation and real-time traffic information, and even has side view cameras and a sixteen-speaker sound system. But what really has me sold is the four-year no-cost maintenance. At almost one-hundred-twenty-five thousand dollars, it should almost drive itself.

I can hear Jett's complaint: "Why in the hell are you buying a new car? There's nothing wrong with your old one."

"Because I deserve it," I'd say.

"You can't stand to keep money in the bank, can you? You just have to spend every dollar you can get your hands on. When you get broke, don't say that I didn't warn you."

Fuck you, you cheap ass asshole. It's my money.

And now, Seymour nods and takes out a purchase order. "Let me take down your information." He asks for my keys. "First, we need to get your car appraised."

"Sure. Another thing: I don't plan on being here for two or three hours. Either you're going to do it, or you're not." Suddenly I feel strong and powerful. Turning down Jett's offer to move back in has left me empowered. For years, I've been Jett's doormat, but now I'm finding my voice.

"My goodness, Mrs. Evans, you're going to be a tough sell."

Seymour and I fill out the paperwork. He runs my credit, and then takes the application up to the new car manager. He comes back minutes later.

"I'm sorry, Mrs. Evans, but we can't come close to your offer."

I get up. "Thanks for wasting my time." I head out the door. Once in my car, I'm pissed. I wanted that silver BMW. I could go to the Audi dealership and get a good price. I know the manager there. But an Audi would be my third choice of vehicle.

Just as I'm about to drive off, I hear a pounding on my trunk. I look over my shoulder and spot Seymour. He comes around to the driver's side. "Yes?"

"My manager wants to speak with you again."

"Why?"

"Because he thinks you two can come to terms about the car."

"Okay, I'll give him a shot." I'm getting excited. I might get my car yet.

I follow Seymour back inside. The sales manager, Hollis McMann, is waiting at Seymour's desk. He extends his hand. "Hello, Mrs. Evans. Thanks for coming back in."

I take a seat. "Please don't waste my time, Mr. McMann. I'm adamant about my offer."

"I understand totally. Let me show you some numbers."

Mr. McMann brings out the invoice sheet for the car I want. He gives me the costs of getting the car delivered, service costs, and clean up. Those costs are close to eight hundred dollars. When you factor in the cost of storing the vehicle on the lot, that's another three or four hundred dollars. That said, if they sold me the car at my price, they'd be losing money.

"I don't believe these numbers," I tell him. "And I don't believe that the cost of this car is really what you say it is. I know all about dealer incentives and dealer cash back. You can make the deal if you want to. I'm sure you've done as much for your friends and family." I get up. "Thanks, but no thanks."

I get ready to leave again.

"Hold on, Mrs. Evans," Mr. McMann says. "You're right about the dealer cash. Can you give me ten minutes? I have to run this by the general manager, Gray Sterling. He has the final say."

"Ten minutes, Mr. McMann, and I'm gone." I take a mint off of Seymour's desk and press my purse into my breasts. I automatically rock and wait. Rock and wait.

Nine minutes later, Mr. McMann is back. "We have a deal, Mrs. Evans. Would you like to take delivery today?"

"Yes, today. I can come back another time for the clean-up. I'm in a hurry."

He shakes my hand. "Thanks for your business."

I nod and rock back in my chair. After my car is ready, I'm going to take a quick drive down to Atlanta. I might do a little shopping at Nieman Marcus and then have some dinner. I should arrive back home at around midnight.

Good. I like that plan. I can visit the twins' place next weekend.

I enjoy a Sprite and a bag of barbecue chips while I wait for Seymour to get my keys. The moment I see my new car shining like wet silver, my smile is as wide as Texas. I get the keys and then transfer my papers and paraphernalia to my new vehicle. And I'm off.

Herman calls. "Is everything okay?

"Great. I just bought a new car. I'm on my way to Atlanta."

"Want some company?"

As I change lanes to pass a car on my left, the car handles like it's floating across the road. I feel like I'm in a cockpit, the ride is so smooth. "No, I need some time alone."

"Did Jett stay long last night?"

"No."

"Charity, I don't know how to say this, but I meant what I said yesterday."

"I'm flattered, Herman, but I can't deal with this right now. My life is in turmoil. I don't know where my future is going. I don't know if I'll have a career in six months. I don't know if I'll be broke in six months. There are just so many variables. I don't want to put any more stress on my mind. Do you understand where I'm coming from?"

"Yes. I'll give you some time."

"Thanks."

"Have a good time in Atlanta."

"I will. Bye."

I get on Interstate 78 to Birmingham, Alabama, to Interstate 20, and then take Interstate 75 into Atlanta. By the time I reach Lenox Square Mall on Peachtree Road Northeast, I only have an hour to shop. But when you know how to shop and which stores to shop at, an hour is all you need,

First stop is Nieman's, where I buy two white blouses, one silk and one lace. I purchase three long gowns and two short ones. I pick up five bra and panty sets, and then head out to Nordstrom's. I try on and select four pairs of sandals and buy a pair of thigh-high fall boots. Finally, I stop by this French boutique, The French Connection, that I've always loved, and purchase two mini-dresses, a pair of trousers, and a matching top.

I'm done and I'm suffering from inundation. I put my purchases in my trunk and drive to Outback Steakhouse. I'm in the mood for a steak and a flaming onion with that tangy sauce that I love. I can never get enough of that sauce. I could eat it every day. I'm tempted to ask the chef for the recipe, but realize that I wouldn't be the first person to ask, and not the last to go away without the recipe.

It's time to get on the road and head home. When I get on the freeway, I call Jamone and tell him where I've been. He and Javed came by the house around nine. They were worried about me. I forgot to leave the lights on. I tell them about the car. Both boys think it was a good move. They want to know if they can take it for a drive next weekend. I say that I have to think about it. They know I'll say yes. After all, I've got insurance, and it's just metal.

When I get home, I turn on the lights and make two trips into the house to haul my purchases inside. I hang up the clothes in my closet and store my shoes on the shelf. I put sachet tablets on my undergarments and store them in my dresser drawer.

I'm still floating on cloud nine, but something is nagging me. I think I've forgotten about something. First, I pour myself a glass of wine, and then I skip up the steps to my office and check my messages.

I flood the room with light. One message is from Arlene. My publisher wants to know how the lawsuit is going. Next, my booking agent calls. He wants to know what happened to me today. I was a no-show at Lemoyne-Owen College and the dean is pissed off at me.

"Damn." I have to e-mail the dean. With my Rolodex still not in sight, I make up my mind to turn my office upside down until I find it.

I sip on wine, rummage, sip on wine, and rummage again. I'm almost finished with the bottle of wine and I feel exhausted. I'm ready to give up when I locate the Rolodex in one of the trash cans. *How in the hell did it get in here?*

I take a seat at my desk and flip through the Rolodex. I find the dean's e-mail address. I turn on my computer and wait for it to boot. That done, I log on to the Internet and my e-mail account.

I exhale, think rationally, and come up with a plausible excuse for missing my engagement this afternoon.

Dean Whitcomb, I'm very sorry for missing my engagement this afternoon. I was very honored to be asked to speak at your prestigious school and be a part of the festivities. However, I'm going through a stressful divorce and the appointment slipped my mind. I hope that you'll allow me to reschedule and give a speech that your students will be proud of hearing. Of course, there will be no fee. Please call me if you have any questions or concerns.

I turn off my computer, shut off the lights, and go back downstairs to my bedroom. I undress, shower, and slip on one of my favorite nightgowns.

I flip on the television set to Lifetime. A movie is on with Blair Underwood and an actress than I'm unfamiliar with. Blair makes me think of Herman.

My home phone rings. It's Jett.

"Where've you been?"

"None of your business."

"Like I told you yesterday, you're still my wife."

"Temporarily," I say.

"Don't ever underestimate me, Charity. You don't know what I'm capable of." He hangs up.

I lie on my back and stare up at the ceiling. Unexpected tears form in my eyes. I have to ask myself, would Jett actually hurt me?

40

The second week of trial is full of surprises. Lynzee keeps staring at me throughout the trial. I could swear that I notice tears in her eyes. Her emotional instability eats away at my heart. From where I'm sitting, I can't tell if she's high on Percocet. I pray that she tossed the prescription and is on her way to being sober again. I wish we could just get our lives back to normal and forget about all of this stupid shit. But that's not going to happen. This trial is real, and the lawsuit is clear.

I don't know how Lynzee's attorney's found so many witnesses to sing her praises. Most of her friends and family members know that Lynzee turned into a Cruella De Ville diva when she became rich. Her attitude was that the world owed her something, and no one could treat her well enough to thank her for gracing the American public with her auspicious talent.

I thank God that Mama didn't live to see her eldest daughter turn into the Wicked Witch of the West. She would have put Lynzee in her place. By the time Mama finished telling Lynzee that she wasn't God's gift to publishing, Lynzee would have been as humbled as an elf.

But as the days pass, I sneak looks at Lynzee and see how miserable she really is. She's never been married, never had a man love her more than he loves himself. She doesn't know what it feels like to have a normal lifestyle with a spouse, kids, and church. She doesn't know what it feels like to sleep in the bed with a man who loves her garlicky breath, and who would bathe her down with baby wipes if she ever became incapacitated.

The only thing she knows is money and power. Now she has neither, and the thought has got to be killing her. I've just learned from Kai that Tyler doesn't want to have anything to do with her mother anymore. Tyler blames Lynzee for talking her into marrying Raymond. She's been miserable ever since. Presently, she's trying to see if she can get the marriage annulled.

Then there's April. Ever since Jett came into the picture, April hasn't had any use for Lynzee either. April doesn't come to the trial to support her mother or show her concern. No, Lynzee is sitting there alone with two attorneys whose only purpose is dragging out this trial as long as they can so that they can get a hefty fee from Lynzee.

Javed found out where Lynzee is staying while she's in Memphis; The Marriott Courtyard downtown. The other night, I sent her a settlement letter offering her three hundred thousand dollars. I still haven't heard back from her.

While listening to Teddy's cross-examinations of Lynzee's witnesses, I can tell that our side is making headway and making her witnesses look like liars. I'm able to discern by the looks that the judge is giving Lynzee's counsel that he's tiring of the long line of witnesses that are basically all saying the same thing. I wouldn't be surprised if he put a stop to it and made them either put Lynzee on the stand or hand the case over to the defense attorneys.

But that doesn't happen, and as each week goes by, the temperature gets hotter and my patience gets shorter.

By the end of August, I learn from the twins that Jett drives by my house several times at night, making sure that Herman's car isn't there. He hasn't stopped the divorce proceedings, yet is all up in my business.

Teddy doesn't do divorce cases, so I have to hire another attorney for the divorce. I retain a female attorney, Molly Russell. She asked for a $25,000 retainer to take the case. I am appalled. When an attorney thinks you have a little cash stashed, they come down hard in your pockets, and there's very little that you can do about it.

I call at least twelve more attorneys. The retainer is around the same amount, and some are even higher, as much as $50,000. I decide to stick with Molly. The thought of having money now is making me sick. Lynzee, Jett, and Molly all have their hands out. Do they think I get fifteen million a book like Stephen King? I still have to pay my agent out of that advance and pay income taxes on that money.

When you get your advance from a publisher, they don't take any taxes out of it. You get a 1099 at the end of the year. A good agent tells you to pay your taxes quarterly, so that you're not shocked by a hefty tax bill at the end of the year. A number of black authors didn't pay their taxes and got in serious trouble with the IRS. Knowing that, I pay my taxes quarterly like any person with common sense would do.

One night, to my shock, I run into April and Jett at Kroger's grocery store. Jett refuses to speak, but April says hello. I say hello back and continue on about my business. It hurts like hell to see the two of them together. I brush back tears and push on. I make it my business to start grocery shopping at Schnucks so that I won't run into them again.

Since April came to town, Jett has only seen his sons twice. I try to tell my sons that their Dad loves them. "Then why doesn't he come by our apartment?" Javed asks.

"Because he's at April's place all of the time," Jamone adds. "You'd think that girl was his woman instead of his daughter."

That hurt, especially since I was thinking the same thing. Why is Jett spending so much time with April? I told him about her sexual proclivities toward women. Didn't it matter? Or was that another lie that Lynzee told?

To my stunned surprise, I get a call from Tyler while I'm in my bedroom watching *24*. I've got on a pair of black-and-pink pajamas and have retired early tonight.

"Hello, sweetie. How're you feeling?"

"Okay, I guess."

"Your baby is due next month, isn't it?"

"Yes, it's a boy."

"I know you're proud."

"Not really. I'm going to give the baby up for adoption. Please don't tell me not to do what my mother did. I already know the repercussions. But I've given this a lot of thought. I want to finish my education at Harvard. You heard about me and Raymond, didn't you?"

"I'm not sure."

"Our marriage was annulled. I'm living in a dorm with a roommate."

"No, Tyler, I didn't know."

"Getting married was stupid. Raymond and I were too young to know what we were doing. All we knew is that we had great sex together." She sighed. "But enough about that. I called you for another reason. I want to be one of your witnesses. I've read all the blogs about the trial, and I know that you need help."

"What? Why?" I sit up in the bed and turn on the light.

"My mother has always been jealous of you. She used to talk about you so bad to me, it was pitiful. She was worried that you'd outsell her one day. I overheard her on the telephone talking to her editor about getting you blacklisted. She's positively guilty of defaming your name and putting your career in jeopardy. I couldn't understand how she could be so cruel. Then I found out about April. And I found out that she didn't dump Uncle Jett, he dumped her."

Now things are beginning to become crystal clear. Why didn't Jett tell me that he broke it off with Lynzee?

"Anyway, April didn't come looking for Mom. Mom sought her out. She wanted to ruin your marriage and career."

How sick. I don't know what I've done to make Lynzee resent me so much. How could I have been so gullible?

"I'm shocked, Tyler. I had no idea that your Mom's hatred of me ran so deep."

"Oh, it's deep. It started when you married Uncle Jett, and

got worse after you got a book contract. Of course, I wasn't born then, but I've heard Mom talking about it enough times to Zedra. Mom doesn't know that I know that she and Zedra have done the wild thing. I almost busted them one time."

"My Lord. I don't know what to say." I write down a few notes on the pad on my nightstand for Teddy.

"So, do you want me to testify?"

"I don't know, honey. You shouldn't be traveling right now."

"I can come after the baby is born. I think he's coming early. My stomach has already dropped." She pauses. "Please, please let me testify, Aunt Charity. It's about time that Mom paid her dues. I know that you've never done anything to harm her. And Aunt Charity—"

"Yes?"

"The reason I stopped calling Javed and Jamone is because I found out the truth about April. The entire cousin/sister thing made me sick. I was so ashamed of being my mom's daughter I couldn't bear to keep up the pretense. I didn't want to lie to my cousins anymore." She begins to cry. "Do you hate me, Aunt Charity?"

"Of course not. None of this is your fault. You're too young to understand the depth of your mother's deception. And you were too young to stop her. So, no, honey, I don't blame you. I thank you for telling me the truth. Especially about your mom contacting April. A few things make more sense now."

"Thank you, Auntie. I've got a new cell phone number. Write it down." She calls out the numbers as I jot them down. "Thanks, Tyler. I'll keep in touch. You call me if you need any-thing."

"I get money from school. I'm doing okay. But the offer for me to testify still stands. I can even buy my own ticket."

"That won't be necessary, honey. Now, you get some rest, you hear? I'll call you back real soon, okay?"

"Okay. I love you, Aunt Charity."

"And I love you, Tyler. Goodnight sweetie." I hang up. Tears spring up in my eyes. I feel pity and hatred for Lynzee all at the same time. Now she's even got her own daughter turning against her. Now she has no one. She only has her millions to keep up the fake pretense of appearing to be happy. What a damn shame.

It's twenty minutes past nine. I call Kai.

"Hey, Kai, it's me. You won't believe who just called me."

I take the next fifteen minutes repeating everything that Tyler told me. Kai isn't the least bit surprised. She's happy that Tyler had her marriage annulled. Kai believes in education, and she didn't feel that Lynzee was doing Tyler justice by allowing her to birth a child so young, especially since she received a full scholarship to an Ivy League school.

"What do you think about her testifying for me?" I ask.

"I wouldn't do it, Charity. If Tyler testifies against her mother, it will cause irrefutable damage between mother and daughter. You don't want to have that egg on your face. Trying to pit mother against daughter is like playing with fire. You'll get burned every time."

"You're probably right."

"How's the trial going?"

"The same. Nothing new. Lynzee is running out of witnesses, and now her case seems weak."

"It's just like Teddy predicted. He knew Lynzee didn't stand a chance. So, Charity, what about the counter suit? Are you going to sue Lynzee for ten million?"

"Gosh, no. I told my lawyer to drop that. I don't need nor want her money. I've had enough. I just want my life to go back to normal."

"How can it with Jett gone and April in the picture?"

"That's a tough question."

"And what about Herman? He told me how he felt about you."

"You talk to Herman?"

"Hell, yeah. I knew that man wasn't gay. I got his number before I left the first time. The only reason I backed off is because of his feelings for you."

"That was gracious of you."

"So . . . how do you feel about Herman?"

"Like he's still my friend. Look, I've loved Jett for thirty years. I can't turn my emotions on and off like a faucet."

"I've seen it done before."

I flip the channel to the ten o'clock news. "Not in this camp."

"I've got to hand it to you, you're loyal."

I scratch my right foot, and then cross my legs. "I'm a married woman. Until I'm divorced, I'm not screwing around with anyone."

"And what if Jett does?"

"Then it's over for good. He won't get a second chance."

"I don't think that's true. I believe you'd take him back."

"You're wrong, Kai. I won't be disrespected by him again."

"Then be ready to rein in your ego. A good-looking man like Jett won't have to go looking for a hot piece of ass. The ass is going to come to him."

After our call is over, I think about what Kai said. Am I being stupid? Should I worry about Jett screwing around on me? Or should I be worried about a woman who's been waiting to steal my man?

41

F inally, Lynzee's attorneys are finished with their witnesses. As expected, Lynzee doesn't testify. Now, it's our turn, and Teddy and our team are ready for a knock-down, kick-ass fight.

Tyler called again. She had her baby son and put him up for adoption. She asked for the second time that she be able to testify. I told Teddy and he said, "We'll wait and see how things go. Maybe we'll use her. Maybe not."

Unlike Lynzee's lawyers, Teddy does plan to have me testify, and I can't wait until it's my turn to get up on the stand. I'll show her jealous ass a thing or two.

After the trial one Wednesday evening, I decide to stop by the twins' apartment. Fortunately, they're both at home. Javed lets me in. The place is a complete mess. There are clothes and empty pizza boxes all over the living room. I drop my purse and start cleaning up the place.

Javed insists, "Mom, you don't have to do this. Me and Jamone were planning to clean the place up tomorrow."

I roll my eyes at him. "Yeah, sure."

Javed peeps outside. "I like the new ride. Can I take it for a spin? I want to see how that baby will perform on the freeway."

I'm in the kitchen now, looking at the mess they've created in there. It's going to take me at least an hour to get this place decent. "Go ahead, Javed. The keys are in my purse."

"Hold up. Let me wake up Jamone. I know he'd want to check out the new Beamer too." He comes back into the kitchen. "Jamone's getting dressed."

Javed puts on his shoes, and I begin the cleanup process. I remove my tan suit jacket and place it on the sofa. When I return to the kitchen, Jamone comes up behind me and kisses me on the cheek.

"Hi, Mom. It's good to see you." Jamone has on a Lakers shorts set, and I'm amazed to see that Javed has on the same outfit.

"What's up?" I ask. "Are you two dressing alike again?"

"No way," they say in unison.

Javed says, "We got a deal on these outfits. It's just a one-time thang."

Jamone opens the blinds and light floods in. "I see the ride, Mom. Javed said you're going to let us take it for a spin?"

"Just be back by the time I finish cleaning up this joint."

They rush outside. I can hear them arguing over who's going to drive first. Finally, Javed takes the lead and Jamone gets in the passenger seat.

I'm in my element cleaning up my sons' place. It feels good to feel needed again. Like I've taught them since they were six years old, they've got good cleaning products, thank God.

By the time I finish cleaning out the microwave, the boys are back. "Look, boys, I don't want to see this place this filthy again. I raised you two better than that. What if I wanted to bring Herman over here to see your place? You'd embarrass the hell out of me."

Jamone hands me the keys. "What's up with you and Herman, Mom? Dad told us that you two had dinner together."

That big-mouth bastard. I put my jacket back on. "Oh, it was nothing. I love Herman like the brother I never had."

Jamone speaks up. "We're not slow, Mom. We see the way that Herman constantly checks you out. Uh-huh. And it's not like a brother who cares about his sister."

Javed nods. "Any fool can see that he's got it bad for you."

I straighten the pillows on the sofa again. "Stop nosing

around in things that are none of your business. I told you that our relationship was innocent, so stop fishing, will you?"

"We will for now," Jamone says. "Did he tell you that we've been to his house? We're working on a new piece for his place. His condo is dope, man."

"No, he didn't tell me."

"Haven't you noticed that our cars are at our studio more often lately?"

"No, I'm in court all day. I haven't seen your cars at the house." I pick up my purse and prepare to leave.

"We should be finished by the weekend," Jamone offers. "He's paying us top dollar for our work. We can't help but wonder if it's because of you."

I walk to the doorway. "Just consider yourself talented artists and that's the reason he's paying you well. After all, haven't you two always told me that your paintings are gaining national exposure and your work is worth more money now?"

"Yes, that's true," Jamone says. He comes over and gives me a hug. Javed follows. "Javed and I just want you to be careful out here. We don't know how long you and Pops are going to be separated, but we don't want you dating anyone else for a long time. You need some time to yourself first."

"Word," Javed says.

"Boys . . . men, listen to me. I'm not going to date anyone until the divorce is final." I put my hand on the doorknob. Jamone's hand covers mine.

"Mom, Javed and I need to hip you to something." They exchange glances. Javed nods at Jamone. "It's about Pops."

I step back, my interest piqued. "What about your dad?"

There is a long silence. Javed and Jamone look at each other again.

"What is it? Tell me."

"We think that Dad's seeing another woman," Jamone says. "We spotted him and this young lady at Horizon's Dance Emporium last weekend."

I'm momentarily speechless. Jett out dancing? And with another woman? "Are you sure it wasn't April?" I ask.

"Yes, we're sure," Jamone says. "We even stopped to talk to

him. He introduced Marla to us. It was kinda awkward. I've never seen Pops at a club before."

"To tell you the truth, it was kinda embarrassing. Pops had to be the oldest dude in the place."

I put my hands on my hips. "And how old is Marla?"

"About thirty, thirty-five," Javed states.

I start to pace the floor. "I'm sorry, guys. I hadn't expected Jett to act this immature. I'm saddened that you guys had to see him like that."

"He gave us a hundred dollars apiece and said, 'Keep this between you and me, will you?'"

Javed looks annoyed. "We told him yes, but we knew what the real deal was: Tell Mom. That was some bold stuff. You two haven't been separated that long."

I stop pacing. "You're right." I know I have to report this to my attorney, but I feel an urgent desire to confront Jett first. "I've gotta go." I force a smile, but inside I'm hurting like hell. "You two stop by and have dinner with me on Sunday."

"What time?" Jamone asks.

"Five o'clock."

"We'll be there," Javed says.

I walk back to the door and turn the handle. I hold my head up high. "See you on Sunday." I close the door behind me.

When I get into my car, I can see my sons looking at me from behind the blinds. I'm holding back tears, and refuse to let them see me cry. I push the ignition start button and slowly drive off.

It seems like my car knows where it's heading. I drive to Jett's job on Mt. Moriah Avenue. I'm so mad I'm seeing purple dots. How could Jett be so insensitive? Doesn't almost thirty years of marriage deserve a little more respect than that?

I get a few whistles about my car. I ask one of the black salesmen, "Is Jett Evans here tonight?"

King Ford is an old dealership. It's blue and silver, like the Ford emblem, but could use some remodeling. Even so, they're one of the top selling dealerships in Memphis. They're purported to have a loyal customer base.

He smiles. "Yes. He just took a break. You want me to get him for you?"

"Yes, please."

"And you are?"

"Charity Evans. His wife." Those words sting my tongue. I feel like the biggest hypocrite alive. After all, I started this bullshit by having Herman over for dinner. But I hadn't expected Jett to retaliate and go dancing with a woman, especially since we haven't been dancing in more than fifteen years. He's got some damn nerve. I can't wait to see his lying ass.

In just under five minutes, Jett comes outside. It's dark now, but I can still see the angry snarl on his face. I roll down my window and say, "Get in." He does, and I drive to the back of the lot. I turn off the ignition and say, "We need to talk."

"About what?" He turns toward me and slips a toothpick in his mouth.

"You and Marla."

"Oh, so the twins told you?"

"What did you expect?"

"Some loyalty."

"Why? You're the guilty one. You've almost cut the boys out of your life and put April before them. How do you think they're supposed to feel? I can tell you, betrayed."

"My sons know that I love them." He looks over his shoulder to see if anyone is watching us. "But what I do with my personal time is none of your business."

"You bastard. You started this bullshit. I didn't file for a divorce, you did."

He rolls the toothpick over his tongue. "And seeing you with Herman let me know that I did the right thing. You two have probably been fucking behind my back for years."

I'm appalled. "You know that's a damn lie."

"Oh, do I?" He caps his hands over his left knee. "I know that you two are entirely too close. I know that you know that I don't like him, but you see him anyway. I'm from the South. Women do as their husbands command. It's in the Bible that a woman should submit to her husband. I've told you that I didn't want him in our home, but you bring him over anyway. Why is that?"

"Because you can't choose my friends. For your information, Herman and I have never been intimate. I've told you for years that we're just friends. A woman can have a male friend, you know."

"Not in my world. I see how he looks at you. I know he wants to jump into bed with you the moment I'm out of the picture." He pauses. "Well, now you've got that chance. You two can go at it like muskrats. I don't give a fuck. Just leave me, my daughter, and my woman out of your business."

"Oh, so now Marla is your woman?"

"Matter of fact, she is."

I feel like the wind has been knocked out of me. How dare this bastard sit in my face and tell me that he's screwing another woman? Doesn't he have an ounce of respect for me? Didn't the thirty years we spent together mean anything to him?

"Okay, then. You've got a lover. I'm going to have to share this information with my attorney. I hope you know you're limiting your chances of getting any money out of the divorce."

He bites down on the toothpick. "I never needed your money. I've got my own."

"That's a damn lie and you know it."

He looks around the inside of the car. "It appears that you're a little greedy. Did you pay for this car with food stamps?"

"Fuck you, Jett. You don't tell me what to do with my money."

"You're right. I never could." He looks out his window. Customers are beginning to look at the vehicles at the back of the lot. They're laughing and high-fiving one another. "Take me back to the front. I've said all I'm going to say."

"Fine." I start up the car. Then I pause. My heart is heavy. I don't want to lose this man. Even though I told him before that he wasn't welcome in my home, Lord knows I still love him. Tears threaten to fall, but I hold them in.

"Jett," I say, "would you consider going to a marriage counselor? Maybe we can work things out. I know that I don't want to give—"

"Hell no. I don't need some white chick telling me how to treat my wife."

"I could find an African American counselor," I offer weakly.

"Same damn thing. I'm a man. Ain't no man or woman alive can tell me how to run my marriage. That's for me to decide."

"Marriage counselors help, Jett. They really do. You said before that you would consider it. Just give it a chance. Please."

I hate myself for begging, but feel that I have no choice. I don't want our marriage to end. I want to live the rest of my life with him, laughing like teenagers, doing our gardening, and going to church on Sundays. Of course, I'll stop drinking again.

"Tell me something, Charity. Are you still drinking?"

I lower my head. "Yes."

"That figures. You've always been weak to alcohol."

"I can stop, Jett. I promise you that I'll give it up."

"No. I'm through." He opens the door, spits out the toothpick, and gets out. With the door open, he looks down and says, "Please don't come back to my job again. I don't need my coworkers knowing any of my business." He slams the door.

I'm outdone. I sit there for a few minutes and pound my head against the steering wheel. How in the hell did this happen? Did my friendship with Herman really set him over the edge? Or just when, when did he really stop loving me?

42

I cry myself to sleep at night. I'm hurt beyond words. I want to follow Jett and bust him with his woman. I want him to see how much he's hurting me.

When I speak to Kai, she totally understands how I feel. She was just in a relationship with a man and found out that he was married. She immediately broke it off. Kai believes that Marla has got to know that Jett is married. The bitch just doesn't give a damn. We both agree that there are some desperate females out here.

The temperature reaches a hundred degrees the last few days in August. Throughout almost all of August, the temperature lingered at ninety-six. Because they don't have any air conditioners, a couple of senior citizens die from the heat. The mayor is visibly upset and starts a drive to give out over three hundred fans to seniors and low-income families.

One of the air conditioners breaks in my home. I'm so used to Jett handling everything that I don't know what to do. I call Herman and he comes over. He checks out the unit, figures out the problem, and calls a reputable heating and cooling company. The unit is fixed and is working like new.

It is the first time that I see Herman face to face since our dinner together.

"I know how the trial is going. I want to know how you're feeling," he asks me.

"I'm okay. A little tired, but fine."

"You know you can call me night or day?"

"I know. Thanks."

We hug each other, and Herman has me laughing with another one of his embalming jokes. I haven't laughed in a while, and it feels good.

"Charity, I'm not going to put any pressure on you," he says, "but do me a favor. I just bought a new plane. Yep, a brand new one. I want to test it out and drive it to the Bahamas. Can you think about going with me?"

I feel a tug of emotion. Here is this man, knowing how much I love my husband, still trying to maintain some contact. I tell him that I'll go with him. My mind could use a diversion.

The trip is planned to take place in three more days. Until then, I'm having non-stop meetings with Teddy. He's found some new evidence that could help our case. He wants to me to come up to his office to discuss the possibilities.

Feeling remorseful, I take the elevator up to Teddy's office late Wednesday afternoon. His secretary asks me to have a seat.

Fifteen minutes later, Teddy comes out of his office looking flustered. He waves me in. "C'mon, Charity. Sorry about the wait."

I go inside and sit before his desk. He takes a seat at his desk that is filled with caseloads and pink message slips. He has on a white shirt with the cuffs rolled up to his elbows. I smell steak and cheese and notice the crushed paper in the trash can. He clears a space and picks up a new pad and pen. "Thanks for coming by. We've got a lot to cover." He puts on his glasses. "Are you thirsty? Can I get you anything?"

"No, Teddy. I'm fine." I rest my purse on my lap and cross my legs.

"We've got a break."

"Oh, I thought the case was going well."

"It is. But we don't want to take anything for granted. I've got a new witness."

"Oh, are we going to use Tyler?"

"No. This woman's name is Cicely Halleron."

"I never heard of her."

"You wouldn't. She went to Chapel Hill with Lynzee and Heidi Armstrong." He flips through a few pages. "It seems that she has some damaging information about Lynzee."

"Oh, what kind?"

"It's sexual."

"Don't tell me that Lynzee was sexually involved with another girl?"

He smiles. "It so happens that she was. But this is no ordinary tryst. This is a threesome, with Lynzee, Heidi, and Cicely."

I know something bad is coming. Do I really want to hear this?

"It appears that Lynzee dressed up in men's clothing, along with attaching a dildo to her pelvis. Heidi objected to Cicely's involvement, but Lynzee wouldn't hear of it. Cicely was a very beautiful girl on campus, and Heidi was jealous of her. To make a long story short, Lynzee told Heidi to either get involved in the threesome or leave. Heidi was hurt and did as she was told.

"This threesome went on for a couple of months before Heidi tired of the attention that Lynzee was showing Cicely. Heidi gave Lynzee an ultimatum: either get rid of Cicely or she was going to kill herself."

"What? What happened to the basketball player?"

Teddy tapped his pen. "There wasn't a basketball player involved. That story was made up for Lynzee's benefit."

"So, Lynzee had prior warning that Heidi was going to kill herself?"

"Yes. It appears so."

"And what happened to Cicely?"

"She transferred to another school after Heidi's suicide. Lynzee graduated a year later and the story died with her departure."

I press my hands against the arms of the chair. "So, you found Cicely and she's willing to testify?"

"That's right. I've got her in a hotel downtown. She's prepared to testify on Friday. I had to give Lynzee's attorney's time to review the evidence."

I shake my head. "I don't know, Teddy. This new information could ruin Lynzee's career for good. I don't know if I'm prepared to go that far."

"I understand Lynzee is your sister and you still feel some loyalty toward her, but let me remind you that Lynzee's done everything possible to undermine you and your career. She's trying to take every dime you've got. She's trying to humiliate you with April, and cause your career irrefutable damage. She tried to turn her daughter, Tyler, against you too. She's responsible for your upcoming divorce. She's caused your sons to have a strained relationship with their father. Do you think you owe a person like that any loyalty?"

I ponder his words for a few minutes before I answer. "I guess not. But we're sisters, Teddy. Blood sisters. I can't forget about that. So she's greedy. So she's a little jealous—"

"A little?"

"Well, she's jealous. I don't know what happened to her to make her feel this way toward me. All I know is that deep down inside my sister still loves me, and if the situation were reverse, she wouldn't use this information to defame me."

"Are you certain about that?" He taps the pen on the pad and glares at me over his glasses.

"Not absolutely sure."

"Then take a proactive stance to salvage what's rightfully yours."

I rise. "That's just it. I've always copied after everything that Lynzee did. When she cut her hair when we were younger, I cut mine. When she got a job, I got one too. When she started dating a basketball player, I did too. When she took shorthand and typing in high school, again, I copied her every move. And finally, when she received success as an author, I copied after her once again. There's no wonder that she resents me. I'm just like her reflection."

"Plenty of young girls look up to their older sisters. It's not unusual for a young girl to want to do everything her big sister does. But Lynzee acted with malice. She should have been flattered. After all, you're a good writer. That alone should have made her proud of you. Instead, she had you blacklisted. That's not the actions of a loving sister."

"I agree. But one of us has to put a stop to this madness. I guess it's going to have to be me." I get up. "I'm going to call Lynzee, Teddy. I'm going to ask her to agree to a settlement. This time I'll offer her a half million dollars. I feel that's only fair."

Teddy gets up. "I think you're making a major mistake. We've got the case won."

"Then let me make it, Teddy. I at least have to try. Our mother wouldn't have expected any less of me."

"And what would your mother say about Lynzee's actions?"

"That she's selfish. That she's an egotistical bitch. And that she is the real opportunist in the family."

"I totally agree."

I slip my purse beneath my arm. "I'm going to go now, Teddy. I'll let you know tomorrow what I've decided to do."

I leave his office dazed and confused. What the hell is wrong with me? Why am I feeling sorry for Lynzee? She's the one who started all of this bullshit.

I take the elevator down to the garage and take a few moments to locate my car. Finding it, I get in. I start the ignition and head for the booth. The moment I pay the fee, my cell phones rings. It's Kai.

"Girl, why haven't you called me?"

"You know I've been overwhelmed by this trial."

"How's it going?"

"My attorney says that we're winning." I exit the garage and make a left on Main Street and a right on Beale Street. I head south on Beale until I get to Riverside Drive.

"How's Lynzee holding up?"

"I'm not sure. I can't tell if she's still taking the Percocet."

"That's a damn shame. You know that Lynzee is one of my favorite authors. That woman can write a helluva novel. And the research that she does on her characters in unparalleled in the business. I don't know a writer out there that works as hard at her craft as Lynzee does."

"Uh, Kai. Did you forget that I'm a writer too?"

"Oh, my bad. You write well, Charity. But as your cousin I have to be honest. Lynzee has got you beat with dialogue and narration."

I continue down Riverside Drive for a mile or so and up on the ramp to Interstate 40. "Thanks for your vote of confidence."

"Girl, you know that I love you. I'm just speaking the truth. You wouldn't want me to lie to you, would you?"

I laugh. "Yes."

She laughs. "Well, I say hell no to that. I wish there was a way that both of you could win."

"I offered her a nice settlement." I turn on the radio. One of Gerald Levert's songs is on. I snap my fingers to the beat.

"And she turned you down."

"Yep. Now my attorney has dredged up some pretty damaging evidence against Lynzee. He thinks that it's going to help win my case."

"Damaging how?"

"About her knowing about her friend Heidi's suicide attempt before she committed the act."

"And you'd crucify your sister like that?" Kai sounds appalled. Lately I've noticed that she's softening up her feelings about Lynzee.

"Wouldn't you?"

"Hell no. I wish I had a sister. We'd be thick as thieves. Nothing could break up our friendship. Not money. Not a man. Not a career. And not even our kids."

I take a hard gulp. "So, you think I shouldn't use the evidence?"

"Like I said already, hell no."

"Why not? She tried to ruin my career."

"Look, you've got a nice house, a husband, kids, and friends who love you. What does Lynzee have? She doesn't have her house anymore. Her and Tyler are estranged, and I'm told that she and April are not speaking either. She doesn't attend church, and she doesn't have any true friends, except Zedra. I feel sorry for her, Charity."

"Lynzee truly doesn't have any real friends anymore. Once she became famous, they became haters."

"Fortunately, you've got friends like me and Herman, who will stick by your side if your publisher pays you twenty thousand a book."

"I know. Thanks, Kai. I truly am blessed to have such good friends."

"Then listen to me. Don't let this supposed surprise testimony hurt Lynzee. She's suffered enough."

"I'm thinking that you're right. But my attorney—"

"Works for you. He has to do what you tell him to do." She pauses. "Now, you do me a favor. You call your sister and you two sit down and talk. I'm telling you, Charity, if you two sit down and talk things out, you'll never regret making this decision."

We say our good nights. I'm pumped up right now. I really want—no, need—to talk to Lynzee. I dial Zedra's number. She picks up on the first ring.

"Hello."

"Don't hang up, Zedra. This is Charity."

"What the hell do you want?"

"Lynzee's new number. Look, I know you don't like me, but I'm trying to help my sister. I really need to speak with her. It's terribly important."

"Why should I give you her number, heffa?"

"Because I'm still her sister. And despite what you think, Lynzee loves me."

There's a long pause. "You're lucky I'm in a good mood. I'm not positive that I'm doing the right thing by my friend, but here's the number." I steer with my left hand, and enter the number in my cell phone with my right. "Thanks, Zedra. Have a good night." I hang up.

It's show time. I dial the number and wait. The phone rings

and rings. The voice mail comes on. I drive along the Interstate and after taking a deep breath, try the number again. Maybe she was in the bathroom. I try again. This time she answers.

"Hello?"

"Lynzee, it's me, your sister. We need to talk."

43

"Talk about what?" Her tone is nasty. "I see how your attorney is turning you against me. I see how easily you can be corrupted."

"Lynzee. Hold on, you're overreacting. I'm trying to not only be your sister, but to be your friend. Now, I know you're staying in a motel downtown. Will you give me the name and I'll come over?"

There's a long silence. "I don't know about this. Maybe you're setting me up for something."

"No, I'm not. I'm trying to help you."

"Why?"

"Because you're my big sister and I love you."

"Do you?"

"Yes," I say.

"After all I've done to you?"

"Yes. You're my blood. I could never stop loving you."

Lynzee cries. "I'm sorry for everything, Charity." Her voice is thick.

"I'm sorry too. It didn't have to come to this."

"Can you ever forgive me about April?"

"Yes. It was partly Jett's fault too."

"I hoped you'd say that. Can you come up to my room?"

"For sure. Are you staying at the Courtyard Marriott downtown?"

"Yes. How did you know?"

"I can't tell all of my secrets, now." I smile. "What room are you in?"

"Three-oh-seven."

"I'll be there in fifteen minutes."

Lynzee opens the door wearing white silk pajamas. Her face is glazed with tears. "Hello," she says.

"Hi." I hug her. "It's good to see you."

"C'mon in. I made a pot of coffee. You want some?"

I sit down at the chair in front of the desk. "No. Do you have anything stronger?"

Lynzee looks perplexed. "You mean booze?"

I nod. "I'm not picky. Anything will do." I shouldn't be drinking, but without Jett's finger wagging in my face, I feel vindicated.

"I've got some vodka, but we need some orange juice. Can you go to the vending machine and buy a bottle?"

"Sure," I say, smiling. "I think I've got some change." I head for the door. "I'll be right back."

I locate the vending machine and purchase two bottles of orange juice. I've got a feeling that this is going to be a long night. Even though Lynzee has agreed to talk to me, I'm still feeling a tad bit nervous. I'm not sure how this evening will end, but I'm praying for a resolution that will suit both of us.

I knock on the door. Lynzee opens it, smoking a Kool. She's got *CSI* playing on the television set. *CSI* is a favorite of both of ours. She's already got two plastic cups half-filled with booze. Like two sneaky teenagers, we gleefully fill up the glasses with juice.

I take a seat on the bed, and we both watch the program for about fifteen minutes while we sip on our spirits. Invariably, we know that we need to be relaxed before we get down to serious business.

I break the silence. "I'm glad that they hired Larry Fishburne to play this role. He's really good."

"I agree. He's making a ton of money, too." Lynzee smiles. She puffs the last of her cigarette and then puts it out.

"You always keep up with the cash, don't you?" I tease.

"I know. It's a bad habit of mine."

"Speaking of bad habits, are you still on the Percocet?"

She looks embarrassed. "Who told you? Tyler?"

"No, but tell the truth. Are you still using?"

"I've been off for three weeks. That shit had me feeling like I was dying. I've already been to rehab twice. I figured I could go cold turkey this time."

I wink at her. "Good for you."

"Charity . . . have you heard from Tyler?"

"Yes." I don't want to hurt her feelings about Tyler's offer to testify. One of these days mother and daughter will come to terms with their problems just like she and I are doing now. "I know about her giving up her son for adoption. I think she made a good decision. She's too young to raise a child."

"And she was too young to get married."

"You're right. Mama would've kicked your ass if she were alive."

Lynzee turns the volume down on the set. "I know. I miss Mama and Daddy so much." She gets up and stands in front of the window. "I never meant to hurt you with this lawsuit, Charity."

"Then why'd you hire an attorney?"

"I was being selfish. I was being greedy. After all, if it wasn't for your book—"

"Your career wouldn't have faltered. You're right. And I'm sorry for writing the book. I wish that I could take it all back."

She turns around to face me. "Do you really mean that, Charity?"

"Yes. I shouldn't have put your business out there like that. That was between you and Heidi."

"Heidi's family tried to sue me, you know."

I sip on my drink. "No, you never told me." I take another swallow. "What happened?"

"We settled. I paid them one point five million dollars fifteen years ago. They tried to come back for more, but we have a solid agreement."

"So, you're saying that you did feel that part of the reason for Heidi's suicide was your fault?"

"Yes, I'll admit that. But I'm not gay, Charity. I like men." She sips on her drink, drains it, and refills our glasses.

"Do you know a woman named Cicely Halleron?"

An evil look comes across her face. "Yes. How'd you find out about her?"

"My attorney found her. She was going to be our next witness. She agreed to testify that you, she, and Heidi had a threesome and that Heidi threatened to commit suicide if you didn't stop fooling around with her."

Lynzee seems to look right through me. "Yep, that's about it. You had all the ammunition you needed to kick my ass. Why didn't you?"

"Because I was tired of us slandering each other back and forth. Somebody had to put a stop to it."

"Well, thank God you've got a conscience." She chugs a shot down. "I was beginning to think that I didn't have one. But that was the Percocet."

"So, you'll agree to settle the case?" I ask.

Lynzee comes over to sit beside me on the bed. "Contrary to what people might think, I'm not broke. I don't need your money, Charity. I've got enough of my own."

"Thanks, Lynzee."

"My accountant managed my money well. The four movies that I made are still paying me good residuals. Two of them play non-stop on Lifetime. That translates to big bucks." She smiles. "My name still has some clout."

"Well, I'm proud of you." We hug for a long moment. "I'm sorry if I ever did anything to hurt you."

She releases me and looks downtrodden. "And I'm sorry about April and all of the trouble that she caused between you and Jett. I read in the paper that he filed for a divorce. Does this have anything to do with April?"

"Yes. It has a lot to do with her. I should have told Jett the moment you told me about her. My friends warned me that Jett would be furious if he ever found out that I hid the truth from him. And they were right. He told me off and left the house that same night."

"This is all my fault. I was jealous of you and Jett and the twins. I lied to you and told you that April contacted me."

"I know that you sought her out." I pour myself another drink. I'm feeling totally relaxed. I enjoy the contentment. "Tyler told me."

Lynzee looks away from me. "It seems that Tyler has more respect for you than she does her own mother."

"That's one thing that I can't fix, Lynzee. It's up to you to get things straight with your daughter. You've made some mistakes, and you need to tell her face to face. No matter how mad she seems now, she'll forgive you. You two are really a lot alike, you know. You both think that you know everything." We both laugh.

Lynzee gets serious. "Now, what about Jett? Any chance of saving your marriage?"

"I'm afraid not. He's dating this woman named Marla. She's about thirty-five. You know what they say about these older men and these younger women. She's going to take him for every dime he's got and then split. Then he's going to come running back to me."

"Will you take him back?"

"Hell no. I'm tired of Jett's controlling ways, and I am hurt that he had an affair before we had a chance at reconciliation. He wouldn't go see a marriage counselor or even talk to our pastor."

"That's sad. I know black men don't like therapists, but it's hard for me to believe that he wouldn't even speak with your pastor."

"He's a stubborn Gemini. Always has been. I know deep down he loves me, but he has too much pride to admit it. I'm just thankful that the twins were grown before we parted ways. At least they got to grow up with both of their parents."

"Do Javed and Jamone hate me?"

"No. They're pissed off at you for what you did to me, but they don't hate you."

"Good. I'm going to have to talk to both of them about what happened. They're old enough to understand sibling rivalry."

"I'm happy for one thing, though. Javed and Jamone have never been jealous of one another. Don't ask me how or why, but they've always had each other's backs. It's the way that I hope that you and I can be from now on." We hug.

"You have my word, Charity," she says, releasing me. "I'll never do anything like this to you again."

She finishes her drink and pours another one. She laughs. "Remember when Mama gave me that ass-whipping for cutting your hair?"

I laugh too. "Yeah. She didn't know that I actually cut it and you were trying to fix it for me."

"And remember the time when you got busted for staying out until midnight?"

"Yeah, I was out looking for your stupid ass. How far did you think you'd get running away from home with no money and no clothes?"

We laugh and laugh. For the next two hours, we talk about old times. We sip and sip and finish the fifth of vodka. I offer to go to the store to buy more, but Lynzee insists that I need to keep my head clear so that I can drive home.

Of course, she's right. I gather my purse. "I hate to say good night. I had such a good time."

"Me, too. I love you, Charity."

"And I love you, Lynzee." Our foreheads touch, and we give each other one final hug.

"I'll call my attorney in the morning and drop the lawsuit,"

"Are you sure, Lynzee? Is this the alcohol talking?"

"Listen, little sister, I can drink your ass under the table, give a speech about unwed mothers, and write three chapters." She smiles. "It's over. Believe it. I'm going to go home on Saturday and see if I can stop in and see my child."

"Good. Then I'll call my attorney and tell him that the case is dropped. He's not going to be happy to hear this, but it's too bad."

I open the door. "Good night, Lynzee. Call me when you get home."

"I will. Good night."

I check my watch. It's eleven-thirty. I open up my cell and dial Kai's number. No answer. I make it to my car and dial again. Still no answer.

I get inside my car and push the button to start the engine. I look around at the inside of my beautifully appointed vehicle. I'm loving every inch of it.

"I knew I'd be able to keep you, baby."

I drive off. My phone rings. It's Herman.

"Hello, Charity."

"Hey."

"You didn't forget about our trip on Saturday, did you?"

"No, I didn't forget. I've got reasons to celebrate. Lynzee is dropping the lawsuit."

"Great. I knew this would happen."

"I didn't."

"I also know that you and I will happen, Charity. Bet on it."

"I'm not good at bets."

"Well, speaking to a man who knows you almost as good as your husband does, consider it a safe bet."

"I never knew you were so cocky, Herman."

"I never used to be, but when a man is fighting for his life, he'll sacrifice anything and everything to get what he needs."

"And what do you need, Herman?"

"Your unequivocal love."

"I think you're wasting your time."

"And I think you're wasting your time trying to deny it. Let me love you, Charity. I'll take you places that you never even dreamed of."

44

Arthur Dinkins and Teddy Bell are two lawyers who are pretty upset with their clients on Friday morning. They both receive phone calls around the same time of day, 9:00 A.M. There will not be a trial today or any other day.

Both of our attorneys plead with Lynzee and me to reconsider our decision. However, we are adamant. We won't sue each other now or in the future. The attorneys have already made a hefty salary since the trial started. Trying to get the lump sum settlement was just plain greed.

"I'm glad that you two did the right thing," Kai says when I call her.

"Me, too," I tell her.

Lynzee calls me on Saturday morning after her plane lands at LAX Airport. She's spoken with Tyler, who agreed to come home for Labor Day weekend.

I say several prayers, hoping that mother and daughter will overcome their difficulties and get their relationship back on track. With only Lynzee and me and one uncle left in Detroit, we have a small family. We can't afford to have our family split up.

Family. Jett's and mine. A couple of months ago, we were the ideal poster of the African American family. Now we're just another statistic.

45

By eight o'clock Saturday morning, Herman rings me up. "Say, lady, are you almost ready to get up in the air?"

"I guess so."

"Good. So, I'll pick you up at nine. I'll have you back home by ten o'clock. And, Charity . . ."

"Yes?"

"Bring a bathing suit. We're going to stop at a resort for a couple of hours. We can sit by the pool and then gamble for an hour or so. Doesn't that sound like fun?"

"Yes. I haven't had a vacation in years. That really does sound like big fun. I'll see you in an hour."

I hurry into my closet and find my sexiest swimsuit, a black one piece. I locate a multi-colored fringed cover-up to dress it up a bit and hide my stretch marks. I pick out a pair of black sandals, and grab a few cosmetics. I put all of my things in an overnight bag and wait by the back door.

This time, I remember to leave a few lights on inside the house and turn the porch light on. I'm wearing rust-colored print jeans with a tan shirt. I've got on a pair of ecru Gucci sandals. I put my hair up in a swanky French twist and hope that I look attractive to Herman.

A part of me doesn't know what in the hell I'm doing. I'm still in love with my husband, but am desiring the attentions of a man I've called a friend and confidant for most of my life. I'm so confused by my actions. If Herman kisses me, I wouldn't be surprised if I kiss him back.

After all, Herman is a very handsome man. He's sexy as hell, smells good, and is articulate in every way. When he pulls up in my driveway wearing a pink linen short set with caramel lizard sandals, I'm tempted to run into his arms. I know better, and refrain from doing something so impulsive.

"Are you ready to go?" he asks me as he stands on the outside steps.

"I'm ready. Here, take my bag please." I hand him my bag, grab my purse, and after shutting the door, lock up behind me.

Herman opens the passenger door so that I can take a seat inside. A few seconds later, he's stored my bag in the back seat and then slipped in behind the steering wheel. He starts the ignition and we're off.

He turns on the radio and Luther Vandross' "A House is Not a Home" is playing. The sound system in his Benz is almost as clear as the one in my Beamer.

Herman doesn't tell me jokes this time. He's dead serious about wooing me, and doesn't mince words.

"I'm not going to rush you into anything, Charity. I plan to wait until your divorce is final before I make any kind of amorous moves. I've waited this long for you; I can wait a little longer."

"I can't promise you anything, Herman. You know how I feel about Jett."

Like a woman needing male companionship and a little sympathy, I tell Herman about Jett's woman, Marla. I tell him how young she is. Herman can understand how I feel. He's astonished that Jett got busted so soon. He thought that it would have taken Jett months before his true nature was revealed. But thanks to the twins, he was openly traduced.

"It was stupid of him to go to a dance venue where the twins might frequent anyway. Do you think that he wanted them to catch him and come back and tell you?"

"You know, I hadn't thought about that." I recline the seat and lean back. "It doesn't matter. He told me to my face twice that it was over between us. I'm nobody's charity case. I'm not going to waste my love on someone who clearly no longer loves me."

"Doesn't it seem strange to you that a long lost daughter could cause this much of a problem in your marriage?"

"That's a good point. Our marriage should have been strong enough to withstand something like this. I can't explain what happened."

"How about Jett's motivation? How deeply does he really love you? Was he with you for convenience sake? Let's say getting his hands on your millions, or was he here till death do us part?"

I sit up. "Funny you should ask that. I'd hate to think that he was only with me because of the money, but the more I think about it, the more your theory seems right on target."

Herman lets me mull over that statement for a while as he navigates his way to the hangar. Once we're there, he parks in his usual place, takes out my bag, and opens the door for me. I see more planes parked than usual. Herman points out the planes and explains them to me. There are three Cessnas, four Bellancas, two Monneys, one Beechcraft, and three Vipers. Smiling, Herman takes me over to his new plane, a white 2011 Cessna 162 with green and black stripes.

He gives me a play by play tour of his new baby. I must say I'm impressed. This time I'm not scared. I know what to expect. And like Herman said before, he's an A-1 pilot. I trust him with my life.

This time he and I put on parachutes. It feels awkward and heavy, but I trust Herman's need for precaution. He helps me strap mine on first, and then puts his on. I don't feel cute wearing this contraption, but I go with the flow.

I wait until Herman puts our things aboard the plane before he helps me up. I get inside and he straps my seat belt. This time he fusses with me like I'm his new baby. I must say that I love all of the attention.

Then it's Herman's turn to strap himself in and put on his headphones. He does a checklist of the statistical instruments and calls the tower. He starts the ignition and pulls out onto the path leading to the runway.

I can hear him talking to the tower, but am too busy enjoying the freedom of going flying again to pay too much attention to what they're talking about.

Minutes later, we're on the runway, getting ready for takeoff. I love the feeling of racing down the cemented stretch of runway that allows the pilot to build up enough speed to lift his machine off the ground and fly high into the sky. It's rejuvenating. It's free-spirited. It's breathtaking.

Once we're airborne, I enjoy viewing the sights below us once again. Everywhere I look, I see beauty. I see cleanliness. I see a miracle.

Herman gives the tower his flight plan to the Bahamas. The weather is perfect and the sky is crystal clear. It's a great day for flying, and I'm happy that Herman chose to spend these precious hours with me.

While we travel, Herman points out the sights below. We pass over Mississippi, Georgia, Florida, and then hover over the Bahamas. At twelve thousand feet, we pass by other airplanes in the expansive sky. A few pilots in single planes wave at us. We wave back. However, by now the weather has changed. The sky has darkened to a steel gray. I hear the rumblings of thunder and feel a tad nervous. For some reason, there is a ton of traffic waiting to land today, and we don't get permission to land. We have to circle the airport again and again before we get clearance.

Suddenly it begins to thunder and lightning. The storm comes on fast and strong, and the small plane is swaying this way and that with the strong winds that come with inclement weather.

"Herman," I ask, "is everything okay? I'm getting kinda worried."

"Not to worry. This baby is built solid."

The moment he gets the words out of his mouth, lightning strikes the left engine. It catches on fire. The plane starts rocking and weaving badly.

"Pronto 348, pull up. Pull up. I'm locating a runway for an emergency landing. Give me a couple of minutes."

"What are we going to do?" My heart is beating so fast, I can barely catch my breath.

"Don't worry, Charity. You're safe with me."

"But I am worried." I look at the blackened sky and wonder how the weather could've changed so quickly.

The sky keeps lighting up with lightning. The smell of smoke and metal burning is beginning to fill the inside of the plane.

"Herman, are we going to run out of air?"

"No, but I'm afraid that we're going to have to make an exit."

My words are shaky. "You mean jump out of the plane?"

"Yep. That's what the parachutes are for. Now, don't be scared. I'll guide you all the way down."

"Don't be scared! Are you fucking crazy? I've never jumped out of a plane before. This shit isn't cool, Herman. I didn't sign up for this. You've got to think of something else."

"We don't have time, and we're out of options. Now, I'm going to slow the plane down to about eighty miles per hour, take the plane below ten thousand feet, steer the plane in the direction of those trees, put the plane on auto pilot, and I want you to follow my lead."

"Herman! Herman! I don't think I can do this!"

"Calm down, Charity. I told you I'll help you."

He opens the passenger door to the plane. We're exposed to the elements, and my French twist is whistling in the wind. I can feel the rain whacking my face and smearing my makeup. However, at this point, I don't give a damn how I look. I just want to be safe so that I can see my sons again.

As he instructed, Herman steers the plane over a clump of palm trees. "We've only got a few seconds! Now, get ready. We're going to have to step out on the landing gear and then drop. Don't be scared. I'm going to hold your hand. Okay?"

"No. It's not okay."

"Charity, you've got to do this. Stop acting like a child. This is serious."

"You think I don't know that?"

"Okay, we're running out of time. We've got to go now." He stands up and unbuckles my seatbelt. He grabs my hand and helps me out the door. I'm trembling like I'm walking on pencils. "Okay, when I say jump, jump!"

"Damn you, Herman," I say through gritted teeth. "I got a feelin' this is going to hurt." I grab my purse.

"Okay, now, jump!"

"Whoooaaa! Dammit, help me, Herman. Grab a hold of me."

We start falling, falling, falling. My body feels like dead weight. Then I see the trees. "We're going to hit them hard, Herman. Dammit, do something!"

46

Whoosh! We hit the palm trees like dead weight. My parachute is swinging back and forth between the tall and short palms. The next thing I know, Herman is yelling my name.

"Charity, are you okay?"

"I think so. Can you make this thing stop swinging?"

Then I feel one final whoosh and I hit the tree hard. I feel the bone in my right leg break. I scream in pain. "Herman, help me! I think I broke my leg."

It seems like an endless time later, Herman is able to disengage himself from his parachute. He climbs the tree and helps me down. It takes him a few minutes to get me out of my parachute. I'm no help. I'm fighting him more than I'm helping him.

Once down, we both breathe a sigh of relief. We look up at the carnage and shake our heads. We're lucky to be alive. Our clothes are torn and ragged. Because the fabric was paper thin, Herman's linen short set looks the worst.

"Ouch," I complain. I check my watch. It's almost three, but it's dark out because of the thunder and lightning.

I balance my weight on my left hip. My right leg is bleeding badly. The excruciating pain is traveling fast from my leg to my brain. I don't know what Herman plans to do. I'm too heavy for him to carry me. "What are we going to do now?" I ask.

Herman speaks quickly. "I noticed from the aerial map that there's a highway about three or four miles to the east of us."

I limp on one leg. "Well, how do you propose to get us there?" Both of us are getting soaked from the rain.

"I'm going to make a hutch out of these branches so that I can pull you."

Before I can open my mouth, Herman has already begun to gather branches and limbs. I have my purse with me, so I open it up and get my cell phone out. It's broken. "Herman, does your cell phone work? Mine's broken."

He's wrapping branches together and moving like a black MacGyver. I never knew that he could be so resourceful.

"I'm sorry, Charity. I left my phone on the plane."

"Damn. We're really in trouble."

"Not to worry," he says, wrapping the branches with long strands of vine and strips from the bark of the banyan tree. "I'll get us out of here shortly and flag down a car. Then we can get you to the hospital to get that leg set."

I decide that it's futile to argue with him. What the hell do I know about survival techniques? So, I just sit and watch him expertly crafting the hutch. In less than two hours, he's finished.

The hutch, interwoven with branches and palm leaves, is approximately six feet long, with two extended poles on one end so that he can pull it.

"It's ready," he says, nearly out of breath. "Go ahead and lay on it."

I do as he advises. I feel him lift me up. "Herman, I know you're tired. Don't tell me that you're not. How are you going to rev up enough energy to pull me four miles?" I can barely see his face in the semi-darkness.

"When I get too tired, I'll stop and take a break. Meanwhile, stop worrying. We'll make it."

I plop my purse across my chest and hold on to the sides of the hutch. I feel Herman lift me up and start pulling the contraption due east. The sounds in the area are ominous. Birds are hovering overhead and squawking, and the sound of crickets is deafening.

I try not to complain as Herman heroically guides the hutch through the brush and toward human contact. It takes three and a half hours to reach the two-lane highway. By now it's pitch black. Thankfully, the rain stops. My leg is throbbing like a toothache and I'm hungry as a grizzly bear. I have to give it to Herman; he hasn't complained once.

I train my eyes to look out for snakes. However, snakes don't really bother me that much. What terrifies me are mice and rats.

There is very little traffic on the road that is glistening like black diamonds. It's eerily deserted. I know that if I were driving down this road, I wouldn't pick anybody up. But I hope for the best.

After seven cars pass us by, the eighth car stops. It's an old Chevy El Camino. The driver's name is Alex.

Herman explains what happened to his plane and how we got to this point. Alex is understanding and offers to drive us to the nearest hospital on Grand Bahama Island. The hospital is about twenty-five miles away. Alex and Herman help me in the back of the El Camino. Even though it has stopped raining, it's very humid out. I'm sweating and crying at the same time.

"Here, Miss," Alex offers. "I've got a pack of peanuts. Would you like some?"

My smile is as wide as the Mississippi River. "Thanks, Alex. I really appreciate it."

I take my time and enjoy each peanut one by one, savoring the nutty flavor and texture. Alex drives about seventy miles per hour and we reach Rand Memorial Hospital Emergency on East Atlantic Drive in twenty minutes.

Herman jumps out and goes into the hospital for a wheelchair. Alex and Herman help me into the chair. Herman and I say thank you to Alex and bid him good night.

When Herman wheels me up to the admissions counter, I fill out the paperwork and then wait for my turn to be called. Herman and I watch television and half listen to the broken English of the Bahamians.

Forty minutes later they call my name. I hand the woman my insurance card. I fill out a few more forms and am asked to wait again. Ten minutes later, my temperature and blood pressure are taken. Then I'm wheeled into the triage area. I'm introduced to a nurse, who checks my leg. Herman is there with me.

"Dr. Williams will be in in a few minutes, Mrs. Evans."

"I'm very sorry for what happened, Charity. I don't have any idea how an engine on a brand new plane can catch on fire." He holds up a hand, "I know, I know. The lightning. Even so, what are the odds that it was going to hit my engine? About ten million to one, I'd venture."

"Talk to the pillow," I say and close my eyes.

The doctor comes in and introduces himself. He cuts off my jeans up to my mid-thigh and X-rays my leg. He tells me it's broken, and that he's going to put a cast on it immediately. "Do you want a specific color?" he asks.

"Pink," I say, smiling.

"I'm going to give you a shot for the pain."

"Thank you."

I get the pain medication and a tetanus shot and they put on the cast. Then they fit me with a pair of crutches. I feel like a mummy as I walk around the small cubicle. I test them out. It's a little awkward, but okay under the circumstances. That done, I'm ready for Plan B. How are we going to get home? Herman already has the answer.

"I contacted a pilot friend of mine back home. He'll be here to pick us up by nine. We should be back in Memphis before midnight."

I rub my leg. It's starting to itch already. "Great. I thought we were going to have to spend the night here."

"No way."

"We're thinking the same thoughts. I want to go home. Now." I put on a pitiful look. "I'm sorry to act like a baby, but nothing like this has ever happened to me before."

"I know, Charity, and you have the right to be angry." He signals one of the nurses. "Can I use the phone again? I need to call a taxi."

Herman manages to get a taxi to drive us to the airport. Once there, we wait for almost an hour before Herman's friend, Vincent, arrives. To tell the truth, I'm scared to get on another plane, but I know that I want to go home.

Vincent tells me not to worry and to take a nap if I would like. He'll have us home in no time at all. We all get aboard the small four-seat aircraft. I think there's no way that I'm going to go to sleep, but I do. When I awaken, Vincent is landing the plane.

Herman and I get out and, working with my crutches, manage to get into his car. We say good night to Vincent and drive off.

I fall asleep again. When I wake up, we're in my driveway. Herman helps me out of the car and to the back door. I get out my keys and Herman opens the door. Thank God I left the lights on.

Once inside, I kiss Herman on the cheek. "Good night. Call me tomorrow."

"I'll call you around noon. I've got a funny feeling that you won't be waking up early." He smiles. "Good night."

I lock up and turn out the lights. I struggle with the crutches down the hall to my bedroom. How in the hell am I going to take a shower with this cast on?

I turn on the television and strip. I leave my pile of clothes on the floor and make my way to the shower. It's awkward, but I manage to get the job done. I lotion down my body and put on powder. I hop into my room and reach inside my top dresser drawer for a gown. That, too, is a feat.

By the time I make it to the bed, I'm exhausted. I lay the crutches across the end of the bed and ease myself between the sheets. I'm wide awake and feel like having a glass of wine. I'm tempted to go get a glass, but feel like the Lord is punishing me for my sins and refrain.

I flip the channels for thirty minutes, unable to find anything that I want to watch. I settle on the Western channel and watch *Gunsmoke*. I think of Jett and how much he loves to watch this show. I've always admired Ms. Kitty, and can see myself in her.

But then I think, *I bet Ms. Kitty never had to deal with a broken leg and a broken husband.*

I turn on my left side and pull the comforter up over my shoulder. My leg feels like dead weight. I toss and turn trying to get comfortable. Finally, I get situated. Just as I feel sleep creeping up on me, the phone rings. It's Jett.

"What was that Negro doing at my house so late at night?"

I get up on my forearms. "What are you doing watching my house?"

"You didn't answer my question. I saw Herman drop you off."

"So what?" I'm starting to feel the pain from my leg. I should have asked for pain pills.

"What happened to your leg?"

"I broke it."

"Doing what?"

"Flying in a plane. Not that it's any of your business."

"Are you crazy, woman? What were you doing up in a plane?"

"Having fun."

"Aren't you a little too old to be doing stupid shit like that?"

"Aren't you a little too old to be dating a thirty-five-year-old?"

"She's thirty-seven."

"Wow. Two years. She's still young enough to be your daughter. You should be ashamed of yourself."

"Look, you started this shit, Charity."

I'm irritated as hell. "Started what? So I didn't tell you that you had a daughter. That's no reason to file for a divorce and start fucking around on me. It seems to me that you were looking for a reason to get out of the marriage."

"That's not true."

"Bullshit. Any other man would've talked things out with his wife. Any decent man would have listened to his wife explain why she held the truth back from him. Any decent man would have understood and stood by his wife. But oh, not you. You had to fly to California and save your child."

"I—"

"You what? You didn't have to move April here. The twins don't want to have anything to do with her."

"That'll change."

"No, it won't. They don't like her, and they don't like how you're treating them. If you keep on acting like a fool, you're going to lose your sons. Is that what you want to happen?"

"No. But I'm sure—"

"You're not sure of shit. You're a damned fool. And I'm glad you filed for a divorce and saved me the trouble. I don't need a weak-ass man calling himself my husband. I need a man who knows how to be a man and stand by his woman."

"Like Herman?"

"Yeah, like Herman. Now, leave me the fuck alone and stop driving by my house. If you don't, I'm going to get an order of protection."

"Don't do that, Charity. I'm warning you."

"And I'm warning you. Stay out of my life." I hang up.

I'm hurt and annoyed. I hate the way Jett keeps toying with my emotions. First he wants a divorce, and then he starts an affair and becomes estranged from his sons. If he's so happy with his life with a younger woman, then why is he worried about who's taking me home at night?

47

For the next few days, I try to get used to the crutches. I make an appointment to see my doctor. He says I won't be able to get the cast taken off until the end of October.

The twins come by every day and make sure that I don't need anything. They're so attentive, it warms my heart. None of us talk about their father. It's almost as if the subject matter is taboo.

Herman had full coverage insurance on his Cessna and expects to get his new plane in six weeks or so. This time he plans on buying a blue-and-white Cessna 172 SP. I tell him that there is no way I'm ever going up in a plane with him again. He laughs, but can understand how I feel.

It's too hard to climb the stairs to my office, so I do what I can on the computer in the kitchen. I check my messages and answer my fan mail.

I call Arlene and tell her that I'm not going to be able to work on the edits for a few weeks. She says that she'll call my editor and explain the situation to her. We're ahead of schedule for the publication date next spring anyway. The truth is I don't feel like writing right now. I can't dredge up the courage to be creative. My mind is convoluted with my own personal drama. I can't get Jett's angry face out of my mind.

* * *

Because of the limitations of my leg, I cancel all of my speaking engagements until the first of November. My agent feels that I can still make an appearance, but I just am not feeling it. I am getting tired of public speaking. It doesn't have the allure that it once did. What's wrong with me?

Another thing I've noticed is my lack of desire to write. I'm more focused on thinking about opening a new business, a bakery. Forget the French bakery, my forte is American pastry. What was I thinking?

I pick up the phone and call the vice president of my bank, Rita Coolidge. I've known Rita since my first book was published. When I deposited my first million dollar check in Bancorp South, Rita called me. She told me that she'd be of service to me whenever I needed any help with banking.

Over the years, I've spoken to Rita five or six times. Now, I need her for an important matter that is weighing heavy on my heart.

"Hello, Mrs. Evans," Rita says. "How can I help you?"

"I want to open up a bakery. I'll bake cobblers, pies, cakes, and yeast breads. I'm going to cook donuts and have petit fours, too. I know I need a business plan, but can you give me any suggestions as to how I should proceed? I've never owned a business before."

"You're right about the business plan. You should call the Small Business Association here in Memphis. They can help you get started. Here, I've got the number." She gives it to me. "Ask for Bonnie Diggins. She's a personal friend of mine." She pauses then adds, "And don't worry about the financing. Bancorp South will help you when you're ready to finance your loan."

"Thanks, Rita. I'll be getting back with you soon."

I'm getting so excited I can barely dial Ms. Diggins' number. Unfortunately, she's unavailable and I get her voice mail.

My mind usually works fast when I come up with a plan. I get out a notebook and jot down my thoughts for the business. I've already got the name, Just Desserts.

As I'm developing a menu, my phone rings. It's Lynzee. I haven't heard from her for a week, and I was a little worried.

"Hello, little sis."

"Hey. What's happening in your world?"

"Oh, lots of things. Tyler's and my relationship is on the mend. She's coming home for Thanksgiving."

"Oh, that's nice. I'm so happy for you guys. You two need each other."

"Yes, we do. But I've got some more news for you. I'm getting married!"

"Are you kidding?"

"No. Michael asked me last night. Of course I said yes."

"Wow. You didn't tell me that you were in a relationship. When did all of this loving happen?"

"We've been dating on and off for about two years. He's a widow, and he's got a grown son, Stephan. Stephan is overprotective of his father, and screens all of his women. Stephan didn't like me at first, but I finally won him over a few months back."

"I'm so happy for you. Now, tell me about Michael."

"He's a businessman. He owns his own automotive business. You know, something like Pep Boys. He's got five franchises here in Los Angeles. He makes good money, but he's not filthy rich or anything like that. But he has good credit, owns his own home, drives a 2010 Mercedes, and plans on opening two more shops by February of next year."

"Sounds like a keeper. How old is he? What does he look like?" I ask.

"He's sixty-one, is about six foot two, physically fit, but has a small beer pouch. He's root beer–colored, still has all of his hair, and reminds me of an older Cuba Gooding Jr."

"Damn, girl. I'm impressed. When do I get to meet him?"

"I was thinking during the week of Christmas. His schedule is pretty tight until then. Can you fly out here?"

"Definitely. Now, what does Tyler think about him?"

"She likes him. I think she's got a crush on his grandson, Keon. Keon's about nineteen. He attends Yale University and is studying law."

"You've really made my day, Lynzee. I haven't had good news like this in some time. Now, when's the wedding set for?"

"Some time near the end of January. Michael has to clear his calendar so we can have a nice honeymoon. He's planning on taking me to Spain."

"Damn. I always wanted to go there." I smile to myself. "Now, what's happening with your job?"

"I'm still enjoying teaching, but I'm thinking about making a comeback in the publishing world. I've got several book ideas. I miss going out on book tours. I miss talking to my fans. I figure if Patricia Cornwell can make a comeback after having a lesbian affair, so can I."

"I feel the total opposite. I'm thinking about taking a break from writing."

"No shit?"

"Yes. But I think you've got such a loyal following that they'd love to read a new book by you."

"My agent believes that we have to start with a realistic goal of maybe selling two hundred thousand or so books, and then build from there."

"That sounds doable."

I tell Lynzee about my plane ride and my broken leg. She's sympathetic and says that she doesn't like riding in small planes either. When I tell her about the bakery, she's excited.

"Well, Michael is on the other line, Charity. I've gotta go. I love you."

"And I love you, honey. Bye."

The doorbell rings. I lumber to the back door. I'm shocked to see that it's Jett. I let him in.

"Can I speak with you for a few minutes?"

"About what?"

"Us."

I must say I'm totally surprised. "Come on in." I lead the way to the kitchen table. We both take a seat.

"How's your leg?" he asks me.

"Fine."

"Can I have some water?" He looks nervous.

I'm not about to get up. "You know where it is."

I watch him going into the cabinets and then to the water dispenser. He looks so handsome in his black jeans, Harley shirt, and cowboy boots.

He comes back to the table and gulps down the water. "Thanks."

"What is it, Jett? I'm kinda busy."

He folds his hands and leans back in the chair. "I was thinking about going to a marriage counselor. I've changed my mind about the divorce. I love you, Charity."

"But—"

"I'm in the process of sending April back to L.A. She really doesn't like the lifestyle in Memphis. California is where her heart is. I'll miss her, but I feel she's making the right decision. It's going to take about three months before she can get transferred."

"Are you sure that's the only reason why you're sending April back?"

"I don't want to talk about it right now."

Now I need some water. I get up, get a glass and fill it, then sit back down. "Why should I take you back? You had an affair."

"It didn't mean anything."

"Bullshit. How would you feel if I had an affair?"

"That's not your personality. I trust you, baby."

"Oh, now it's baby. You've got some nerve. What's the matter? Is your money running low? You getting tired of selling cars?" I'm starting to get pissed. He's called me out my name, treated me like dirt, had an affair, and now he wants to kiss and make up.

"No and no. Matter of fact, I'm the top salesman at King. If you took me back, I would still keep my job. My boss is even considering moving me to a management position."

"Right now, I have to say no, Jett. You've hurt me too badly. If it wasn't for the affair, I would take you back in a snap. But after Marla, I'll never trust you again. I'm sorry."

"Baby, we can see a faith-based marriage counselor. Matter of fact, I already found one. She's a black woman about forty.

Her office is in Germantown. All I have to do is call her and she'll fit us in her schedule."

"I can't do it."

"Please reconsider, baby. I know you haven't stopped loving me. We've got too much history to give up on our marriage now. And I know the twins would be happy to see us get back together."

"The twins want what I want."

"I've already spoken with them."

"When?"

"This morning, before they went to class. I'm sure they'll be calling you sometime today."

"I wouldn't doubt it."

"Please, Charity, give me a chance. I'll be the husband that you always wanted. I don't want your money. I don't need anything from you but your love."

"Love? I don't even know if you know what it means."

Jett reaches inside his pocket and removes a business card. "Her name is Allene Jackson. Please call her." He gets up. "I'm not going to force you to do anything that you don't want to do. All I'm asking for is a chance." He leans down and kisses me on my forehead, and then leaves.

I pick up the card. I stare at it for a long while. I can't help but wonder if Jett is really trying to make a go of our marriage. I feel all kinds of conflicting emotions. This past year, knowing about April has been hell. I felt like the proverbial ugly step-mother. Perhaps I was wrong when I didn't confront him right away, and in the end, he turned on me because I withheld information about his daughter. I think about our past, the present, our future together. I'm torn.

Am I a fool to want him back?

48

Thank God, Dr. Robinson is ready to take off my cast. I've suffered long enough. I sit on the patient's table and watch as he uses a saw to cut off my pink cast. I'm praying that he's careful and doesn't accidentally cut my skin.

But I needn't have worried. He does his job expertly, massages my leg, and writes me a prescription for Motrin. I thank him and stand up. My right leg feels weak, but I'm able to walk okay.

"I'll see you back here in three months, Mrs. Evans."

"I'll be here."

I pay my bill and make a future appointment. I carry the crutches out to my car and put them in the trunk.

I managed to get in touch with Bonnie Diggins. We've met several times over the past couple of weeks, and now, we're almost finished with my business plan. I put an ad on Twitter for a general manager and two bakers in the Memphis area, who are creative and dedicated to their craft.

I've got dozens of hits. I take my time interviewing potential candidates and going out with my realtor to find the perfect location for the bakery. Presently, I've found two locations that I love and they're both in Midtown.

The twins love the bakery idea and want to work there part-time while they're in school. I've got to say, I love the idea.

I've searched my soul about Jett and our marriage. I've

picked up that card for the marriage counselor dozens of times, but can't make myself call her. A part of me wants to go, but another part of me wants to end the marriage and move on with my life.

Jett calls me two or three times a week. He still professes his love and says that he'll wait on me. He's in no hurry.

It seems that Herman is trying to speed up his game plan. We have dinner at a restaurant at least once a week. This week he wants me to accompany him to an auction downtown at the Peabody Hotel.

He's interested in two things. The first is an original poster of "I Am a Man" from the 1968 sanitation strike. His other desire is to outbid other buyers for a South Carolina plantation owner's Bible that includes deeds of sale for slaves, with handwritten records of births, deaths, and marriages of his slaves.

On the night of the auction, I select a lavender silk chiffon sheath with side splits and a jeweled neckline. I accent the dress with a copy of Oprah's pear-shaped diamonds and Richard Tyler rhinestone pumps.

When he picks me up, Herman is wearing a silver Hugo Boss tuxedo with white shirt and silver rhinestone bowtie and cufflinks. He's wearing gray alligator square-toe shoes that shine like liquid paraffin.

I pick up my matte silver clutch and follow Herman outside to his car. Once we're inside, I look over to my right. I freeze. I could swear that I see Jett's F-150 parked on the end of the cul-de-sac.

"Did you see who I saw?" Herman asks me.

"Yes. I saw him."

"What's he trying to prove?"

"That he loves me." I turn my head away, ashamed by my emotions.

Herman glances over at me while he steers the car through the subdivision. "And how about you? What are your feelings for Jett?"

"I'm not sure. I loved him for almost thirty years, bore him two sons, and thought I'd spend the rest of my life with him. But things changed."

"I understand that when you love someone, those feelings don't leave overnight, but I'm hoping that time will depict Jett's true nature. I'm confident that you will see that I can make you happier than you've ever been in your life. I have such plans for our future."

"Herman, don't. You're moving too fast. Slow down. I'm not going anywhere."

Herman turns on the radio. Of all the songs to hear, "Since I Lost My Baby" comes on. Call me a romantic, but the words bring tears to my eyes. I know that a part of me still loves Jett. A part of me wants him back. But there is a part of me that is crazy about Herman. I don't want to give him up. We have so much in common. He makes me laugh. He makes me strive to be the best I can be.

He understands my desire to open up the bakery. He's given me several good ideas. He's even accompanied me to put down a deposit on a building that I found. He thinks the location on Cooper Avenue is the perfect spot for a bakery too.

For the past week, I have been cooking some of my special desserts and trying them out on Herman. Since he watches his weight, he only samples forkfuls. But he is very satisfied with the cobblers, cakes, and rolls. He even suggests the name of a contractor that can renovate the building and get it up to code.

I've been Twittering and blogging like crazy. I love this invention. I've been keeping up with the three people who I think can turn my business into a successful venture. The tentative general manager is Moses Landon, and the two bakers that I'm most impressed with are Heidi Hefner and Enrique Faison.

I've had the three of them over to my house on two occasions to show me their stuff. I must say, I made wise choices. As a businesswoman, I had the good sense to interview five more potential employees, but they were not up to par.

I'm thinking that if everything goes as planned, I can open the bakery the week before Christmas. It's perfect timing. After most women have cooked up a storm for Thanksgiving, they will be all worn out for Christmas and will probably be overjoyed to buy their confections from a good bakery.

Advertisement is key to making my bakery known to the public. I find the ideal young man who's Internet savvy, as well as being the owner of one of the best advertisement agencies in Memphis.

And now, we've made it to the Peabody. Herman valet parks the car and we go inside. Hundreds of bejeweled men and women crowd the lobby. Overhead signs directing guests to the auction room are displayed in bold purple paint.

"I'm getting nervous, Charity," Herman says while guiding me through the crowd. "I really want that poster."

I pat his arm. "Don't worry. You'll get it. Times are hard out here now, and people's wallets aren't as thick as they used to be. You happen to be in a business that is recession-proof."

He smiles. "That's true. I've got more business than I can handle. I'm thinking about hiring an assistant. Do you think Javed or Jamone might be interested?"

"Heck no. No offense, Herman, but I don't want them involved in that type of work." I feel bad for a quick minute, but Herman's known me long enough to know what I really mean. "If everything works out the way I plan, my sons will be working for me."

We follow the crowd to the auction room and find seats. People are talking and laughing, and making several trips to the wet bar.

"Would you like anything to drink?"

"No. I stopped drinking."

"Good for you. Then I won't have anything either."

"No, go on. I'm not tempted. I've prayed about it, and I'm straight."

"Believe me, I don't desire alcohol either. I only drink on special occasions, like weddings or New Year's Eve. You caught me off guard when we had that champagne at your house a while back."

"Sorry about that." The seats are beginning to fill up. The auction is set to start in twenty minutes.

"You know, Charity, I've got a business plan too."

"Oh. What type of business?"

"A charter plane service to the casinos in Tunica, Missis-sippi."

He goes on to explain that there's a wide open market for charters. The profit potential is ridiculously lucrative. He wants to get in before the market becomes oversaturated.

"I don't plan on being a mortician for the rest of my life."

"Wow. You've stunned me. I thought you loved your job."

"I love the money." He smiles. "But the charter service will allow me to do what I love and make money. It's a win-win sit-uation."

"I'm very impressed. How soon do you think this will hap-pen for you?"

He shrugs. "I'm thinking I can have everything up and run-ning by next summer."

The auctioneer beats the gavel. "Ladies and gentleman, Gazelle Auction Galleries are proud that you've selected our company to purchase some of our most valuable items tonight. If you will look at your pamphlets, you can see the order in which each item will be auctioned." He smiles. "Is everyone ready to begin?" He pounds his gavel again. "The first item is a rare collectible. It's a poster of one of three hundred to four hundred printed for a march on City Hall. The 'I Am a Man,' poster is something that transcends being a mere placard. Those words are basically the quintessential thing that the civil rights demonstrations were about." He pauses and as-sesses the crowd. "Can I get an opening bid of five thousand dollars?"

A few people raise their hands. Herman is one of them. I scan the crowd, checking out Herman's competition. Since there are almost four hundred items to be auctioned, not everyone is interested in the poster.

"Thank you to the gentleman in the seventh row. Now, can I get a bid of seven thousand five hundred?"

Again Herman raises his hand. Hesitantly, the other gentle-man raises his hand too.

"I'm getting a little edgy," Herman admits. "I can afford to go a little higher, but I want to save money for the Bible."

"I don't think you have anything to worry about. I can see that gentleman counting his duckets with his fingers. Trust me. He's on a budget too."

The bidding continues, and now I'm getting nervous. I didn't know that Herman had such deep pockets.

It turns out that Herman is able to buy the poster for thirty-four thousand dollars. He's blissful. He was prepared to spend thirty-five thousand.

We wait patiently until his next item of choice comes up for bid. It's the two hundred twenty-fifth item. The bid starts at five thousand dollars. A bidding war goes on between four people. In the end, Herman loses. He'd budgeted for thirteen thousand dollars. The Bible was sold for fourteen thousand five hundred dollars.

"C'mon. Let's go," Herman says after the Bible is gone. "Unless you want something."

"No, I'm fine. My house is filled with trinkets and such. I don't have any more room for artwork, sculptures, masks, or Bibles." I tug on his arm. "I'm ready to go." I check my watch. It's ten-thirty. I text my three employees from my cell phone.

The poster is wrapped gently in plastic and secured with yards of strong string. Herman puts his prize in the trunk. We head home with little traffic to slow down our drive. Herman and I talk about our businesses until we reach my house. He drives to the back door and parks. Then he turns to me.

"Since you don't drink, Charity, can I come in for a soda? I'd love to finish our conversation. I have so much more to share with you." He kisses my hand.

My heart races. I know that if I let him in, it could possibly lead to something else. My heart says yes, but my instincts say no. "Not tonight, Herman. Maybe another time."

"Okay. I won't push it."

He walks me to my door. After I unlock the door, I turn my head to say good night, and he kisses me dead on the lips. I'm hungry for love, so I kiss him back. The kiss deepens. I feel myself standing on my tiptoes to enjoy every moment. He wraps his arms around my waist and I find myself giving in to him. Then I see Jett's face and pull back.

"Um, I think we better call it a night before one of us gets in trouble."

"I enjoyed that, Charity. You and I would be good together."

Don't I know it? I didn't miss the bulge in his pants grazing my inner thigh. I've seen him dance. I know that he can work his pelvis like a provocateur. But I'm still a married woman, and no matter how low Jett stooped, I won't renege on my marriage vows.

"I enjoyed it too. We've got a lot to look forward to. Now, I'll talk to you tomorrow." I slip inside the door. "Good night."

He waits for a beat and then leaves. My heart is palpitating like an ingénue's. I know it's too soon to think about a new relationship, but could the therapists possibly be wrong about dating before a year? I feel that Herman and I would be good together. I'm going to sleep on that thought tonight.

I turn out the porch light and walk into the kitchen. I ignore the wine that's calling my name and elect to enjoy a cold glass of apple juice. I chug it down and put the empty glass in the sink.

I take a deep breath, sit down at the desk, and turn on my computer. I type in Twitter.com. In minutes, I'm enjoying a conversation with my crew. Heidi and Enrique have come up with five new recipes. Moses likes the choices and has a few ideas of his own.

Afterward, I head down the hall to my bedroom. I remove my dress and hang it in the closet, put away my shoes and jewelry, and hop into the shower. I still feel heated from Herman's kiss and find myself caressing myself. I hold my head back and imagine Herman making love to me. The image is so clear, I can almost touch it. I'm wondering if it's the newness or the excitement of another man's touch. Am I really over Jett? The phone cuts off my reverie.

I jump out of the shower, grab a towel and answer the phone. "Hello?"

"It's me." Jett's voice is husky.

"What is it, Jett? It's late."

"I hate to bother you with this, but I feel I need to tell you. Have you heard from Marla?"

"No. Why should I?"

"She tried to commit suicide. She took an overdose of sleeping pills."

I'm stone cold. "I don't know why you're telling me this. Why should I care?"

"Because Marla blames you for our breakup."

"Oh, so you stopped seeing her?"

"Over a month ago. She won't accept the fact that it's over."

"I'm sorry to hear that, but I can't do anything about it."

I hate myself for being so cold, but I feel scorned. I don't give a hot damn about Marla. Maybe she should see a therapist.

"Just don't be surprised if she calls you."

"Thanks for letting me know, but I think I can handle it."

There's a long silence. "By the way, since you didn't call Allene, I decided to see her. I've been going to counseling for a month now. I wish you would agree to go with me."

I have to say that I'm impressed. I didn't think he had it in him. The love I still feel for him makes me want to tell him yes, but the bitch in me argues, "Hell no!"

"I'm sorry, Jett. I appreciate you're trying, but I feel that it's really too little, too late." I hang up.

I fall on the bed and let the towel drop to my sides. I lay back and think about Jett. He's the only man that ever made love to me. I have to admit that the sex has always been great. More than great. Fantastic. What he does with his hands and hips is magic. It would be so easy for me to let him back in. It would be so easy for me to tell him to come home. But the devil is amused and tells my heart no.

I wonder, how long can I allow the devil to reign over my heart?

49

Usually, the temperature is still in the seventies or eighties in November. However, we're having a bit of a cold spell. For the past three weeks my leg has been killing me. Dr. Robinson prescribed some Motrin 5, but that hasn't helped. The pain is excruciating.

When I speak with Kai, she tells me about her friend, Gail Norman.

"Gail told me that it felt like ice picks were coming through her neck and shoulders. She tried every massage therapist she could find. Nothing worked."

"Damn. That's not encouraging news."

"The therapist told Gail that she had a tendency to fibromyalgia. She told her that if she didn't do something about stretching and relaxing, she was heading in the direction of full blown fibromyalgia. I think that's what you have."

"What solved Gail's problem?"

"Yoga. She does it five or six times a week. Why don't you try it? I'll drive down and come with you."

"Okay. That sounds like a great idea."

"I'll locate the best yoga instructor and give you a call back."

"Thanks, Kai. I owe you one."

One Saturday morning, the twins come over. They wake me up from a deep sleep. I don't usually hear them when they're working in their studio. Painting is a quiet hobby and requires very little running around for inventory. The twins have enough paint in the storage shed to last them for two years.

"Mom, get up," Javed coaxes. He's nudging my shoulder.

"Geez." I prop myself up on my elbows. "What got you guys up so early? What time is it?"

"Seven-thirty," Jamone offers. "I've already made coffee."

I throw back the covers. "Okay, you two get out until I get changed. I'll meet you in the kitchen in five."

Stretching, I lumber into the bathroom and wash my face. I brush my teeth, and then scrounge through my drawers for jeans and a sweatshirt. I put on a pair of socks and scurry into the kitchen.

Jamone hands me a cup of coffee. "It's just how you like it. Plenty of cream." He smiles.

Javed is sitting at the table twiddling his fingers. I look back and forth between the two. They have an odd twinkle in their eyes.

I take a seat at the table. "Jamone, sit down." I wait. "Okay, you two, what's up?"

"We were wondering . . ." Javed says.

Jamone hits him in the arm. "We were wondering if you've spoken with Pops lately."

I sip my coffee. It's perfect. "Yes. Why?"

"He told us about the marriage counselor," Javed states.

"Yeah, so?" So, now Jett's got the boys on his side. I'm intrigued.

"We think you should go with him to see Ms. Allene. The two of us have been there already. She really knows her stuff."

I'm taken aback. "You two saw her?"

"Yes, Mom." Jamone rubs my elbow. "Dad wanted us to give Ms. Allene your perspective about y'all's marriage."

I jerk my head back. "So, you two spoke for me?"

Jamone says, "We did the best we could, but we think that you should talk to her. Javed and I want you to give Pops another chance."

Javed says, "We know you still love him, Mom."

I nearly choke on my coffee. "And who told you that?"

They nod their heads together and speak in unison. "We know."

"I appreciate you guys trying to get me and your dad back together, but this is my choice, not yours. I have no plans to see Ms. Allene. I have no plans to reunite with your father. I'm sorry. Too much damage has been done."

Jamone refills my coffee cup. "Just hear us out. Pops is sending April back home. And that *beyotch* is not happy about it at all. She likes it here."

"And how would you know?"

"I spoke to her last week." Javed looks contrite. "She came over to our apartment. She wanted us to be friends. Jamone and me told her that we didn't want to have anything to do with her skank ass."

"Boy, was she pissed," Jamone says. "She blames you for making Pops send her back to L.A."

"Your dad can't make her leave."

"I think so," Javed says. "Dad found out that she's an alcoholic and smokes marijuana. He threatened to tell her boss at the airlines if she doesn't leave."

"So, now I've got two broads that hate my guts."

"Two?" Jamone asks.

"Didn't your dad tell you about Marla?" They look confused. "She tried to commit suicide recently. She blames me for breaking her and Jett up."

"Word, Mom. Me and Javed can put fear in those broads for you. We can threaten to F them up if they come anywhere near you. For sho'."

I shake my head. "Don't bother. I'm not in the least bit worried about those women."

"Good," Javed says. "Now, back to Pops. Can't you give him a second chance? He loves you like his shadow, Mom."

"He should. I've never done anything to hurt him."

"And he's sorry for hurting you," Javed says. "Everybody deserves a second chance. My English professor married her husband five times."

I laugh. "Fool. Is she still with him now?"

"Yep," Javed says. "They're getting ready to go on a honeymoon to Hawaii. My teacher is even thinking about having another baby."

"I'm happy for them. But you two are wasting your time."

"Mom?" Javed says. He comes to sit down before me and puts his head on my lap. "We just want you to be happy, and we know that Pops always puts a smile on your pretty face. You just can't throw away thirty years. Heck, you two are more like brother and sister than husband and wife." He hugs my waist. "Please promise us that you will go see Ms. Allene. Please."

I really am touched. One session wouldn't kill me. Why the hell not? "Okay, I'll go. But I want you two to do something for me."

"Anything, Mom," Jamone says.

"Wash my car. I went through some mud when I went to see a contractor two weeks ago. I haven't had time to take it to the car wash."

"It ain't no thang. I'll get right on it," Jamone says.

"And I want it detailed inside and out." My windows need cleaning. I can't stand a dirty car. Especially one that I'm paying notes on. "Okay, and do a good job on my wheels too."

Javed says, "We know how you like it, Mom."

I get up. "Okay, I've got to make a few calls. Call me when you finish."

From halfway down the hall I can hear the boys laughing and getting silly with each other. I'm glad that I could put a smile on their handsome faces.

I go back into my bedroom and make up my bed. When I finish, I sit on the edge and pick up the phone. I call Kai.

"Hello, lady."

"Hello to you, too," I say. "Why haven't I heard from you?"

"Because I've been sick."

"What's wrong? Do you have the flu?"

"No, I'm pregnant. Four months."

I jump up and do a jig. *Thank you, Jesus.* "I'm so happy for you, Kai. I know how much you wanted a baby."

"Yeah, but there are complications. He's engaged to someone else. He says he's committed to her."

"Ouch."

"Hell, I should have figured out what was going on. He never answered his home phone at night. Only his cell."

"Then fuck 'im. You're getting what you need out of the deal. Is he going to be around to help with the baby?"

"He says he is, but I'm not counting on him. Can I ask you a favor, Charity?"

"Sure."

"When I go into labor, can you drive down here to be with me?"

"All you have to do is ask. Of course I'll be there."

The contractor that Herman hooked me up with is a genius. He draws up the plans to my specifications and begins working a week later. He hires two extra men on his crew so that he can meet my deadline in December.

Meanwhile, I make a list of all the baking goods and utensils we need. Moses is in charge of gathering everything else we require. After running a background check on Moses and finding his record to be clean, I gave him an American Express card with the business name on it. He's now a registered user on the account.

My advertising guy, Edward Jefferson, has everything in place and has already sent out an e-mail blast with the name of my business, the address, and times of operation. He's got ten radio spots set up to run a week before the grand opening. We've got a billboard on Interstate 40. When I first saw the sketch, I was impressed, and the finished product is awesome. Edward even has advertisements on the side panels of several Memphis Area Transit Authority buses.

I know that Lynzee wants me to come down to visit Michael during Christmas week, but I want her to come down the week before for my grand opening. I'm trying to work up the nerve to ask her.

One Friday afternoon I'm working on the bakery business. I realize that I haven't bought the books and ledgers I need to keep inventory and keep a current client list. I get in my car and head out for Office Max across the street from Wolfchase

Galleria Mall. Suddenly, I have an urge for a cappuccino. I swing by Starbucks and park my car. Alexander's Restaurant is directly across from it. As I head for the door, I spot Herman and a woman holding hands. They're laughing and joking. She kisses him on the cheek.

Needless to say, I'm furious. I forget about the cappuccino and get back into my car. I watch Herman open the door for this woman and minutes later, drive off.

Then I think to myself, we're not a couple. What's to stop him from getting some booty? I'm not giving him any, and he is a grown man. Still, my feelings are hurt. I thought that Herman told me that he could wait. Seeing him holding on to that woman's hand shows me that he doesn't intend to wait for me anytime soon.

I'm mad, but I'm still on a mission. I go to Office Max and purchase all of the books I need. When I get home, I text Moses and tell him what I purchased. He's coming over tomorrow morning to pick up the ledgers.

I'm still madder than a caged tiger. I don't waste any time calling Herman.

I get his voice mail. For the next half hour I continue to call; still, no answer.

I think about the twins. I think about Jett, Marla, and April. Lord knows that I still care about my husband.

I retrieve the business card that Jett gave me. I dial the number. Allene answers on the second ring.

"Hello?"

"Hello, Ms. Jackson. This is Charity Evans. I'd like to know when you'll have time available to meet with me. I'm Jett Evans' wife."

"Thanks for calling, Ms. Evans. I've been hoping to hear from you." She pauses. "Let me see. . . . I can see you at four o'clock on Monday afternoon."

"Good. I'll be there."

Who am I kidding? I was just waiting for a chance to prove Herman's infidelity. But then again, who's to say that Jett is still being faithful? Am I being over precautious, or am I destined to be like Kai, and end up with no man at all?

50

The twins and I spend a quiet Thanksgiving Day at home. Jett tried to persuade me to let him join us, but I refused. I've been to the therapist that Jett found. She wanted to see me alone, so she could get my perspective on our marital problems. Like the boys said, Ms. Jackson is nice. What I like about her is that she admits that there is no easy fix for a broken marriage.

I'm still attending yoga classes. My pain still hasn't come back yet, and I'm thankful to Kai for suggesting the classes. Another plus from the yoga is fitness. I'm back in a size eight. I plan on staying that size, and take seventeen suits to the tailor's and have them sized down to a slim eight. The tailor is happy for all of the business. I'm happy to look like myself again.

The twins intend to help me decorate the bakery two days before the grand opening. I put Jamone in charge. After all, he claims to be the creative twin in the family and knows what a classy opening affair should look like.

Herman finally calls. I'm tempted to not answer his call, but I want to see how good a liar he is.

"Hey, there," he begins. "I've been trying to contact you for over a week. What did you do for the holiday?"

"I had dinner here at home with my sons." I exhale. "What about you?"

"My cousin, Jennifer, has been here for a week. I flew her in from Las Vegas. We celebrated our holiday dinner at Tunica. She's trying to get a job there as a public relations specialist. Jennifer's been in the business for fifteen years."

Was that the woman he was with? "Oh, tell her that I said hello."

"She wants to meet you. I've told her everything about you. Matter of fact, she's one of your fans. She's read all of your books."

Damn. This sounds legitimate. I scan my memory, trying to remember her face. I hope I can recognize her if I see her again.

"Charity . . . are you still there?"

"Oh, yes. I'm just flattered about your cousin is all."

"Okay. How about the three of us meeting for dinner on Saturday night? We can go to Alexander's. That's where I took Jennifer, and she made me promise to take her back."

Then it was her. Stupid, stupid, me. Now what am I going to do? I'm trying to get back with Jett, but still holding out hope for Herman. I need help.

"Saturday is fine. What time?"

"How about six?"

"I'll meet you two there."

"I can pick you up."

"No, it's better if I meet you there." I don't need Jett seeing Herman's car in my driveway.

Later that evening, I call Lynzee. I explain to her my dilemma with Jett and Herman.

"You've had a bad year, little sis. I'm glad you're seeing a therapist. She can help you sort out your life. You've got a lot of important decisions to make."

"I know. I want to use my brain and not my heart to make the right decision about Jett and me. I really care about Herman, but I know the timing is all wrong."

"I agree. Like usual, you're moving too fast. Slow down. Life's not as complicated as you think."

"Thanks, Lynzee. I'm so used to rushing everything, even writing my books. It's time that I slowed down."

"Thank the Lord you're finally getting it."

"I love you, Lynzee. Thanks."

"And I love you, too, Charity."

She expresses how sorry that she is for getting everything started with April's presence. "I was strung out on Percocet when I first called April. I'm embarrassed to say that I hated your guts back then, Charity. I wanted to do anything I could to hurt you."

"You love me, you hate me, Lynzee."

"Yes, I felt both. But my hatred of you at the time out-weighed the love. I didn't want Jett back. But I knew when you told Jett about April that he would have a positive reaction. Men are suckers for their daughters, you know."

"I'm finding that out to be true. Jett seems crazy about April."

"And she told me that she loves him too."

"Do you still talk to April?" I ask.

"Not really. I leave her messages. I tell her that I love her. I tell her that I didn't mean for things to turn out this way. She leaves me messages and says that she hates my guts and she doesn't want to have anything to do with me."

"Does that bother you?"

"A little. But after I found her, she and I never really got to know each other. Once I found out that she had an addiction like I did, I pretty much didn't want to have too much to do with her."

"Why didn't you try to get her clean?"

"I couldn't get myself clean. How was I going to help her? Plus, Tyler was going through changes then with Raymond. It was all too much for me to deal with."

"I see."

"Besides, I was more focused on competing with you, little sister. I felt threatened by you. I was thinking of anything and everything I could do to you to end your career."

"And now, since you're going back writing again, can this

happen between us a second time? We ain't the Brontës, you know."

"No way. I've learned my lesson. And I don't care if your sales are greater than mine. I'll be so proud of you. That's the truth, Charity. I would rather you become the number one African American writer than some of these other haters that I know."

"Thanks." I pause. "Now, what are we going to do about April? Jett is sending her back to L.A. in January. Do you think she'll contact Tyler or do anything negative to hurt your career?"

"It's not likely. April can't take a chance of losing her job and ending up on the streets. As you probably know already, not only does she have an alcohol problem, she's hooked on marijuana. Maybe one of these days I'll be in a position to help her emotionally. That is, if she'll accept it."

"What about her adoptive parents? Have you spoken to them lately?"

"Not since I found April. They've washed their hands of her. It appears that she burnt her bridges with them years ago."

"What'd she do?"

"She set their house on fire. They didn't have homeowner's insurance, and they lost everything. Presently, they're living with his sister. All of April's pictures of her growing up and her prom are gone, and they said that they prefer it that way. They never want to see her again in life."

"So, she has no one?"

"Not if Jett turns his back on her."

"I don't know what to say, Lynzee. I've tried to have feelings for April, but I don't. Hell, I'm human. We all have flaws. Having her use Jett's love as weakness disgusts me. I don't trust her. I don't respect who she is."

"Who could blame you? Your marriage is in shambles because of her."

"No, Lynzee, because of you."

"I can't deny it. You're right. I admit that everything is all my fault. If I could fix any of it back the way things were before, I would. I know I've asked you before, but can you please forgive me, Charity, for causing so many problems in your life?"

"A part of me wants to say no, but because our Mama raised us better, I have to say yes. Yes, I can forgive you, Lynzee."

Lynzee starts to cry. "I told Michael about my Percocet habit. I told him about me and you. I told him about Tyler's marriage and the adoption. He knows everything."

"That's good that you're being honest with him. Your relationship should be stronger because of it." I pause, but I have to ask. "Does he know about Heidi?"

"Yes. He understands how college girls get into relationships like that. He chastised me for knowing about her threats to commit suicide and not doing anything about it. But he said when someone really wants to kill themselves, there's really nothing that I could have done about it."

"That's true." I sigh. "Enough of that morbid shit. I need you to do something for me."

"Name it."

"I'm having a grand opening of my bakery on December seventeenth. Can you come down and celebrate the opening with me? I'd like to put your name in the publicity promotions. Maybe you can read from your new book."

"You want me to be a featured guest?"

"Yes. It would make me proud."

"Then hell yes! I'll fly in on the sixteenth. Is that okay?"

"Yes. I'll pick you up at the airport. Get an early flight so that I can kick your ass at Boggle before we go to bed." I laugh and Lynzee laughs with me.

I meet Herman and Jennifer at *Alexander's*. She's a pretty girl, with a beautiful personality. When we sit down at her table, she immediately launches into a dozen questions about my books. She makes me laugh because she's so serious about the characters. I answer her queries the best I can, because I've actually forgotten some of the characters in my first two books. I pique her interest with my latest book about the Afghanistan war. She loves the topic.

We eat dinner and almost freeze Herman out of the conversation. He's courteous and lets us talk. He seems amused. But when it's time to leave, Herman tries to kiss me again. I pull away. He's hurt, but says he'll call me tonight.

Herman called and I told him about my therapy sessions. I thought he would be mad, but he was actually happy about it. He told me that he'd rather that I be sure about the divorce than have regrets. He said that he was open to talk about the sessions if and when I felt the need to. If I don't, that's fine with him too. I truly treasure Herman's friendship. He's one of a kind, and I know that he really cares about me.

I'm finding that I'm getting butterflies thinking about him, too, especially intimately. I've had sexual dreams about Herman that have me waking up sweating. Guilt consumes me, and I need two Excedrin P.M. to get back to sleep. I'm going to do what Ms. Jackson suggests and read the Bible more. Maybe reading about marriage and love will help me sort out this dilemma.

51

I'm scheduled to have another session with Allene Jackson. It's the first time that Jett will be in attendance. Jett is there when I arrive and Allene takes us right in.

She gets out her notepad. "Jett have you been attending church?" He nods yes. "And you, Charity?"

"I haven't been in months."

Allene says, "I want you to try and attend church this Sunday. Can you do that for me?"

"Yes." Jett will be there. Does she expect us to sit together?

Jett and I are sitting side by side. Allene is sitting at her desk. She glances back and forth at both of us before she asks the question, "Now, who wants to be the first one to voice their complaints about the marriage?"

"I do," I say without hesitation. "I believe that Jett and I had a beautiful marriage before he found out that he had an illegitimate daughter. After that, he resented me and our marriage soured. He lost his trust in me. I lost my trust in him when our sons caught him out with a younger woman. Now my trust for him is gone, and I don't know if it can ever be repaired."

Allene looks at Jett. "Your turn."

Jett looks humbled. His head is lowered and his hands are shaking. "Like Charity said, we had a wonderful marriage. I never loved a woman the way I loved her. I trusted her with my life. Then I found out about my daughter, a daughter who always wondered about the paternity of her natural father. I found out that Charity lied about knowing the truth. I abhor a liar. Have no patience for liars. I felt I had no choice but to leave. The hurt was that deep. Charity knows that I always wanted a daughter."

"Tell me why you hid the truth from Jett, Charity."

"From the beginning, I had a premonition that this child would cause problems in our marriage; that her presence would ultimately challenge the love Jett felt for me and my sons. I mean, talk about a dysfunctional family. Having a cousin and a sister in the same body is a little hard to digest. I know me, and I know that I would never be able to accept this child. I knew that it would be an ongoing competition between us to claim Jett's love. I admit that I was wrong for withholding the information from Jett, but I only did it to save our marriage."

Jett begins to cry. I have to freeze my emotions to not reach out and hug him. I now know how much I still care for this man. After all, what other black man do I know who's in love with Willie Nelson's songs? None.

"I have to say that I believe you two really love each other. I believe that your marriage can be saved. Are you willing to work on it? Charity?" I nod. "Jett?" He nods.

"Well, that's enough for today. I want you two to talk before you come see me again. I want you two to think of five things that will help make this marriage solid again." She rises, and I follow Jett out of the office.

I'm too embarrassed to look Jett in the eye. I head for the door. I don't want to say good-bye. It sounds so stupid for me to say that to my husband, a man who I feel that I need back in my life for good.

I open the door, and Jett puts his large hands over mine. He looks deep into my eyes. "Marla has lost it. She quit her job. She's talking about kicking your butt with a baseball bat. I'm worried, Charity. Maybe you should have one of the twins stay with you for a while."

"No. I know how to protect myself. Besides, I still have the gun you bought me." I pat my purse. "I keep it with me at all times."

"Good. I don't know if I could go on if something happened to you." His eyes fill with tears again. "I wish I could go home with you. You need my protection."

A part of me wishes he would. I kiss his cheek. "I'll be fine, Jett. I'll see you at church on Sunday." I smile and leave.

I get into my car. I lied to Jett. The truth is I can't find my gun. I hid it from myself. I put it up in a safe place and forgot where I put it. I don't want to alarm the twins and ask them to help me find it.

First it was April; now it's Marla who wants to harm me. Is Jett's love really worth all of this drama?

52

It's just like I felt when Zedra threatened me. I'm getting a crook in my neck looking over my shoulder. When I go to the grocery store, I rush in and rush out. When I get gas, I lock the gas switch and sit in my car until the tank fills up.

I think Jett told the twins about Marla because they find a reason to stop by the house every day. Even though I'm only a little bit scared, I feel safer knowing my sons are around.

"Mom," Javed says, "can you pick up Jamone and me on Sunday? We want to go to church with you."

I smile a mile wide. "Certainly, son. Service starts at eight. I'll be at your place at seven-thirty."

"Okay. We'll be ready." He flashes a smile. "I've got good news."

"Tell me."

"Ms. Spherion wrote an article about Jamone and me. We're on the cover of the January issue of *Queen Magazine*."

I laugh. "Isn't a woman supposed to be on the cover?"

"Yeah. We've got that handled. Jamone and I painted a portrait of Michelle Obama in her inaugural ball gown. It's stunning. We're holding the canvas on the cover."

"Oh, that was smart."

"Javed thought of it. We're hoping that Mrs. Obama sees the cover and commissions Jamone and me to paint a portrait of her and her family. Wouldn't that be the bomb?"

"Yes. And you two would soon be rich. You'd have more work than you could handle."

He blushes. "That's the plan."

I hug him. "I'm so proud of you guys. You've never given me any trouble."

"You and Pops never gave us a reason to." He puts his arm around my waist. "Now, what's this I hear about you and Pops having a talk on Sunday night? Have you got your five things already?"

I pop him in the head.

When Herman calls me, I tell him the truth. "I think that I'm going to reconcile with my husband."

"Are you sure?"

"I think so."

"I'm disappointed, Charity."

"I thought that you might be. I came this close to doing the wild thang with you. You know you had me all hot and bothered on several occasions."

"No, I didn't. When?"

"When you kissed me at the door that night, I thought I was going to faint."

"I thought my zipper was going to bust open." He laughs.

"And when you had me up in your plane the first time, I felt so close to you. I wanted you to take me home and make love to me that day."

"Damn, Charity, why are you telling me all of this now when it's too late? Or is it?"

"I'm sorry, Herman. I just had to let you know how you were making me feel. I don't know if we can remain friends."

"I thought you'd say that."

"We're too close to each other now."

Herman's voice is serious when he says, "I meant it when I said that I love you. I do and always will. And I'm not talking about a friendly kind of love. I mean the kind of love that a man shares with his woman, an Adam and Eve kinda love."

"I know, Herman. And I'm sorry. I care deeply for you, too, and I always will." There's a humbling silence. "I want you to find the right woman who will love you the way you deserve to be loved."

"I found her already."

"No. I'm serious. You need a woman who can help you with your career. You're still starting the charter service, aren't you?"

"Damn right. I've got my business partner and we're developing a business plan. Do you think you can agree to let me take you up on one of our new Cessnas? It will seat twelve."

"We'll see."

"That's all I ask."

"God bless you, Herman."

"God bless you, Charity. Good night."

On Sunday morning, I rise at six. I prepare myself one of my favorites, blueberry pancakes. I don't need any bacon or sausage, just milk. I scarf down three cakes and savor every bite. I clean up the kitchen and Twitter my crew. They're all up and eager to celebrate the grand opening. I concur.

I get dressed and design an artful French Twist on my silky tresses. I select a pink-and-orange Christian Dior suit with jumbo orange, pink, and lavender beads. I put on Jimmy Choo tan pumps and grab a caramel-colored Birkin bag.

When I pull up, the twins are already coming out of the door. To my delight, they're dressed alike in black pants, black-and-gray ties, and white shirts. They have on black leather gym shoes.

"Hi, sons," I say when they get in the car. "I love your look."

Jamone says, "We thought you'd like it."

"Can I drive, Mom?" Javed asks.

"Okay. I'll get in the back and let you two sit in the front." We switch places. "Now, don't speed and you won't hear my mouth."

"I feel you."

True to his word, Javed doesn't speed as he drives the seventeen miles to Greater Community Faith Church of God in Christ on Fisher Avenue. Javed parks and stores the keys in his pocket. I keep silent as I grab my purse and Bible. When we enter the church, we spot Jett standing in the middle section. The choir is singing, and the pianist and drummer are bringing up the heavenly harmony on the right side of the stage.

The choir sings three more songs before one of the missionaries reads the day's announcements. One of the deacons speaks next. He talks about the upcoming Christmas program and says he hopes that all will attend. The youth choir is putting on a play on December nineteenth. The floor opens for testimony.

I hear testimonies about how prayer helped a family member beat cancer. I hear testimony how the church helped people get off of the streets. I hear testimony about how a woman's college-bound son's $3200 medical bill was paid. Then I hear Jett.

"I want to thank God for my family being here today. I want to thank God for giving me another chance to save my marriage. I want to thank God for giving me the courage to tell my wife how much I love and need her. I've committed some hurtful sins in my life, and I hope I will be forgiven for them. I ask that the church pray for me and my family. Thank you." Tears are streaming from his eyes.

My eyes mist with tears too. I know that Jett meant every word that he said. He rarely testifies.

Six other members testify before the choir sings another selection. Finally, Pastor Bolton approaches the pulpit. He breaks out in *Beautiful Zion*, a hymn that the entire church knows and joins in on. Some of the members get excited and break out dancing. The pastor is feeling a heavenly inspiration, and joins some of the members in a dance of his own. The music booms and booms, then finally filters down to a soft beat.

The pastor goes back to the pulpit. His message today is "Faith." For the next forty-five minutes, the pastor reads scriptures from Luke and Daniel. The congregation follows along in their Bibles and holds up their hands when the pastor asks, "How many of you know what I'm talking about this morning?"

"When it's all said and done, you need to have faith in order to have salvation. For those that are married, you need to make your marriage like a threefold cord of love and trust, with God at the center."

It seems like the pastor is speaking directly to Jett and me when he makes his closing statements. He speaks about marriage, trust, love, salvation, and faith. Jett and I exchange glances. Then we smile at each other.

Just then, an alarm goes off outside. One of the ushers goes to the door. She comes back in and says quietly, "Anybody own a silver BMW?"

Javed rushes to the door. Jamone follows. Then Jett and I leave the church. The alarm on my car is blaring. The driver side window is busted out. Sitting right on the front seat is a pile of hot shit.

"Don't look, Mom," Javed says.

"I'll get some cleaning products," Jamone says. "I'll be right back."

Jett looks at the pile of shit and yells in the air, "You bitch!"

"Calm down, Jett. We're still at church," I tell him.

I don't have to look at the seat. I can smell the feces from where I'm standing. I stand in the back of the car and watch and wait until the twins clean up the mess. It seems like it takes forever to get all of the glass shards up. Javed leaves a pile of paper towels on the seat so that I don't get my suit wet.

People from the congregation are ogling and shaking their heads. I can't much blame them. It's a sorry sight to see.

"I'm sorry, honey," Jett says.

"It's not your fault." I get in the car. "Call me later."

The twins hop in. I push the ignition button and we drive off. On the way home, Javed says, "I think it was April who did that foul shit."

"No," Jamone offers, "It was Marla. Dad told me that that woman is out of her mind. Somebody is going to get their butt kicked."

"How'd they get in the car? I thought it was difficult to break into these vehicles."

"It is, but she broke the window out, remember?" Javed says seriously.

I speak up. "Listen, I don't want you two to do anything. Nobody was harmed. So someone put some feces in my car. So what? It's over. Let it go."

"You're wrong, Mom," Javed groans. "It ain't no telling what this ho might try next."

I pray that Jett can talk to Marla and convince her to leave me and my belongings alone.

But my prayers aren't answered. Jett goes over to Marla's apartment and punches her in the mouth. She calls the police. Jett is arrested. Hours later, I'm at 201 Poplar bailing Jett out of jail.

He's breathing hard and stone cold mad. "Marla claims that she didn't do it. Then she started bragging about what she planned to do to you. She said, 'I'm gonna fuck that bitch up.' That's when I punched her in her mouth. You know the rest."

I drive Jett to his apartment. "You know you haven't mentioned April's possible involvement."

"April wouldn't do anything like this. She doesn't like you, but she wouldn't hurt me. She knows if she hurts you, she hurts me."

"That sounds sweet, Jett, but Lynzee told me that April set her adoptive parents' house on fire."

"When?"

"Fifteen years ago."

"See? She's changed. April wouldn't do anything like that now. I'd be willing to bet money that she wouldn't."

"Okay, Jett. You know your daughter better than I do. I'm going to say good night. I've got to get up early tomorrow."

"How's the bakery business coming along?"

"Everything's running smoothly. I'm scared that something's going to happen."

"Don't wish bad luck on yourself." He gets out. "Good night, Charity. Thanks for bailing me out. I love you."

"Good night, Jett. I'll call you in an hour or so about the five things. Remember?"

He winks at me.

I drive home reeling. Why didn't I tell Jett that I loved him too? Why didn't I tell him that no matter what those women do, nothing can tear us apart this time? But then I think: What if one of those fools tries to hurt one of my sons? My heart feels heavy. I've got to go home and find that gun. No matter how long it takes, I'm not going to bed until I find it.

53

I'm so tired it feels like my eyelids are sandbags. No matter, I'm still on a mission. My dresser, chest of drawers, and armoire are all yanked open. I even take all of the towels and bedding out of the linen closet. Nothing. My mind is so convoluted, I can't think rationally.

Then it comes to me. I put the gun inside one of my hat boxes. But which one? I get a stool and go through every box. I find it in the box with my black mink hat.

The closet is a mess, the linen closet is a mess, the bedroom is a mess, but I leave everything just as it is and fall down on my bed holding the gun. In seconds, I'm fast asleep.

When I awake, I won't let anything deter me from doing my yoga. I spend an hour in the exercise room and do my thing. I'm sweating in thirty minutes. In sixty, I feel rejuvenated.

Smelling like a raccoon, I take a shower. When I get out, I phone Jett, and we talk about the five things we think will help strengthen our marriage. It's a good conversation, and I'm feeling closer to Jett than I have in a long while.

Before we hang up, Jett says, "I'd like to know if you can do me a favor."

"What is it?"

"Go dancing with me."

"What? On a Monday night?"

"Sure. I'd like to take you dancing to this new club. It's

called Tryst. They only play old school songs. Remember the record we danced to when we first started dating?"

"Yeah. It was 'Dedicated to the One I Love.'" I sigh. "I still love that song."

"Me, too." He pauses. "C'mon, baby. We deserve to have some fun. I want to hear you laugh again. I miss hearing your laughter. Nobody laughs like you."

I love the way he calls me baby. When he says it to my face, it makes my knees weak. When he says "baby" over the phone, it makes me swoon. "I'd love to go dancing with you, Jett."

"Thank you, baby. I'll pick you up at nine."

"I'll be ready." I smile as I hang up. Things are really coming together between us. Jett knows that I love to dance. It's a shame that it took us getting separated before we spent a night on the town. But no matter, I'm happy to put on my dancing shoes. I think I've still got it.

Throughout the day, I text Moses and turn on the music, practicing my dance moves. I'm tempted to call the twins to help me out, but they'd only laugh at me.

I start dressing at quarter to eight. I don't want to rush. I want to wear my thigh-high boots and a mini. I scan my closet and find the perfect dress. It's a multi-colored mini with a deep plunging front neckline. I select what I feel is the coolest jewelry to accent the dress. I hang my dress over the closet door and take my time applying my makeup. I notice a line around my mouth that I haven't seen before. Damn. I continue and finish. I get out the curling iron and bump my shoulder-length hair into a stylish bob. Neat. I slip into my dress, put on my beads and thigh-high boots, and step back before the mirror and assess myself. Yep, I look ten years younger.

I check my watch. It's twenty minutes to nine. I'm getting nervous and can't stop sweating. I have to touch up my makeup twice before Jett calls me.

I think it would be better if I meet him there. He gives me the directions and I punch it into my navigation system. Jamone took my car to Abra's Collision Shop on Brunswick Road and had the window repaired. Meanwhile, I feel for the bulge in my Hermès bag, and then start up my car and head on out.

I groove to Alicia Keys on the drive over. By the time I arrive, I'm in a pretty good mood. I valet park and wait for Jett at the front door.

The parking lot is jam-packed. Middle-aged men and women wearing their finest walk past me and enter the establishment. I smell different perfumes and savor the fresh, clean scents. I enjoy smelling women's and men's cologne. I even own a bottle of men's Gucci fragrance. I think it makes me smell like a wild child.

Jett arrives two minutes later and valet parks. I'm surprised because he's usually too cheap to do so.

When he gets out of the car and comes into the light, I give him the once over. I whistle. He's wearing a beige silk shirt with silver and iridescent pin-striped beading. He has on beige silk slacks and the matching alligator shoes that I bought him last year.

"Wow, Jett. You look fabulous."

He gives me a whirl. "And you look stunning, you pretty young thang."

We both laugh.

"You ready?" he asks.

"Certainly. Let's do it."

Baby Face's "Whip Appeal" is playing when we enter the club. Tryst is decorated in black and white. With several lighted three-dimensional dice and playing cards on the black walls, the décor is the junk. Dozens of tables with black tablecloths, white leather club chairs, and white magnolia candles are spread out across the huge room. The lighted dance floor is packed with men and women doing their thing.

"C'mon, that's our jam," Jett says. "Let's dance."

We slow dance to "Whip Appeal" and then speed up the pace when Marvin Gaye's "What's Going On" comes on. We take a breather and find a table. A waitress comes over and takes our orders of Sprite on the rocks. She frowns. No big tip here tonight.

We drink half of our sodas and get back on the dance floor. Jett is dancing like he never stopped, and I enjoy watching him swivel his hips and pop his fingers. We continue to dance to Smokey Robinson and the Miracles, Gladys Knight, The Supremes, Chuck Berry, Little Richard, The Jackson Five, The Four Tops and The Temptations.

When we finally sit back down, I'm exhausted. "I'm having a ball, Jett, but I've got on new boots and my feet are killing me."

"Are you ready to go?"

I nod. "Can we come back?"

"Anytime the feeling hits you."

We exit the building and hand the valet our parking tickets. It's raining like salt pellets. The temperature has dropped ten degrees. My car is up first. I kiss Jett on the cheek and get in my car. "Call me tomorrow," I say. When I get inside, the music is so loud it hurts my ears. I turn it down. I slowly drive off, waiting for Jett to get into his vehicle.

I weave around the parked cars and head toward the street. All of a sudden I feel something gnawing at my heel. The gnawing is faster and faster. I turn on the overhead lights and look down. "Eeeeek!" It's a rat. I kick at it, get out my gun, and shoot it. *Bang! Bang!* "Yikes!" I scream as I yank the car in park and exit my car.

Jett is right behind me and comes to my rescue. "What's wrong, baby?" He puts his arm around my shoulder.

I'm shaking like I've got the shingles. "It's a–a–a rat . . . in my . . . car."

He releases me and gets into my car. In seconds he's found the rat. He exits the car, goes into the back of his truck, and gets a rag. He goes back to my car and picks up the rat. He walks over to the edge of the property and tosses it over the fence.

When he comes back, I'm still shaking. "I'm not getting back in that car, Jett. Who could have done something this nasty?" I start crying.

"I'm not sure." He holds me tight. "C'mon, get in my truck."

I let him lead me to his truck and he helps me get inside. People behind us are blaring their horns. Jett puts his hand up like a stop sign and hurries to get in my car. He drives it to an empty space and parks it.

"Take me home, Jett. Please." I can't stop crying. I'm terrified of rats and mice. How could someone be so cruel?

Jett puts the pedal to the metal and we arrive at my house in twenty minutes. He walks me to the door. "Please come in, Jett. I don't want to be alone."

He follows me back to our bedroom. I sit on the edge of the bed. Jett sits next to me. "I'm not getting back in that car. You're going to have to get rid of it." I'm dead serious.

"Baby, it's all right. I'll take care of it. I'll catch a taxi to the club tomorrow and bring it home. Then you can decide if you still want to trade it in."

I grab his waist and hold him tight. "I don't want to be alone tonight. Will you stay with me?"

He pushes me back and looks me in the eye. "Are you sure?"

I nod. "Take me in your arms, Jett, and show me how much you need me."

"All you had to do was ask," he says and begins to unzip my dress.

54

Jett turns out the lights. "No, leave them on," I tell him. "I want to look at you." I clasp his face with my hands and guide him to my lips. I kiss him lightly, and then it deepens to a long, fencing match of moist tongues. Jett has kissed me many times, but somehow this feels new.

Gently, he releases himself from me. He stands, but my languid arms refuse to release his neck. He lifts my lithe body and my mouth covers his. As he begins to disrobe me, I help him, squirming in his arms to remove the loose mini, with an eagerness that feels irresistible.

"Let me help you," I say, and begin to remove his clothing. There is no rush, no hurry. We both know what to expect, how we will feel.

He allows me to kiss him again as his eyes worship my face. His elongated finger outlines my full lips. The flat of his palm strokes my cheek. The tip of his long fingernail traces my hairline from beneath one ear to the other. All the while, his eyes remain transfixed on mine. I look deep into the eyes that look like bronze crystals, bewitching me until I have no independent thought, no feelings other than those that begin and end with him.

We take our time exploring each other's bodies with such freedom and intensity and eagerness that instead of exhausted, we feel energized and enraptured. My hunger for him at this moment has grown into a greedy, insatiable desperation.

It's so quiet, yet I hear the music inside of my head: jazz, rhythm and blues, and reggae. I want to move my body to the beat of the music and take Jett on a journey to the Milky Way and back.

I feel my body slipping into a trancelike state where intelligence and wit are rendered powerless, becoming enraptured, humble slaves to the magnetic rule of emotions and sensitivities. When his hands slide behind my neck and he entangles them in my tousled hair, I tilt my head back and open my eyes wider, allowing the exotic sensations to wash over me and bathe me in a pool of anticipation.

We fall into the bed.

Jett takes his time loving every pore of my body. Though I try to reciprocate, he gently pushes me back so that he can take the lead. Then he moves back up to my breasts and slowly but masterfully caresses every millimeter with his artful tongue.

I can feel the moisture on his manhood that mirrors the moistness between my legs. I am ready to feel the mahogany log that is wedged between us. Inspired, I grab a hold of it, and gently guide it inside of me. Slowly he probes, sliding, slipping just an inch in and out of me. I groan and arch my buttocks up higher to feel the length of him. He begins a rhythmic dance of his hips that leave me breathless. I work my hips in the exact rhythm of his. The thrusts increase and deepen. Then abruptly, I feel his legs tense, and then suddenly he slams inside me all the way. His thrust is so deep, so fast, my heart skips a beat. Seconds later, I feel a convulsive orgasm slice through my languid body.

Then he lifts himself up and begins a new dance, this one more methodical, more heated, and more stimulating for this physical aphrodisiac. His breath becomes short as he picks up speed. He begins to push harder and harder, faster and faster, until he stiffens. I hear a catch in his throat, and with every quiver that stabs through me, I begin to feel each pulse as he comes inside of me. He collapses his elongated body on top of mine. Our breaths mingle together. Our hearts bounce each beat back and forth and back again. We exhale, and surrender to the magical moment that wraps me in the solitude of his loving arms. I feel strangely calm.

"Are you satisfied, baby?"

"I'm good—no, great." I smile to myself, knowing that I am coming back to me, the way I used to be. Mainly because I've made love to my man and today is Monday, not Friday. Call me corny, but Lord knows that I love this man.

Jett wakes up first the next morning, and kisses me tenderly. He rises and heads for the shower. When he returns, he changes back into his clothes, minus the boxers, which he throws in the hamper. I love the thought of him drawer-less, with his love muscle free to flip-flop this way and that. I eke out a feline smile.

"Baby, I called a taxi to take me to get your car. I'll be back in an hour."

"Okay. I'll be dressed by the time you get back." He kisses me again and exits the room.

After Jett leaves, I stretch out, rubbing the sheets where we made rapturous love, burying my head in the pillow, and breathing in his erotic scent. I close my eyes and envision his handsome face. I imagine his long body lying like a suction on top of mine. I try to reproduce the sensations that he unearthed in me, try to imagine the sensations that I produced in him. My heart feels full.

I finally rise at nine. I take a long, relaxing bath and turn on the Jacuzzi. I allow the jets to massage the muscles that Jett caressed late last night. I exit and clean the oversized tub.

I dress in pale blue sweats and put my hair into a short pony tail. I apply a tad of blush and put on a smidgen of lipstick. I make up the bed and head into the kitchen. Thankfully, Jett already has the coffee on. I fix a cup and sit down at the desk.

I'm still daunted about the rat last night, but try not to dwell on something so depressing. I made love to my husband last night. I have a lot to be thankful for.

As I sip my coffee, I text Moses, Enrique, and Heidi. The four of us plan to meet at the bakery at 4:00 P.M.

After I finish my third cup of coffee, Jett comes home. He rings the doorbell since he no longer has a key. I make a mental note to give him one today.

He's changed into jeans and a white sweatshirt, and looks irritated. He says, "The more I think about who put that rat in your car, the madder it makes me. I think we should go downtown and file a complaint against both Marla and April. At least the police can stop by their apartments and interrogate them. The police really don't handle matters like this one, but maybe they'll do us a favor because of your celebrity status."

"I'm game to go downtown, but I'm not budging on that car. I want to get rid of it. Today."

"I'll take care of the car." He takes a sip of my coffee. "Are you about ready to go?"

"Let me get my purse." Knowing I'm going to the police station, I tuck my gun beneath the mattress.

I gather my purse and meet him at the back door. When I hand him a key, his smile is enigmatic.

Jett drives my car, and I drive his truck. We drive down to 201 Poplar, go down to the lower level to the Citizens Disputes Office, and file a complaint. Jett shows the supervisor pictures of the rat. They really seem indifferent, but they take the complaint because I am somewhat of a celebrity.

The supervisor assures us that someone will speak with Ms. April Tempest and Ms. Marla Lawson today. A policeman will stop by our house later and give us an update.

That done, we head for the BMW dealership. I find Seymour and tell him about my problem. He's happy to get another sale and helps Jett and me pick out a silver-blue 2011 model. They appraise my car, and allow for the insurance to fix the damage. Less than ninety minutes later, I drive down Germantown Parkway in my new car.

It's noon when we get home. Jett calls the twins and asks them to help him get his clothes from his apartment. They are overjoyed.

For the next two hours, Jett and the twins move Jett's clothes and personal items back into our bedroom closet. I take a moment and look at the closet when they finish. His clothes look like they belong there. It makes me smile.

Bringing the Harley back takes another hour. After they finish, the twins want a play by play scenario of last night's happenings.

We are all in the living room. The Christmas decorations are in a big box in the corner. The fake seven-foot tree is lying on the floor beside it. The twins are going to help me decorate the tree and staircase this weekend. Right now, the television set is turned to the news.

"Where was Pops when you found the rat?" Javed asks after I tell them what happened.

"He was behind me. After I jumped out of the car, he came to my rescue and threw the dead rat across the fence."

"Dag, Mom. I wish I could have seen that," Jamone says, shaking his head.

"Why?" I ask.

"So I could've helped you. I've never shot a gun before." Jamone makes a trigger out of his finger and thumb.

"Okay. It's over. I've got a new car, but we still don't know who did it. It could be Marla. It could be April." I shrug. "The police are speaking to both of them today."

"I think it was Marla," Jamone says, "that ho is crazy."

"I think it was April," Javed adds. "She ain't got good sense either. Plus, she gets high. She was probably laughing her a—"

"Javed?"

"You know what I mean." He changes the channel on the TV.

"How'd they get in? I heard you have to use a laser key code to get inside of one." Jamone looks at me and then at Javed.

"These thieves out here now are high tech. Or the perp could have bribed the valet."

I frown. By now it's three-thirty. "I'll see you two later. I've got a meeting with my new crew at the bakery."

They both say, "See ya."

* * *

I pull up to the bakery and admire the new sign for Just Desserts that was put up this morning. I open the door. The crew is already there. We all say hello.

Moses is an imposing figure. He weighs about three hundred twenty pounds, has a bald head, average features, and a Santa Claus belly. He won't be thirty until next spring. "Looks like we're going to be good to go on the sixteenth, Charity."

"Remember, our trump card over the other bakeries is our pies," I say.

"I believe my Tang pie will be a favorite," Enrique says. "It tastes like a Creamsicle. It's real popular in the summer, but since the weather is so nice, I'll think it'll work this season."

Heidi has a chocolate strawberry pie recipe that's been in her family for sixty years. She also has a honey walnut pie that's equally appetizing.

Moses has a lemon icebox pie. He says the recipe came from a can of Eagle brand milk. He also chooses to share his mother's secret recipe for a hot fudge pie.

"Remember, we beat a little egg white and brush it on the bottom of the crust to keep it flaky and keep our filling from soaking in," I add.

To make our customers happy, Moses suggests that we give our customers a baking tip once a month. This month is making perfect pie crust. The secret is in the use of ice water. Two hundred recipe cards are on top of one of the glass cases that will showcase the bakery items. The cases are shiny and well designed.

"Yes, I think we're fine. The only thing left to do is to check the appliances and make sure they're in working order."

"Charity, do you think we need to purchase a van?" Heidi asks. "You know, just in case we start catering." Heidi is Caucasian. She has wispy brown hair, large eyes, a pointy nose, and narrow lips. Heidi has been baking for almost twenty years. She has a wonderful recipe book handed down from her great grandmother.

"Maybe later. Not right now."

"I think we'll be catering by next summer," Enrique says. Enrique is Italian. He's got wavy black hair, with a Christmas tree head, sharp features, and a goatee. He's a handsome rascal, and should bring plenty of young girls into the bakery.

"Possibly." I scan their faces. "Now, does everyone have their lists?" I've asked each of them to prepare a list of special ingredients that they need.

"Now, you guys look around and see if there's anything else that needs to be done."

Moses goes off on his own. Heidi and Enrique naturally gravitate to each other. They speak in low tones and check out everything in the shop.

Heidi turns on the ovens and makes sure that they're working properly. She checks out the industrialized mixers that are on the counter. They work just fine.

Enrique is more concerned about the baking utensils. He goes through the cabinets, one by one, making sure that we have everything that was on the initial list.

Then Moses checks the linen. "We don't need to run out of dishtowels when we're halfway through with our pastries. I really think that we need to order a dozen more, just to be safe."

A washer and dryer are also located in the back of the shop, so that we can keep the linen clean and fresh. We agree that we will take turns each week washing and cleaning the pots. Every one of us loves to bake, but we've all agreed that we hate to clean up the mess.

"I'm still considering hiring Javed and Jamone to wash out the pots and bowls. They can clean up after we finish baking. That way they won't be in our way," I say.

"That'll work," Moses adds. "Your sons seem like good kids. We welcome the addition to our new family." They all nod and smile.

Thirty minutes later, we all meet in the entryway. "Everything looks cool," Enrique says. Heidi nods.

"I don't see anything out of place," Moses says. He rubs his thick hands together. "I'm just ready to get started."

"Okay, everybody. I'll meet you guys back here at 4:00 A.M. Thursday morning."

Satisfied that all is well, I leave the bakery and say good-bye to my crew. On the way home, I hear about my rat incident on the radio.

"Breaking news: Local *New York Times* bestseller, Charity Lavender," the DJ says, "and her husband, Jett Evans, were enjoying a night out at Tryst last night. It seems that someone wanted to spoil their evening by putting a live rat on the floorboard of Charity Lavender's car. Fortunately, she noticed the rodent before driving off, and exited the car. Thankfully, she's doing fine. The police are investigating."

When I arrive home, the police are there talking with Jett in the driveway. He waves me over.

"This is Lieutenant Chalmers and Lieutenant Samuels. They spoke with Marla and April."

Lieutenant Samuels speaks first. "My partner and I interviewed both women. Neither one of them have alibis for last night. We warned them that this is a misdemeanor and if something like this happens again and they're caught, they will be prosecuted."

Both lieutenants look dead serious. "I see you have a new vehicle, Mrs. Evans," Lieutenant Chalmers says.

"Yes, I bought it today."

Lieutenant Chalmers writes down my license tag number. "We'll put your car into our system and advise the other officers to be aware of anything unusual happening to your vehicle."

"Thank you." I shake their hands.

When they leave, Jett hugs me. "How's my baby?"

"Now that you're here, I'm perfect."

55

I've been ripping and running like crazy, making sure that I don't forget a single item for the grand opening.

The twins put their artwork up last night, and it looks spectacular. The colors in the paintings bring out the lemon sherbet coloring of the walls. I love that the bakery is so bright and cheery. It's like bringing the sunshine inside.

The alarm wakes me up at three-fifteen on Thursday morning. I dress in jeans and a Lakers jersey. I kiss Jett good-bye, grab my purse and keys, and head out to my car. I've started walking all around my vehicle and looking inside before I get in. Everything looks okay.

I get in and start up the engine. I back out of the driveway and lower the garage door. Twenty-five minutes later, I park my car right out in front of the bakery. I go inside and turn on all of the lights.

My crew arrives one by one, five minutes apart. The menu is scripted on two white boards behind the glass cases. A duplicate is listed inside the kitchen area. The four of us wash our hands, put on our aprons, and get to work.

We make five kinds of cobblers, ten pies, fifteen cakes, bread, rolls, donuts, and crepes. We even have a small section of French pastry.

In less than ninety minutes, the bakery smells heavenly. None of us are tired. We're gaining energy as we fill up the glass cases and stock the shelves.

The helium-filled balloons are already in the bakery section and some are blown up outside as well. There's a "Grand Opening" banner beneath the "Just Desserts" sign. In the right-hand side of the bay window is a large photo of Lynzee.

Jett calls me at noon. I give him an update on our progress. He says that he'll order pizza for dinner. He tells me he loves me for the third time that day. I tell him how much I love him too.

By six o'clock that evening we're finished. We clean up the kitchen and prepare to leave. I ask Moses to check inside of my car for me. He does and says that it's fine. I told my crew about the rat incident. They were all appalled.

I go home and change. I have to pick up Lynzee at the airport at eight. I arrive at Memphis International Airport at seven forty-five. I listen to Alicia Keys' CD again while I wait.

Around eight-twenty Lynzee comes out with a man. I'm almost positive it's Michael.

I hop out of my car and greet them. "Hello, guys. Welcome to Memphis." Lynzee makes the introductions. Michael is just like I pictured him: a mirror image of Cuba Gooding Jr.

Michael puts their luggage in the trunk. Then we're on the road, chatting and laughing like sisters should be doing. I'm happy, once again, that Lynzee decided to drop the lawsuit. There's no telling where either one of us would be right now.

I've learned that when siblings truly love each other, there's no such thing as sibling rivalry. Love trumps the negative every time.

By the time we park the car and unload the luggage, it's nine-thirty. I'm going to have to do an all-nighter. The crew and I have to be at the bakery at midnight, so we can have all the fresh-baked confections ready by six A.M.

I introduce Michael to Jett who shows them where they'll be sleeping. Jett helps Michael with the luggage. You'd think they were staying a week instead of three days.

While they're upstairs talking man talk, Lynzee and I get out the games. We play Boggle first. While I'm kicking her ass, Michael comes down.

"Can I play?"

"Sure," I say. "Have a seat." Jett says good night. He has to get up early for work tomorrow.

It turns out that Michael whips my natural ass at Boggle. I'm pissed and amazed at the same time. When we play Scrabble, Michael once again leads everyone in points. By eleven forty-five he's the clear winner.

"The twins are going to pick you two up tomorrow and bring you down to the shop."

"What time?"

"Around nine."

"We'll be ready."

After showering and dressing, I head out to the garage. I do my usual checking around the car. Satisfied, I get in. I exit the garage and drive the twenty-five minute trek to the bakery. When I walk in, it smells like success. I get to work.

There's plenty of space, but every now and then we bump into one another. We laugh and continue on about our business. Our baking is being done as professionally as I've seen it done on the Food Network.

By five forty-five, we're all finished. We remove our bakery aprons and put on our embroidered ones. It's still dark out, but Moses unlocks the door at six sharp.

A few customers are waiting. "Good morning," one woman says. "How much for a dozen donuts?"

I give her the price.

"Oh, that's cheap. I'll take a full dozen."

I put each of her selections inside a silk screened pastry bag. She thanks me and says she'll be back tomorrow.

Customers stream in like ducks on a pond. I say *cha-ching* to myself every time someone makes a purchase.

By eight o'clock, the place is packed. When Lynzee, Michael, and the twins arrive at nine, they can barely get inside. I make an announcement about Lynzee being my featured guest. A horde of customers make a line to get her autograph.

When the shop is less busy, Lynzee and Michael come into

the kitchen and look around. They like what they see. Heidi and Enrique are busy baking fresh pastry, and Moses is writing away on the books.

After Lynzee autographs dozens of books, I give Michael, Lynzee, and the twins samples of some of the desserts. They stuff themselves and applaud the chefs.

Jett stops in around noon. He says hello to everyone and gives me a kiss. He stays and eats a donut before he leaves and goes back to work. He drops Michael and Lynzee off at home.

At three, I'm getting tired. We've turned off the ovens, finished baking for the day. By five, I can hardly wait until closing. My eyes are beginning to stick together.

At five forty-five, we begin storing the unsold items to be sold as day-old baked goods tomorrow.

It's pitch dark outside, and I don't notice that the twins are missing. As Moses is tabulating the receipts for today, Javed runs into the shop. He has April by the neck.

He slams the door, huffing and puffing. "This bitch was ready to throw a Molotov cocktail into the shop! I told you that this bitch was the perpetrator all along."

Jamone comes in. "Yeah, we caught that ho. I already called the police on my cell phone. They should be here any minute."

I look at April's filthy face. "Why'd you do it, honey? I never did anything to hurt you." Her tattered clothes reek of gasoline and smoke.

She almost spits in my face. "You took my daddy away from me, bitch. I hope you die."

Javed shoves her thin body down into a chair. "You're the one who should worry about dying. You're going to spend some time in prison, girl. There ain't no telling what them crazy freaks gonna do to you in there."

"Fuck all of y'all," April sneers. Then she turns to me. "How'd you like that shit on your seats? And that rat?" She laughs. "Priceless."

I'm so shocked I can't speak. I call Jett and tell him what's happened. He's on his way.

Sirens are blaring outside the bakery. Two patrol cars pull up. People are looking inside the bakery and wondering what's going on. After they put April in handcuffs, I ask the twins to go outside and make a statement.

A reporter shows up and puts the event on Channel Thirteen News. It'll be shown at nine.

Then Jett drives up. I go outside. They're putting April in the squad car. He says, "April, I trusted you. Now you've broken that trust. You need help. I'm willing to take you to see a psychiatrist when you are released from jail, but then you and I are going to part ways. It's going to take some time before I can trust you with my family again."

"I'm not seeing no fucking shrink." She spits on the floor. "Fuck you, then," she snarls.

The officer slams the door. A few minutes later, the squad car drives off. Jett comes to give me a hug. "You told me that you thought it was April. I didn't believe you. I'm sorry."

"Don't be sorry. Just be glad that our life is richer and our sons are happier than they've ever been. We've got a successful business, I've got a successful writing career, and you're doing well at King Ford. What more can any human ask for?"

"Sex."

56

I'm tired as a mule when I get home from the bakery, but I feel energized about my man's upcoming presence. Lynzee and Michael have turned in early, and I'm thankful that I don't have to keep them occupied. If they're lucky, they'll be entertained by each other.

I think about my sons. I hope they've learned something from Lynzee and me. Money doesn't guarantee happiness, and lies have a way of catching up with you. It's best to be honest with the one you love, no matter what the cost. And most importantly, don't sell your soul for a house. Like Jett said, it's just mortar and brick. A mansion doesn't make a home. A home is where your heart is, and mine is here with my husband.

Before Jett gets home, I rush into the bathroom and take a shower. By the time I finish, Jett comes into the bedroom and shuts the door.

"Baby?" he calls out.

"I'll be right there, sweetie," I tell him.

I drop the towel on the bathroom floor and walk into the bedroom naked. I stand before him.

Jett spins me around and shakes his head. "Your ass still looks like you've been sitting on a pile of rocks."

I tap him on his nose. "I don't know when the last time you

checked, but your butt looks like you've been sitting right beside me."

We both laugh.

"Seriously, I need you, baby," he says.

"And I need you." I help remove his clothing. My eyes hold his as we cast off every item of clothing. Nude, he takes my hand and guides me between the sheets.

I think of Alicia Keys' song, "Love is My Disease." She tells her lover that when he's gone, it feels like her whole world is gone with him. She says that she thought love would be her antidote, but now it's her disease.

I don't know how I can ever get used to being without you. Baby, I'm addicted to your love.

I wish that Jett would say those words to me. I'd melt like butter in a hot skillet. But my man isn't as romantic as I would like him to be, so I had the forethought to turn on "Hang On in There, Baby," one of my favorite songs by Johnny Bristol while we're making love.

He kisses me deeply, and massages the small passage between my legs. I sigh in anticipation of what I know I'm about to receive.

In an insane rush, we come together. We require no further arousal, no additional petting or caressing to incite the fires of our sexuality. Our two bodies are so inflamed and eager that in an instant, we are joined in a fiery union. It isn't sweet. It isn't pretty. It isn't like any first time before. But it is explosive, somewhat dangerous, and something that neither one of us will soon forget.

Bliss.

"More," I say, unable to disengage myself from him for even a second. "More," I whisper in his ear, biting his neck and licking his ear. Then I feel him enter me again. To hear him whispering my name and feel him fill me so pleasurably with an emotion so powerful, it can only be described as religious. For me, this is the climax, the reason that I'm alive, to experience that special capitulation when I feel loved and complete.

"I love you, Charity. Always, forever."

"And I love you, Jett. Forevermore."

We fall asleep in each other's arms, tenderly entangled, not willing to let go of the sweetness of our union.

The windblown raindrops splattering on the window merge and flow downward. I feel Jett stir, and place my arm protectively around him. "Baby," he utters so softly I can barely hear him. To my ears, it's an aria. I'm in his arms once again, and all that is carnal, and material, and tangible evaporates into an intoxicating mist of emotions.

I regret not trusting my man's love for me. I am ashamed that I kept truths from him that affected his life and future. I had no right to keep him from his blood daughter. It was his decision to make, not mine. Knowing that, I believe that our marriage can survive any problems in the future, because our future is one of togetherness and trust.

There is no reality to my sensations, and the peace I feel is incarnate. There are no nerve endings to feel cold or heat or pain or pressure. It's as if Jett and I stepped inside an illusion, leaving time and truth behind. We are no longer two individual souls. We are a single, inseparable presence that can never be broken.

I've learned that nothing is stronger than real love. "Commitment" is a word that seems overused, but is ultimately the key to having a good marriage or relationship. When you make that commitment to your spouse at the wedding ceremony and say, "Till death do us part," mean it. Mean it for the rest of your natural lives and God will bless you. I know he blessed Jett and me, and we couldn't be happier. The product of that love lies in the future of our sons, Jamone and Javed.